Shot Twice, and *Still* Coming

The Death Merchant took the key out of the door and dropped the ring and the two keys into the left-side pocket of his topcoat. The enemy was capable of anything. He'd kidnap his own mother if it served the agency! And if he had a mother.

Camellion was about to slide in on the seat when it happened: one! two! terrific slams in the broad part of his back, the savage blows comparable to being hit twice with a sledge hammer.

By the butt of Buddha. I've been shot!

The Death Merchant's lightning-fast reflexes saved his life. Even many pros would have fallen instant victim to surprise and would have paused. Camellion did not. No sooner had the double pain stabbed in his back than he was throwing himself forward across the front seat of the car.

Once again, the Death Merchant was in a striking position, ready to kill—or be killed.

THE DEATH MERCHANT SERIES:

- #1 THE DEATH MERCHANT
- #2 OPERATION OVERKILL
- #3 THE PSYCHOTRON PLOT
- #4 CHINESE CONSPIRACY
- #5 SATAN STRIKE
- #6 ALBANIAN CONNECTION
- #7 THE CASTRO FILE
- #8 BILLIONAIRE MISSION
- #9 LASER WAR
- #10 THE MAINLINE PLOT
- #11 MANHATTAN WIPEOUT
- #12 THE KGB FRAME
- #13 MATO GROSSO HORROR
- #14 VENGEANCE: GOLDEN HAWK
- #15 THE IRON SWASTIKA PLOT
- #16 INVASION OF THE CLONES
- #17 ZEMLYA EXPEDITION
- #18 NIGHTMARE IN ALGERIA
- #19 ARMAGEDDON, USA!
- #20 HELL IN HINDU LAND
- #21 THE POLE STAR SECRET
- #22 THE KONDRASHEV CHASE
- #23 THE BUDAPEST ACTION
- #24 THE KRONOS PLOT
- #25 THE ENIGMA PROJECT
- #26 THE MEXICAN HIT
- #27 THE SURINAM AFFAIR
- #28 NIPPONESE NIGHTMARE
- #29 FATAL FORMULA
- #30 THE SHAMBHALA STRIKE
- #31 OPERATION THUNDERBOLT
- #32 DEADLY MANHUNT
- #33 ALASKA CONSPIRACY
- #34 OPERATION MIND-MURDER
- #35 MASSACRE IN ROME
- #36 THE COSMIC REALITY KILL
- #37 THE BERMUDA TRIANGLE ACTION
- #38 THE BURNING BLUE DEATH
- #39 THE FOURTH REICH
- #40 BLUEPRINT INVISIBILITY
- #41 THE SHAMROCK SMASH
- #42 HIGH COMMAND MURDER
- #43 THE DEVIL'S TRASHCAN
- #44 ISLAND OF THE DAMNED
- #45 THE RIM OF FIRE CONSPIRACY
- #46 BLOOD BATH
- #47 OPERATION SKYHOOK
- #48 THE PSIONICS WAR

ATTENTION: SCHOOLS AND CORPORATIONS

PINNACLE Books are available at quantity discounts with bulk purchases for educational, business or special promotional use. For further details, please write to: SPECIAL SALES MANAGER, Pinnacle Books, Inc., 1430 Broadway, New York, NY 10018.

WRITE FOR OUR FREE CATALOG

If there is a Pinnacle Book you want—and you cannot find it locally—it is available from us simply by sending the title and price plus 75¢ to cover mailing and handling costs to:

Pinnacle Books, Inc.
Reader Service Department
1430 Broadway
New York, NY 10018

Please allow 6 weeks for delivery.

____ Check here if you want to receive our catalog regularly.

#48
DEATH MERCHANT
THE PSIONICS WAR
by Joseph Rosenberger

PINNACLE BOOKS   NEW YORK

This is a work of fiction. All the characters and events portrayed in this book are fictional, and any resemblance to real people or incidents is purely coincidental.

DEATH MERCHANT #48: THE PSIONICS WAR

Copyright © 1982 by Joseph Rosenberger

All rights reserved, including the right to reproduce this book or portions thereof in any form.

An original Pinnacle Books edition, published for the first time anywhere.

First printing, January 1982

ISBN: 0-523-41644-X

Cover illustration by Dean Cate

Printed in the United States of America

PINNACLE BOOKS, INC.
1430 Broadway
New York, New York 10018

Dedicated to

**"The Fox"
&
"Wild Bill"**

Morituri morituros salutant....

Chapter One

Inefficiency was close to the top of Richard Camellion's *Things-To-Hate* list, and the fact that he was now a part of that incompetency—even though through no fault of his own—made him grit his teeth in frustration.

He had been in New York City only a day and a half, and everything had gone smoothly, until a few hours ago, until the Oldsmobile Omega he had rented had developed engine trouble on Wyck Expressway, the multilaned route that led to John F. Kennedy International Airport. The engine had finally quit cold two and a half miles from the airport. Try hailing a taxi on any expressway! Camellion might as well have tried to stop a passing airliner!

There he had stood, on the concrete, the cold late fall wind whipping at his British trenchcoat, vehicles zipping by him like large bullets. Finally, two cops had stopped and, giving him disgusted looks, had helped him push the pile-of-junk from Detroit to a parkway. As friendly as a couple of cobras, the two bluecoats had driven the Death Merchant the rest of the way to Kennedy International. They hadn't gone out of their way to do him a favor. New York cops do not even do each other favors. The two patrolmen were stationed at the airport—or Camellion could have walked.

Even though Camellion was an hour and ten minutes late, he hurried to the American Airlines gate that handled Flight 64, the flight from Chicago to New York. As he had expected, Flight 64 had been on schedule. The passengers had deplaned and were gone—and so was Doctor Wayne Davis and his secretary, Miss Ursula Czerweny, as well as the two Central Intelligence Agency Case Officers who had accompanied them from Chicago.

Courtland Grojean had foreseen the possibility that, due

to an act of Fate, the Death Merchant might be delayed. To offset any break in Camellion's schedule and to insure that the Death Merchant made contact with the four from Chicago, the Chief of the CIA's covert section had instructed the two Case Officers to take Dr. Davis and his secretary to the main concourse and wait close to the United Airlines ticket counter. Should Camellion be late he would then find the four in the main concourse.

How would they know him? They wouldn't. He would know them; he would recognize them from photographs given to him at United States Embassy in Tokyo, a day before he had caught a Pan Am flight to Los Angeles, U.S.A. To further help Camellion's identifying the four, Howard Utall and Martin Kenninger, the two Company men, had been instructed by Grojean to carry copies of the *Chicago Sun-Times* and to have the newspapers resting on their laps, with the headlines upside down, pointing outward, toward the Death Merchant.

The only thing wrong was that Utall and Kenninger weren't waiting close to the United Airlines ticket counter. Neither was Ursula Czerweny. Nor Dr. Wayne Davis—the prize package that Utall and Kenninger (with the help of Camellion)—were to deliver to the Pforzheimer Science Foundation in Mt. Vernon.

Feeling like the poor relation who had been left out of the will, Camellion took off his Sunsensor dark glasses and casually looked up and down the long concourse alive with people of every age, race, color, and costume.

I should have worn an undershirt! Underneath his blue broadcloth shirt, he wore a full chest-back-and-sides bulletproof garment made of the special Pen-Stop process. Not one of the better, but the best bullet-resistant garment in use, anywhere in the world. The Armour-Hide Super Contour Garment could stop a .44 magnum slug at twenty feet—unless the projectile was a Lee Jurras .44 projectile. But . . . the "vest" did have a tendency to make the back of the wearer itch.

Black attaché case in hand, the Death Merchant walked twenty feet to his left and found a seat on a bench next to a couple of young soldiers bug-eying the centerfold in a *Playboy* magazine. Carefully, he placed the attaché case between his feet. Very important to Camellion, the case contained two "Custom Hunter" Auto Mag pistols, each with a 10½" barrel.

Camellion knew that Dr. Davis and the three others had taken Flight 64. They had been aboard the American Airlines plane. . . . *And I don't think they got out and walked away—not at 20,000 feet. Or they didn't take the flight, in which case Grojean lied to me! I don't think he did.*

Camellion sorted various other possibilities. There weren't too many of them. The four had gone to one of the slop shops to eat? To the restrooms? Impossible. The two CIA men were career employees. They wouldn't amble off to eat. . . . *And it wouldn't take them all this time. They'd stick their heads in a furnace if the Fox ordered them to. Those two followed instructions. They would sit and wait.*

Conclusion: a flaw had developed in the operation. Somehow, The Other Side had gotten to Dr. Davis, his secretary and the two intelligence officers. The KGB! Only agents of the Sword and the Shield could have grabbed the four. Even though the Czechs and the Bulgars were intensely interested in the whole field of the paranormal, or Psi (i.e. the entire range of psychic phenomena—or Psychotronics as Psi was called behind the Iron Curtain) only the intelligence service of the Soviet Union had the worldwide capability to set up a snatch-and-grab-job in John F. Kennedy International Airport. . . . *And the Mafia. But the Mafia is interested in the long green, and not even the Big Boys would dare go up against the Company.* . . .

Or—could there have been a sudden change of plans on the part of Grojean? Had there been a last minute development that had necessitated CIA people in New York meeting the four from Chicago? Sure, it was possible. It was also possible for the sun to flare into a nova and destroy the Earth in a few seconds.

But not very probable. . . .

The Death Merchant was convinced that the KGB had grabbed Dr. Davis, his secretary and Grojean's two spooks. How the KGB had accomplished the task without notice, without shots being fired. . . . *The pig farmers must have employed a jim-dandy dilly of a ruse!"*

Stroking his gray, fuzzy beard, the Death Merchant made up his mind. He would make one more patrol around the concourse, just to be sure, although he felt he would be wasting his time. From the very beginning, even while he had been in Indonesia[1], he had had a gut feeling about this mission, which the CIA had dubbed *Operation Basilisk*[2]. Another irritation he had to contend with was that he was unable to phone Grojean or Melbert, Grojean's aide, from the airport. All phone calls that went to the Chapel of Prayer Funeral Home in Mt. Vernon had to be scrambled.

One more sashay around the concourse, then rent a car and drive to the safe house in Mt. Vernon. There wasn't any other course of action to take.

Camellion picked up the attaché case, got to his feet and started to walk, his eyes darting over the faces of the people in the crowd. No where did he see anyone that even faintly resembled any of the four from Chicago—not that he expected to.

Twenty minutes later, he was at the Avis-Rent-a-Car counter, telling the clerk about the rented Avis Oldsmobile that had died on Wyck Expressway. He wanted to rent another vehicle, one that wouldn't fall apart ". . . when I'm halfway to Manhattan."

The clerk, a busty brunette in a white silk tunic and black crepe pants, looked troubled as Camellion handed her the keys and the acceptance slip. She looked at the name on the piece of paper.

"I can't understand it, Mr. Higgdon," she said apologetically. "Our cars are always in good condition. I'm very sorry for the inconvenience you went through. What time did the engine stop running? Do you remember?"

"An hour and forty-five minutes ago," Camellion said. "At two thirty. It wasn't all that much of a problem, miss. Those things happen."

The young woman flashed her best smile at Camellion and expertly faked great concern. "I'm glad you feel that way. But the car shouldn't have broken down. I apologize for the delay. Is there any particular kind of car you prefer? This is a busy part of the afternoon and not too many models are available."

"Make a suggestion." The Death Merchant noticed that the young woman wasn't wearing a bra. He also noticed the heavy scent of perfume emanating from the woman behind him. He turned slightly and glanced at the woman. In her

---

1. See Death Merchant book #47, *Operation Skyhook*.
2. A legendary reptile that is hatched from the egg of a seven-year-old cock and has a fatal breath and glance.

late thirties. Heavy features, little makeup. Round horned-rimmed glasses that gave her the appearance of an owl. Dressed in a blue pant suit and stroller coat to match, she reminded Camellion of a grammar-school principal on a short vacation. The woman smiled slightly and shifted her heavy handbag to her other arm.

Camellion turned back to the clerk whose crimson lips formed another phony smile. "I have an '81 Camero. It's like new. It has cruise control, AM/FM stero and—"

"A car that runs well," interrupted the Death Merchant pleasantly, again noticing how the woman's breasts struggled within the confines of the silk blouse—*two grapefruits topped with cherries!* He wished too that the woman behind him would step back five paces. He hated the smell of strong perfume.

The clerk filled out the record sheet, then handed Camellion the keys and said that the Camero would be in Section G-3 of the parking lot. "The license number is written on your receipt, Mr. Higgdon. It's a blue and white car. Do you know how to get to Section G-3, sir?"

Camellion nodded. Continued the young woman, "The car will be in Section G-3, in ten minutes, sir. It will take you that long to get to the parking lot."

"Fine. I'll get a bite to eat first. Please make sure the car is there."

That damned stinking perfume. It smells like refined pampas poop!

With a couple of cheeseburgers and a glass of milk turning to chyme inside of him, Camellion walked to the large parking lot, thinking of the fantastic implications involving Operation Basilisk, a mission that was only a Lilliputian part of the silent war being fought between the United States and its allies and the Soviet Union and the nations of the Warsaw Pact—*a psionics war, a deadly conflict that was a race to learn the secrets of the psychic world, of the preternatural, and apply those secrets to methods of defense and attack*.

It was not generally known to the American people, but there were scores of men and women in the Pentagon whose sole job was to investigate "unreality," to deal pragmatically with the realm of the paranormal, with what the average man would call "damn nonsense." This very top secret group was the "psychic task force"[3], with one mission—to investigate military applications of psychic phenomena and develop defenses against psionic and/or psychotronic weapons.

There was one reason for the existence of this psychic task force: fear . . . a deep dread of the grim fact that the Soviet Union was not only developing such psychic weapons but was years ahead of the United States. The situation was so critical that Charles Rose, a North Carolina Democrat who served on the House Select Committee on Intelligence, advocated launching a "Manhattan Project" type effort to develop psionic weapons. Said Rose, "The Soviets are up to their ass in this stuff and we shouldn't fall behind."

Truth is usually stranger than the most fantastic of fiction. This is especially true of psionics that can be described as the interaction of mind and matter. Or when applied to the military: weapons systems that can operate on the power of the mind.

Two subdivisions of the field had been under investigation for a number of years. Mind-altering techniques were well advanced . . . procedures and techniques that included manipulation of human behavior through use of psychological weapons effecting sight, sound, smell, temperature, electromagnetic energy or sensory deprivation.

The other area of experimentation involved parapsychological phenomena known as OOBE—out-of-body experience, remote viewing (collecting date/information from afar), bioinformation (or extrasensory perception), depending on the source and technique employed.

The CIA and the Pentagon were convinced that the Soviets were way ahead of the U.S. in parapsychological research[4]. In fact, there was conclusive evidence—*and Grojean wouldn't give me the source of this evidence!*—that the Soviets had further developed techniques to control and actively employ their knowledge of parapsychology. Included in the Soviet research has been investigation into

---

3. This is fact. (see *Discover* magazine, March 1981 issue.)

4. Also reports prepared by the Office of the Surgeon General, and entitled, *Controlled Offensive Behavior*—USSR. Unclassified, 1972. *Soviet and Czechoslovakian Parasychological Research*. Unclassified, 1975.

such areas as *telepathy* (the mental awareness of information over a distance), *precognition* (the knowledge of future events), *telekinesis* (movement of matter with the mind), and the transfer of bioenergy from one body to another.

The CIA and the ONI (Office of Naval Intelligence) had verified in 1980 that the Soviets had made progress in:

The transfer of energy from one organism to another. This involved the ability to heal or cause disease over a distance—and death for no apparent cause. To accomplish such assassinations by mind power, Soviet scientists were working on Photonic Barrier Modulators that, if successful, would be able to kill from thousands of miles away.

"In contrast, we're working on Hieronymous[5] machines," Courtland Grojean had confided to the Death Merchant.

With the Hieronymous machine concept, one needed only a photograph of a tarket for ammunition. Drop a photograph into the slot—say the photograph of a submarine, or of the President of the United States—press a button—and the sub sinks, or the President could have a "stroke."

In his machine-gun rattle voice, Grojean had dropped another bombshell. "The Soviets have been at this game a long time. We have a great deal of evidence that the first victim of their Photonic Barrier Modulator was the *Thresher*."[6]

Telepathic behavior modification. The Soviets were working on techniques and methods that would induce hynotic states up to distances of 1,000 kilometers.

Psychokinesis (mind over matter), or what the Americans called telekinesis.

U.S. scientists were making progress with remote viewing with the application of OOBE travel, or out-of-body travel, a phenomena that was not at all uncommon. Literally thousands of people have had the experience of "floating" outside of their physical bodies, yet being able to view themselves with total awareness and complete

---

5. Dr. T. Galen Hieronymus, the inventor of the Hieronymous Machine, a device for detection of emanations from materials.

6. The submarine *Thresher* sank and broke up in 1963.

consciousness. Very often the phenomenon is associated with extreme danger, such as illness or accidents.[7]

The intelligence-gathering capability available through OOBE travel is obvious. In the safe house in Mt. Vernon, Grojean had let Camellion read a very *TOP SECRET/G-6 GRADE PERSONNEL/EYES ONLY* report entitled Psychological Evaluation on Tested Subjects Involved in Project Invisible. Subjects, tested in a U.S. Naval Laboratory, had actually penetrated the Soviet Union and the People's Republic of China while in "bodiless" state and had actually retrieved extremely valuable data from strategic sites!

"How did the scientists know the information was accurate?" Camellion had asked. "I presume it was confirmed?"

"It was," Grojean had replied. "Six months later."

While the Americans and the Soviets were experimenting in any number of directions, both sides were concentrating on the ultimate weapon, the psychotronic device that could induce illness and/or death at long range, with little risk to the operator. Such a weapon would be silent, impossible to detect, require no special psychic ability to charge the generator and need only a human operator as the power source.

Dr. Wayne E. Davis, of Hancock, Wisconsin, had invented such a device—the *Alpha One Psionic Unit*. And the device worked. *It could kill!*—although that is not why the scientist had perfected the machine. Dr. Davis's sole goal was to diagnose and *cure* disease; and he had done both with dogs, cats, and rabbits, at a distance of a bit more than 70 miles, the distance from Hancock to Madison, the capital of Wisconsin.

Like the nosy old maid on the block who sees and knows everything, the CIA had learned of Dr. Davis's experiments. Company contact men had immediately appealed to Dr. Davis's patriotism with giant doses of "Mom," "flag," and "the Russians are right around the corner." Knowing that Dr. Davis was a deeply religious man, the Company

---

7. Including the author. As a Security Officer, I once was forced to kill three men. I was slightly wounded. All of it happened in less than a minute. After I fired the last shot, I found myself standing across the room, looking down at the three corpses and at *myself*—twenty feet away. "By God, I'm dead!" I thought. A moment later, I *returned to my own body*.

tossed a verbal below-the-belt punch—did Dr. Davis want to see the United States fall to Godless atheists? Did he want to see the churches closed and the publishing of Bibles banned?

Horrified at the thought of the enemies of Christianity loose on holy American streets, Dr. Davis agreed to cooperate with the CIA. He agreed to test the Alpha One Unit in a kill situation. The first test was highly successful. Six rabbits were killed at a distance of 10 miles. The Alpha One Unit first induced extreme high blood pressure in the rabbits. *Eighty-six minutes later, all six bunnies died of intracerebral hemorrhage—stroke!*

The second test was conducted at a distance of 110 miles. Again the test animals died of stroke!

There was a single fly in the ointment. Dr. Davis would not reveal the secret of the Alpha One Unit to CIA scientists. In spite of all their pleas and arguments, Dr. Davis would not reveal how the device worked, steadfastly maintaining that he wanted to "think about the moral aspects" before permitting his machine to be used for military purposes.

Frustrated to the extreme, the CIA talked to Dr. Davis's two assistants, Bryan Lee Walsch and Raya Walsch, the man and wife team who had been with Dr. Davis for almost 17 years. Could they, would they talk to Dr. Davis and try to get him to cooperate fully with the CIA?

No, the Walschs would not. "If we did, which we won't, it wouldn't do any good," Bryan Walsch said angrily. "Wayne's his own man. He makes his own decisions."

Ursula Czerweny, Dr. Davis's secretary, wouldn't even discuss her trying to get the scientist to reveal the secret.

The Company had more ideas than a politician has excuses. Would Dr. Davis be willing to go to Mt. Vernon, New York, and demonstrate his machine to the members of the prestigious Pforzheimer Science Foundation? Yes, he would. But he would not give them the secret either.

Grojean had explained the real purpose in getting Dr. Davis to go to Mt. Vernon. The CIA hoped that the foundation's scientists could persuade Dr. Davis to cooperate fully with "his government." Patiently, they would explain to the "obstinate Puritan" (as Grojean referred to Dr. Davis) how the Soviet Union was way out in front of the U.S. in the development of psionic weapons that most certainly would be used to destroy the United States. Is that what Dr. Davis wanted? Did he want to see America destroyed by the forces of hell?

Should that strategy fail, the CIA would have to apply pressure, and get rough, if necessary.

Grojean had wanted Camellion to accompany Dr. Davis from Hancock, Wisconsin, to O'Hare Airport in Chicago. Tied up with a mission in Indonesia, the Death Merchant had not been able to fly back to the United States in time. Camellion had time only to fly to NYC from San Francisco and to confer with Courtland Grojean in a private supper room at Kenny's Steak Pub West, a restaurant at 221 West 46th St. in the heart of New York City's theater district. From Kenny's the Death Merchant had driven straight to the John F. Kennedy Airport.

Only now there wasn't any Dr. Davis to escort to Mt. Vernon!

Camellion glanced at the lead-colored sky. The wind had quickened and rain was only a few hours away. Good. Camellion despised sunshine the way an Arab "loves" icebergs! Even daylight was depression to the Death Merchant. Night was the only time to live, love, and die. . . .

He didn't have any difficulty in finding Section G-3, mainly because he had been in and out of John F. Kennedy Airport several dozen times or more. Soon he spotted the '81 white-topped Camero, parked beside an '81 Buick Regal 4-door.

He checked the license number, then walked around to the door on the driver's side and, holding the attaché case in his left hand, unlocked the door with one of the keys in his right hand.

Camellion had another suspicion. It wasn't for nothing that men close to Courtland Grojean called him "The Fox." Could Grojean—*Without saying anything to me?*—have arranged a phony kidnap, to prove to Davis how dangerous the Russians are—and then miraculously rescue him and the three others?

The Death Merchant took the key out of the door and dropped the ring and two keys into the left-side pocket of his topcoat. Grojean was capable of anything. *He'd kidnap his own mother if it served the Agency! And if he had a mother?*

He was about to slide in on the seat when it happened:

one! two! terrific slams in the broad of his back, the savage blows comparable to being hit twice with a sledge hammer.

By the butt of Buddha! I've been shot!

Shot twice in the back, shot by an auto-pistol equipped with a noise supressor and, from the feeling of the twin stabs, by high velocity projectiles, slugs that had been stopped by the titanium toughness of the Armour-Hide Garment.

The Death Merchant's lightning fast reflexes saved his live. Even many pros would have fallen instant victim to surprise and have paused. Camellion did not. No sooner had the double pain stabbed in his back than he was throwing himself forward across the front seat of the Camero, attaché case still in his left hand. He pulled in his legs and, with his right hand, unlocked the right front door and pushed it open. His legs were still on the seat and the upper part of his body was slithering out the other side of the car when two more bullets struck the left door, both projectiles ripping through the outer side with loud zings but stopping when they struck the inner sheet of metal.

The Death Merchant slid from the seat, closed the right door, got down between the Camero and the Buick Regal and pulled a Heckler & Koch VP70Z DA auto-pistol from a left-side shoulder holster. He got to his knees and looked underneath the Camero. He was just in time to see a pair of legs moving from across the way, approaching the left side of the car. The owner of the legs moved slowly, then quickened his steps.

Camellion realized that the slugs had been fired due south of the Camero. He knew from the way the projectiles had left when they struck his back. The Camero was parked at the end of a line of cars in the G-3 Section. Then, to the south, was a driveway and another line of vehicles. Twenty-five feet south of the Camero was the first car of the next horizontal line. The shots had to have been fired from the left side of that car, a Cadillac. He was also very much aware that the loud cracks from the West German pistol would bring airport security men on the run. However, common sense demanded that it was better to worry about airport security than to end up dead in the marketplace.

He sighted on the legs—now moving much faster—and fired four times, the loud noise of exploding cartridges shattering the tranquility of the late afternoon air.

Bohumil Fatalipeyli, the KGB gunman, was also shattered. All four VP70Z 9mm X 19 Parabellum projectiles striking him in the ankles and knocking his feet out from under him. With a cry of fear and alarm, the Russian crashed to the ground. He didn't have time to do anything else. The Death Merchant instantly killed him with a couple of slugs in the right side.

The Death Merchant got up, took a deep breath and darted around the front of the Buick Regal, all the while knowing that he was taking one enormous chance and that he would be very lucky if he didn't stop a slug. He almost did. A bullet missed his left shoulder by less than a sixth of an inch. A second 9mm projectile, fired from a silenced SIG automatic, cut through the Gore-Tex-tm material, at the right bottom, of his British trenchcoat.

Then Camellion was on the right side of the Buick and opening the attaché case. In no time at all, he had a stainless steel Custom Hunter Auto Mag pistol in each hand, his fingers wrapped around the buffalo horn eagle grips.

Zerrrringggg! Zerrrringgg! More enemy slugs from silenced weapons ricocheted from the front of the Buick as an angry Death Merchant moved to the right rear of the vehicle—*Damn!* He didn't like being shot in the back, although he conceded that it was the most sensible way to gun down a target. *I'm going to teach you trash that you should never insult an alligator until you've crossed the river! One, two, three! I'll be damned if you snuff me! DO IT!*

He reared up and began to pull the triggers of the Auto Mag pistols, the large weapons bellowing big booms. A storm of .44 magnum projectiles ripped into the right side of the red Cadillac coupe, forcing the three Russians, crouched to the left of the vehicle, to have a fatal appointment with their own mortality. A .44 Jurras Flat Point bullet bored through the red car, hit Lavrenti Biski in the stomach and knocked him all the way back to the next car in line. His consciousness fading, Biski had hardly hit the ground when a .44 JFP projectile stabbed Sergei Aluevski in the left upper chest, ripped through his lung and tore out through his back, ripping apart the intraspinatus fascia muscle in the process. His mouth a swimming pool of blood, Aluevski uttered a strangled, choking sound and started to go down for the very final count. He jerked violently and gurgled loudly again as another .44 JFP projectile crashed through the vehicle and struck him just above the right knee.

Elana Vulkovitch, armed with an unsilenced .32 Walther PP, was more than astonished. She was terrified over the botched-up hit and the sudden deaths of the three men with her. Slugs were tearing through the Caddy all around her, but she didn't know what to do about her trapped situation, her will power frozen in icy fear.

Fate took over. A bullet struck the Cutlass Supreme behind her, glanced off with a screaming whine, shot back in her direction at an angle, struck the left end of the bumper of the Caddy, streaked upward and sliced across the tip of her nose. Reflex took over. Elana Vulkovitch jumped to her feet, in that barest sliver of a second forgetting about the Death Merchant, who certainly had not forgotten about her.

When she jumped up, Camellion saw her face for only a moment, but that blink of an eye in time was long enough for him to recognize her. It was the very same woman who had been behind him at the Avis-Rent-A-Car counter—*the same woman who smelled like a Hong Kong whorehouse!* And, long enough for him to give Elana Vulkovitch the small gift of a .44 bullet, squarely in her chest—the iron fist impact almost lifting her off her feet before the meeting of bullet with flesh and blood and bone smashed her to the ground.

The men who are best at killing develop sharp instincts in matters of survival—or they don't live very long. It was this finely honed intuition that told the Death Merchant he had silenced the enemy, although he couldn't be one hundred percent positive. Nonetheless he had to take the chance. He had to get the hell out and away.

He dropped the Auto Mags into the attaché case, closed the case, pulled the VP pistol from his topcoat pocket, cautiously stepped around the front of the Buick Regal and, with the VP ready to fire, exposed himself, full length, to the Caddy. Nothing happened. Whoever had tried to kill him was dead. Yet his problems were far from over and Camellion knew it. To the east, he could see people ducking behind cars in the distance and men pulling down their women to protect them.

Pure trouble was to the west, the direction of the airport terminal building. A half-dozen security officers, some with revolvers in their hands, were running in his direction, urged on by bystanders pointing at Camellion and shouting, "He's one of them! We saw it all!"

Camellion wasn't surprised. Shooting the Auto Mags had been synonymous with blowing a trumpet in a marble orchard at midnight.

Needing time, the Death Merchant pushed the switch on the VP to full automatic, swung the machine pistol to the west and, aiming low, fired off the last 14 cartridges in the magazine. A brief *BLRRRRRR* and the weapon was empty, the hollow-point projectiles striking the ground only a few feet in front of the security men, who jumped for cover behind cars, their scattering giving the Death Merchant time to run to the Camero and get behind the wheel. By the time the security guards were on their feet, he had backed out the car and was turning to drive south.

He wasn't worried about the people who had seen him. If fifty people had seen him, there would be fifty different descriptions. Even those who gave the correct description would describe a man who was in his late fifties or early sixties, had a gray beard and mustache, was wearing a dark trenchcoat, a navy corduroy hat, and carrying a black attaché case. Well and good. A false ID on the part of witnesses would help him escape from the area. A description of the car he had rented would go out. The cops would bottle him up on Wyck Expressway.

Camellion calculated that he had no more than ten minutes to get the hell out of the parking lot, drive to the other side of the terminal building, park the Camero among airport employee vehicles, get out and lose himself in the terminal building. He could kill a lot of time in restrooms and in restaurants. A few hours later, he could grab a taxi and get back to the city.

Fingerprints in the car? The cops would find only smudges. The coating of dexerfamalene on his palms would insure lack of prints.

He thought again of the woman he had killed. Weird! How had the Russians spotted him? He'd have to do some hard thinking on that.

With an expert yank, he pulled off the beard, then the mustache, and, as he drove with his left hand, stuffed them into the inside pockets of his tick-weave Harris Tweed jacket with his right. The corduroy hat went under the seat. He pulled off the gray hairpiece and pushed it into the left-side pocket of his jacket, making sure that not one strand of the genuine hair was exposed outside the flap of the pocket. Finally, he partially slipped out of the topcoat, driving with one hand, switching from one hand to the other as he freed his arms of the sleeves and pulled the coat down around his waist. *Damn the Russians! The pig farmers ruined a $400.00 topcoat and a $275.00 jacket!* A sly, crooked smile twisted itself across his mouth. The police would naturally expect a man on the run to get rid of his outer coat in an effort to make ID-ing him more difficult. But the police would not anticipate any "criminal" to be so pessimistic as to carry two coats, in case he had to ditch one. Another coat was an absolute must for another very good reason: There were two bullet holes not only in the back of the trenchcoat but also in the back of his tweed jacket. How would he look, walking around inside the terminal with two bullet holes in his back?

Camellion opened the attaché case on the seat beside him, took out the two Auto Mags and, one by one, stuffed them in his waist band, after which he awkwardly tightened his belt until he felt that he was about to squeeze himself in two. He next reached into the case and pulled out the cocoa brown plastic raincoat neatly folded in the lid and held in place by wide bands of rubberized material.

All he needed now was 50.1-percent of luck. . . .

He slackened speed, turned the steering wheel to the left and guided the car around the corner of the building. He then had to force himself to drive at a 35-mph limit to avoid attracting attention. People walking by the building and men and women in other cars didn't give him a second glance. Another five minutes. Three hundred feet to go. Park in that slot between the station wagon and the van. Good cover. No one was apt to see him putting on the raincoat. Finally, walk the hundred feet to the building. Just a little luck . . . a single pinch. . . .

The Death Merchant chuckled, thinking of the old axiom that the defeated always remember the battle longer than the victor. Not this time! This time the defeated would not remember anything. The Russians who had tried to kill him were dead—*Whether they were pig farmers, or even non-Russians working for the KGB, now they're food for the worms or the hot breath of a crematory.* . . . No matter, it was this kind of excitement, with a liberal sprinkling of uncertainty, that made life worth living, that gave meaning and purpose to existence.

He began to hum, the words to the tune rolling through his mind. . . .

Glory, glory hallelujah. Teacher hit me with a ruler. So we socked her in the beanie with a rotten tangerriney, and her teeth came marching out. . . .

Chapter Two

Mount Vernon, State of New York, located on the Bronx and Hutchinson Rivers, adjacent to the Bronx, is a solid chunk of American history. Among other things, the area (before the township was named Mount Vernon) was the scene of several Revolutionary War battles. It was here that Glover's Brigade, on October 18, 1776, probably saved Washington's army from defeat by General William Howe. After the war ended in defeat for the British, the township was named Mount Vernon, after the home and the burial place of George Washington's home in Fairfax County, Alexandria, Virginia.

Today, with a population of about 75,000, Mt. Vernon has diversified industrial development that includes book publishing and the manufacturing of clothing, chemicals, and electrical instruments. A dredged portion of the Hutchinson River serves as a port, and the city is a major petroleum-storage center.

In the north part of the city is Barret Avenue (named after a Revolutionary War hero), a clean, tree-lined street that runs from east to west. Morrison Way (named after an old trapper who died of too much booze in 1781) stretches from north to south. On the southeast corner of Barret and Morrison is the Chapel of Prayer Funeral Home, one of the finest mortuaries in Mt. Vernon, offering a full range of "Personalized Services Affordable To All . . . Prearrangement Counseling . . . Beautiful Spacious Chapel . . . Cremation . . . Special Prayer Rooms . . . Out of State Shipment (and free coffee)."

For the past 13 years the owners of the mortuary have been Mr. and Mrs. Orvel P. Hutchinson; however, Orvel Hutchinson is not a mortician. He attends to only the business end of the burial or cremation racket. Two licensed undertakers do the embalming and cosmetic work needed on fresh cold cuts.

The funeral home is constructed of light brown sandstone, the architecture ultramodern, as is the two story residence of the Hutchinsons next door to the mortuary—to the west. On the mansard roof of the house is an amazing array of antennae, all short-wave stuff. There's a Hy-Grain TH5DX with a 5-element tri-band beam, a Cushcraft A 147 11-element Yagi, a Cushcraft 20-15-10 A-3 meter beam antenna, two loop antennae and a Sanserino Loop antenna that can be tuned to different operating frequencies. In the backyard, close to the marble birdbath, is a Rohn BX48 sixty-foot tower that has 9 square feet of antenna.

These antennae surprise no one on Barret Avenue, no one who knows Mr. and Mrs. Orval Hutchinson, for it is well known that Orv Hutchinson is a ham radio nut. As Ethel Hutchinson has often remarked, "Orv's always at his sets." Laugh. Laugh. "Why I sometimes think he loves his hobby more than he loves me."

Mrs. Hutchinson knows the real reason why her husband is interested in short wave radio, even if she can't tell her friends the truth. That truth is that Orv is a Case Officer—a "career employee"—in the United States Central Intelligence Agency. The second half of the truth is that the Hutchinson house is a CIA "safe-house," code named Green Ripe Melon-16-b in operational files of the company's clandestine section—all of it proving one thing: the best place to hide anything is right under someone's nose. . . .

Courtland Grojean, his over-fifty face faintly clouded with annoyance, folded the *New York Post* and placed the newspaper on the rug beside the Victorian-portrait chair in which he was sitting. "Higgdon, you were very lucky," he said to Richard Camellion, who was seated some distance away in the attic whose slanting walls had been soundproofed. "The New York police haven't the faintest idea who 'Leonard Higgdon' is. They're totally baffled."

Of all the men in the room, Grojean was the only man who knew that "Higgdon" was Camellion and that Camellion was the infamous Death Merchant.

Camellion stopped rocking in the rocker and stared across the room at the chief of the Company covert section. "That's what the papers say. What do the Company's contacts in the NYPD say?"

"Essentially the same thing as the newspapers," replied Grojean. "The police are stumped. The prints in the car and on the attaché case were smudged. They're tracing the trenchcoat and the attaché case. I assume they can't be traced to you?"

"They can't be," Camellion said in a relaxed manner. "The only thing that could connect me with the hits at the airport is the 'Leonard Higgdon' signature on both the Avis registeries. It's impossible to completely disguise one's handwriting. But before the police could do any comparing of signatures, they'd have to find 'Higgdon.' And he no longer exists."

The immaculate Grojean, dressed in a navy cashmere jacket, gray flannel slacks and Scottish plain-toe black oxfords, carefully lighted a cigarette before speaking. "The police also suspect that the man who escaped Kennedy International wore a disguise." He permitted himself a rare twist of a smile. "As you already know, they're not certain whether the 'terrorist's' name is 'Higgdon' or Santa Claus. But damn it! did you have to use those magnums?"

The Death Merchant crossed his long legs and leaned back in the rocker. "No problem. I removed the two barrels from the AMPs and put on new barrels. The old barrels will never be found. Neither will the barrel from VP. Neither will 'Leonard Higgdon.'"

Roger Barnkoff, sitting in, and moving the swivel chair by the radio table from side to side, spoke up in a low voice, "If it's any consolation, the cops don't know any more about the four corpses at the airport than they do about Higgdon. All their identification was false—drivers' licenses, social security, home addresses, everything. Those four Russian sons of bitches might as well be aliens from another planet."

On the uphill side toward 35, Barnkoff was a specialist

from the CIA Office of Technical Development. Slim, he had pleasant features, a quick smile but large ears.

"We can't be positive they were KGB," interposed Fred Thumm, another Case Officer, who was at a card table, playing solitaire. He paused with a card and tilted his head slightly. "It's only been seven hours, and the cops still don't have the prints. I mean our contacts still have not tipped us off if any IDs have been made on prints."

"The police have the four bodies. Who knows what their pathologists might come up with?" said Wilbert Donovan, one of the three ONI agents in the large attic room. "Since the shoot-out took place at Kennedy International, the police have got to be thinking of the international terrorists angle."

The Death Merchant's cool gaze rested for a moment on Grojean, then swung to Thumm, a slender man of medium height who had long sideburns, a shaggy black mustache and hands whose fingers were constantly inspecting some item. Camellion would have bet that Thumm even twirled his thumbs in his sleep.

"Anything on the dental IDs of the four?" Camellion asked. "Or hasn't that report come in yet?"

"Nothing yet." Grojean stated, crossing his legs very carefully. He hated wrinkles. "We won't get a complete report from our contacts until sometime tomorrow morning. It doesn't make too much difference. What matters is that two of our people and Dr. Davis and his secretary are missing. The only answer is that the four were kidnaped. We must presume, for the time being, by the KGB. Only some of the KGB from the Soviet delegation at the UN could have pulled off such a grab. If anyone thinks differently, I'd like to hear from him right now."

"If it was the KGB, the agents who met your people at the gate must have had a perfect excuse for luring them away," theorized Jacob Hall, who was in charge of the New York City office of Naval Intelligence. Tall, stout, with hooded eyes and a full-faced short and curly beard, he leaned forward and peered accusingly at Grojean, as much as to say, *your men goofed!*

The imputative look in Hall's eyes was not missed by Grojean, who merely said, "Correct. In order to fool my two men the gimmick the KGB used had to be more than good. It had to be perfect. However, this speculation is a waste of time. It isn't helping us find Dr. Davis and his ALPHA ONE unit.

"The Ruskies could have them stashed anywhere," Roger Barnkoff said, his voice almost angry. "Let's face it, Grojean. The KGB outsmarted us on this one. We'll never find Dr. Davis and his secretary. Our two men are probably dead by now, or will be shortly."

Jacob Hall frowned in resentment. "Maybe that's how you CIA people view the situation. The ONI takes a different view. We're going to make every effort to find Dr. Davis and his device, although I personally am skeptical of the Alpha One Unit. It sounds like a lot of science fiction bullshit, but we're still going to follow it through, all the way."

"What makes you think we're not?" snapped Fred Thumm.

Courtland Grojean wrinkled his nose in displeasure and wished that the outspoken Barnkoff were in his department so that he could demote him. Yet he couldn't deny the logic of Barnkoff's reasoning. The specialist from the Office of Technical Development could very well be right! For twenty-six years Grojean had pitted his wits against the various intelligence services of the Communist world, particularly against the Main Enemy—the KGB, the world-wide espionage and sabotage apparatus of the Soviet Union. A coldblooded man who was almost as much at home with death as Camellion, Grojean was not one to indulge in false hope or wishful thinking. By now Dr. Davis was probably on his way out of the State of New York, on the first leg of a journey that would take him to Mother Russia.

Grojean looked at a man sitting on a metal folding chair to the right and slightly in back of Camellion. Wearing a red turtleneck sweater, the man was tall and muscular with a wide and long face and a great mane of crisp, frizzled, and very black hair, sprinkled with gray and rising from a lofty brow. At the age of 34, Merle Hamilton Duvane was the best CIA "street" operator in New York City. He was also something of an educated freak. Like his proper Boston father, Duvane had an M.B.A. degree[1] from Harvard University's business college but, hating business, preferred a career in the CIA. Much to the consternation of his father,

1. Master of Business Administration.

the vice president of a Wall Street brokerage firm and a member of the Association of MBA Executives[2].

"Duvane, have you heard any unusual rumors from your contacts in the United Nations?" Grojean said in a cultured tone. "Anything at all about the Soviets?"

"We can forget that route," Duvane said evenly. "There aren't any rumors. You know how the Ivans operate. We only get sniffs of what the KGB wants us to smell and almost always its disinformation."

Duvane got to his feet and started toward the refrigerator on the other side of the room, saying, "Why don't we backtrack? Maybe we'll get a clue in that manner."

"Such as?" asked Grojean.

Reaching the refrigerator, Duvane opened the door and took out a can of Diet-Rite Cola, then turned to face Courtland Grojean. "We've speculated all over the place as to how the KGB could have known about Dr. Davis and his gismo device. How did they know that Davis and his secretary and our two men were coming to New York? The KGB had to know days in advance in order to set up the kidnap deal." He pulled the metal tab from the top of the can. "We might also ask ourselves how the KGB targeted Higgdon at the airport?"

"See here, you're not suggesting there's a hole in the dike, are you?" Luke Drayer, another ONI agent, asked. "If you are, it's damned unlikely."

Duvane, walking back to the folding chair with the can of cola in his hand, didn't seem to notice the edge to Drayer's tone, or the way Drayer, Hall, and Wilbert Donovan, the latter the third ONI agent, were staring at him expectantly.

"I'm giving possibilities." Duvane sat down and crossed his legs. "The KGB doesn't have a crystal ball, and don't tell me they used ESP to learn about Davis and his gismo. You tell me how they found out without penetrating some sector within our sphere?"

"I think I know how they made me at Kennedy International," Camellion said candidly. "First of all, the KGB had to know that an individual was meeting Dr. Davis and the other three at Kennedy."

"But they didn't know what you looked like—the four

---

2. Located at 305 Madison Avenue, New York, N.Y. 10017

you were to meet as well, as the Russians—not even how you would be dressed!" thrust in Roger Barnkoff.

Grojean's even gaze fell on the Death Merchant. "No one but us and the four on Flight 64 knew you would be meeting Dr. Davis. Not even Doctor Pforzheimer of the foundation knew you were to meet the plane. No one but us was privy to that information."

Camellion folded his hands in front of him. "The KGB had to have been told by one of the four that I was supposed to meet them near the United Airlines ticket counter. The only other answer is that someone within the CIA or ONI is a traitor."

"That's damned nonsense!" Jacob Hall savagely bit off the end of a cigar. "You're being paranoid, Higgdon. None of us here would even dream of selling out to the damned commies."

Luke Drayer addressed himself to the Death Merchant. "Come to think of it, now that Higgdon is 'dead,' what are we supposed to call you?" He grinned like an imp. "I don't suppose you'd care to tell us your real name?"

Camellion smiled slightly, his eyes raking Drayer, who had curly dark brown sideburns, wore aviator-style glasses and had a reputation for both organization and rhetoric.

" 'Chester Giffwangle,' " Camellion said. "Call me Chet." He turned toward Courtland Grojean. "I won't be able to leave here until I have a complete identification packet. How soon can you arrange it?"

Grojean's attention turned to Roger Barnkoff, who was the Assistant Chief-of-Station of the main New York City Company station.

"Tomorrow afternoon," Barnkoff said quickly. "I'll radio S-1 before I leave here. A special messenger should have the package here no later than noon tomorrow. Chet, I'll have to take several photographs of you before I go, for the driver's license and one of those state ID cards that private companies print—OK?"

Nodding, Camellion got back to Hall. "Duvane's right. We have to consider all possibilities. No one in this room might be a Russian lover, but there must be a couple of hundred people, in both the CIA and ONI, who have information on *Operation Basilisk*. We can't close our eyes to the very real possibility that one of them sold us out for a price. It wouldn't be the first time that money became a stronger attraction than duty and honor and love of country." He shook a finger at Hall. "And you can't deny it."

"I'm not!" snapped Hall. "But nothing you have said explains how the KGB made you at Kennedy International. None of us could have contacted the KGB. We didn't even know what you looked like until you arrived here an hour ago; and when you left Grojean and Melbert at Kenny's steak house, you weren't wearing a beard and a trenchcoat, and you weren't carrying an attaché case either."

"I guess good old Chester Gerwangle didn't—"

" 'Giffwangle!' " corrected the Death Merchant.

"Whatever—but apparently you didn't trust Grojean and Melbert," finished Wilbert Donovan, who was slim, tanned, and still had a rather boyish figure. He always spoke in a high voice and always at a machine-gun rate of speed.

The Death Merchant reflected for a moment. "The KGB was able to target me by using simple deduction. One of the four on Flight 64 had to tell the KGB that I'd be waiting for them around the United Airlines ticket counter. I was there. I sat and waited. I looked around. I walked all over the main concourse. It wouldn't be difficult for trained agents to spot me. We know that they did. The bitch who followed me over to the Avis counter proves as much. She wanted to find out the model of the car I'd be using and where it would be parked. Once they had that information, it was child's play to set up the ambush."

Duvane scratched a bushy eyebrow. "Look, Wiggle Waggle or whatever you're calling yourself, none of that is going to help us find Davis and the other three. As I understand it, Davis is the only man who knows the full secret of the Alpha One device. "He stopped short and looked at Barnkoff. "Or do we have enough on the unit to proceed without him?"

Barnkoff shook his head. "We could build three-fourths of the device, but without Davis, we couldn't possibly complete the machine, much less make it work."

Barnkoff explained that while the Alpha One Unit was basically of the Hieronymous design, Dr. Davis had added a few modern refinements. In the Hieronymous machine, a metal coil or plate was used to detect the correct frequency setting, this accomplished by having the operator stroke the plate with his fingers; simultaneously, he turned the various capacitors and resistors with the other hand. He knew he had reached the correct frequency when he felt a sudden stickiness or drag. The trouble with the arrangement was that the frequency was difficult to detect, the length of time varying from one operator to another. In place of this stroker plate, Dr. Davis installed a Galvonic Skin Response device, which turned out to be immensely more sensitive to minute physiological changes and effects in the operator and thus resulted in a much more reliable and sensitive detector system. In addition, Dr. Davis provided prewired circuits from both the input and the output sections of the machine to phono plugs outside the casing.

"In its most basic explanation, psionics is a combination of psychic awareness of physiological stimulation and biophysical interaction with L-fields," explained Barnkoff. "And before any of you ask me what L-fields are, I'll tell you. The L-field is the field of life. It's the L-field that makes a fertilized egg of two human beings grow into another human being, or the egg of a frog into a frog. Before the existence of L-fields was established it was hard to understand why a particular group of neurons should be lodged in the gray matter of the cortex and not in the spinal cord; and why the branches of the neuron—the dendrites and axons—apparently move to their ultimate destinations without mistakes. Now we know that all this is ordered and controlled by the L-Fields."

"Hold it." Duvane held up a hand. "I asked if we needed Davis. I didn't want a lecture."

Barnkoff shrugged. "Have it your way."

The buzzer on the door sounded and a red light on a small control panel, by the radio transceivers, began flashing.

"That must be Stephen," Grojean said. "Let him in, Barnkoff. It's the button below the light."

Barnkoff swung around in the swivel chair and pressed the button. The electric lock in the door clicked. The red light went out and the low buzzing ceased. Stephen Melbert, Grojean's aide, opened the door and entered the attic room. A man with a broad massive chin, a pale face, and whispy white hair (although he was only in his middle forties), Melbert looked more like a college professor than a man who had spent his entire adult life in the dark twisting tunnels of international espionage.

Dropping down in an armchair, Melbert came right to

the point. The New York police had identified two of the gunmen the Death Merchant had killed—through fingerprints. One of the would-be assassins was Victor James Hedman, a small-time hood from Brooklyn. The second triggerman was Manlin "Manny" Rich, a gunsel who lived in Queens. Both men had rap sheets so long they could have been grocery lists for an army division—suspicion of assault, assault with a deadly weapon, breaking and entering, blackmail, and (Manny Rich only) hijacking. Hedman had served four years in Dannemora for a stickup. Rich was on parole from the Atlanta Federal pen—interstate transportation of a stolen vehicle.

"You're positive?" Grojean said to Melbert. "Rather, you're sure our contact with the NYPD was positive? She had better be, for the thousand dollars we paid her."

"She was." Melbert frowned as some of Hall's cigar smoke drifted across his nose. "Get this. The police are not going to release the news to the press that they'd identified two of the gunmen, not just yet. The Commissioner's secretary said that they're picking up all of Hedman's and Rich's friends and associates in an effort to get a lead on the other man and the woman. The last she heard, the police hadn't learned anything."

"Did she give any information about scars and other marks on the bodies?" inquired Camellion.

"I asked her. There weren't any," Melbert said. "Why are scars so important?"

"Russian doctors cut into a body differently from doctors in the West."

"I'm beginning to wonder if any of them were Russians," Duvane said thoughtfully, digging into an ear with a forefinger. "On the other hand, it's not even conceivable that two dirt-bags like Hedman and Rich were anything but shooters. That still leaves the third man and the woman, and if the New York cops can't paste an ID on them, we won't be able to either."

"No matter which direction we take," commented Drayer drearily, "we're up against a stone wall."

The Death Merchant leaned back in the rocker, folded his arms, tilted back his head and studied the cream-colored ceiling.

"The items that were in the pockets of the four at the airport," he said. "How difficult would it be to obtain them from whatever police property room they're in?"

Grojean's voice was noncommital. "Why? I think if the police couldn't find anything important among the effects, we'd be wasting our time if we tried."

"See here, Giffwangle. We already know that the identification carried by the four was totally false!" pointed out Jacob Hall, pulling at his short beard.

The Death Merchant lowered his head, leaned forward and peered intensely at Courtland Grojean. "We don't have a single clue where Dr. Davis is. The items might give us a lead. We might find something the New York police overlooked." His voice became frigid. "It's a chance. What else do we have?"

Grojean hesitated a second or two. "It will take three or four days, and at the price it will cost the taxpayers, you had better come up with something."

"Make it two days," Camellion said. "We're not even crawling. The Russians are racing."

Four days and $65,000 later, a special messenger from the New York main CIA station came to the Chapel of Prayer Funeral Home. The woman carried a large blue tote bag which held everything that had been in the pockets and handbag of the men and the woman the Death Merchant had killed.

There had been some developments during those four days. The newspapers reported that two of the gunmen killed at Kennedy Airport had been identified as minor New York hoods. The police also admitted to the press that they had questioned scores of people who had associated with Hedman and Rich. None of the persons questioned had been able to give them a lead. What the police did not reveal to the press was that one Arnold Quincy, Manny Rich's best friend, had disappeared. The police were quietly tearing the city apart in an effort to locate Quincy, who, like Rich, was so crooked he had to put on his clothes with a corkscrew.

Camellion opened the large brown envelopes that had belonged to the unidentified man and the mystery woman and dumped the contents on an aluminum folding table. A wallet, a billfold, both containing forged identification; cigarettes, a cheap lighter; the usual junk that a woman carries: lipstick, tissues; a penlight; a brass-colored stamp keeper paperweight in the woman's envelope; a fingernail file; a white linen handkerchief; some loose change. The woman had carried $650 in American money in her purse, the man $537; some loose change. Absolutely nothing in writing.

Leaning over the table, Duvane said, "It's odd that there isn't a single key among the effects."

"No," Camellion said, opening the large brown envelope marked, Hedman, Victor. 78349. "Keys would lead to locks, specific types of locks. Those locks could point to the Soviet Union.

He dumped the contents of the envelope on the table. More junk. But nothing of value. While Duvane slit the billfolds of the unidentified man and woman and the other men watched, the Death Merchant used a razor to cut apart Hedman's billfold. Result on all three billfolds? Zero.

Courtland Grojean (who wouldn't think of leaning over the table and wrinkling his coat) watched expectantly, a severe expression on his face. He had authorized a $65,000 cash payment to the two police officers who had stolen the items from the property room—and by God! Camellion had better find a clue.

"It's a waste of time," mumbled Jacob Hall. "It's pretty damned obvious to me that the cops went through everything."

"Patience. Dissatisfaction is the basis for all progress," the Death Merchant said and poured the contents of Manlin "Manny" Rich's envelope on the table. There was a billfold, a pocket comb, cigarettes, lighter, a box of aspirin, a stick of chewing gum, a ring of keys and a ticket stub to a porno movie house off 42nd Street. All the identification in the dead gunsel's well worn billfold was false. Rich had lived in Queens; yet on the ID card his address was listed as 4161 Eagle Street, Utica, New York.

Carefully, taking his time, Camellion began searching the pockets and the various compartments of the billfold. Empty.

"A sheer waste of precious time," Hall muttered.

"Hall—shut UP!" Grojean said imperiously, his eyes on the Death Merchant, who, using a single-edge razor blade was cutting off the inner flap that covered the "secret" money compartment of the billfold. The compartment itself was empty. He had cut off the flap at a point where it had been sewn into the top edge of the back of the billfold. Now he looked at the billfold. It didn't feel right; the back was just a wee bit too thick. On close inspection, the Death Merchant saw why. The back piece of leather had been carefully slit and the edges glued together, some of the glue having been pressed out between the two sections, having hardened on the top edge.

"You've found something?" inquired Luke Drayer.

Slowly and with extreme care, Camellion took the razor blade and reopened the back of the billfold. Inside the two sections were two one-hundred-dollar bills and a slip of light blue paper. Camellion opened the slip of paper. It was a receipt from the Jefferson Animal Hospital in Queens for $425.00, the cost of an ear operation on and the care of a German shepherd named "Thor." The receipt was made out to Manlin Rich and listed his Olive Street address in Queens.

Camellion gave the receipt to Grojean, who looked at it and started it on its inspection route among the men.

"That's a lot of money to pay to get a dog operated on," commented Roger Barnkoff.

"A better question would be why Rich had the receipt sealed in the wallet," Grojean said thoughtfully, stroking his pointy chin. "It's reasonable to assume that Rich wanted the receipt in a safe place or he wouldn't have sealed it in the back of the billfold."

"The receipt represents the dog," Camellion remarked, a slight smile on his face. "The animal is very important to him, or rather, was. Nothing is important to Rich now. He must have really loved the dog, so much so that he wanted the receipt with him for psychological comfort. The two C-notes were 'escape' money within the city, in case something went wrong."

"But that receipt is not going to give us a lead to Dr. Davis," Will Donovan said slowly.

"We don't know that. Not yet," Camellion said. "We haven't followed through on the lead yet." He looked at his wristwatch. "It's only one-twenty-seven. We have plenty of time."

"To do what?" One hand in his coat pocket, Grojean stepped closer to the Death Merchant. "At this stage of the game, we can't afford to take unnecessary chances."

"We can't afford to play it totally safe either," Camellion said. I'm going to have a talk with the vet at the animal hospital. Duvane, Donovan. I want you two to go with me. . . ."

Chapter Three

The Jefferson Animal Hospital on Roosevelt Avenue, in the Jackson Heights section of Queens, was one of those pet places that catered to the general public, as long as the owner of a pet had the cash. As the signs in the three waiting rooms (one for cats, one for dogs, one for birds, ducks, etc.) clearly stated in big red letters—POSITIVELY NO CREDIT.

Richard Camellion and Merle Duvane got out of the Caprice Diesel Wagon and started up the concrete sidewalk to the entrance of the animal hospital, confident that no one would recognize them—even if any person had known them. The Death Merchant had used his talents in the makeup department to completely disguise himself, Duvane, and Fred Thumm. Thumm was replacing Donovan who, with Jacob Hall, had to return to New York City on ONI business.

The Death Merchant had used flesh-colored sensolexisene facial masks and, in conjunction with plastic putty, liners, and various colored "flesh pencils" and other material from his makeup trunk had transformed himself, Duvane, and Thumm into persons that in no way resembled him and the two other men.

With wavy blond hair, a blond mustache, and a broad chin, "Sergeant Hance" walked with a slight limp. Appearing to be about fifty, Hance had a broad nose and a large mouth. A mole was on his left cheek. By like token, "First Grade Detective Walter Simds," no longer resembled Merle Hamilton Duvane. Camellion had had trouble with Duvane's enormous mane of hair, a head of hair so thick that fitting a hairpiece over it had been impossible. Cut it off? Camellion might as well have asked the Company man to slice off his penis! Camellion had done the only thing he could do under the circumstance. "Wear a hat and keep it on," he had ordered the cold-eyed CIA man. It had not been difficult, however, to change the shape of Duvane's face. Thumm's face had been even easier,

Camellion and Duvane came to a wooden sign set in the small yard—JEFFERSON ANIMAL HOSPITAL. DR. LEROY J. JEFFERSON, DVM. WE TREAT YOUR PETS WITH LOVING CARE.

The Death Merchant chose the door marked Dogs, opened it and walked into the waiting room that was filled with people and their pets of all breeds, sizes, and colors. Camellion went right up to the counter in the opening of the wall to his right. Beyond the opening was the desk of the receptionist and the bookkeeper's office.

The Death Merchant did not smile. "Is Dr. Jefferson in?" Camellion asked the receptionist. "It's important that we see him immediately."

The middle-aged women with three chins looked up and let him have an icy who-do-you-think-you-are look. "Sir," the receptionist said frostily, emphasizing the sir. "A lot of people and their pets are waiting to see Dr. Jefferson. I suggest you take a number card from the wall and await your turn like everyone else."

"Look, sister! We're here on police business," Camellion said harshly. He pulled a badge case from his topcoat pocket, flipped it open and thrust out the blue and gold badge in front of the startled woman's face. Blinking, her lower jaw fell and she stared at the badge, the words NEW YORK CITY POLICE DEPARTMENT, HOMICIDE DIVISION, jumping out at her.

"We want to see Dr. Jefferson about a dog he treated," Camellion intoned gravely and pulled back the badge. He and Duvane stared hard and demandingly at the woman.

"I'll call the doctor," the woman said nervously, picking up the telephone receiver.

A few minutes later, Camellion and Duvane were in Dr. Jefferson's office, a small room at the end of the hall's examining cubbyholes. In less than half a minute, Dr. Jefferson, looking worried, hurried into the office from a rear door, the bottom of his green smock flapping around his legs. A nervous little man with an enormous half-bald head and a squint to his gray eyes, he tried to affect a pleasant smile.

"I'm Dr. Jefferson. How can I help you gentlemen?"

After introducing himself and "Detective Simds" and showing his badge (genuine . . . but "borrowed" from the NYPD), Camellion said, "Doctor, we're investigating the deaths of the three men and the woman who were shot at Kennedy Airport yesterday afternoon. I'm sure you read about it in the papers or saw it on the news on TV."

"Yes, yes, it was terrible." Dr. Jefferson began squeezing the fingers of his left hand. "It simply isn't safe to be on the streets nowadays."

Camellion pulled the receipt from his pocket and handed it to Jefferson. "This is your hospital's receipt. As you can see, it's made out to Manlin Rich, one of the men who was killed at the airport. It's dated day before yesterday. I presume the signature is one of the women out front?"

Dr. Jefferson looked at the receipt, handed it back to the Death Merchant and nodded. "Yes." He swallowed nervously, then cleared his throat. "Myrna is my receptionist. She's the one you spoke to."

"About Mr. Rich and his dog, Thor," urged Duvane, giving the vet his best cold-fish stare. "Tell us about Rich."

"He had an appointment Wednesday afternoon, with his dog Thor. Thor's a two-year-old German shepherd, a very handsome animal, full bred. The animal had a cyst in his right ear. We removed it. In fact, the dog is still here. He's healing nicely. I don't know what else I can tell you."

"Was that the first time Mr. Rich brought Thor to you for treatment?" Camellion said, licking his lower lip.

"What can you tell us about Rich?" demanded Duvane.

"Oh, no," Dr. Jefferson said. "Mr. Rich has been bringing Thor here regularly ever since he got the dog. He's brought him here for checkups and for his rabies and distemper shots." Dr. Jefferson began squeezing the fingers of his right hand. "Actually I don't know anything about Mr. Rich. I don't mind telling you I was surprised when I read in the papers that he was an exconvict and made his living in a questionable manner. All I can tell you is that he brought his dog to me now and then, but he never talked about himself, only about his dog. He really loved that animal." He paused and looked for a long moment at Camellion. "Come to think of it, Sergeant Hance, there was something odd about his last visit, the day before yesterday."

"In what way?"

"Well, sir, the removal of the cyst was a simple operation. The cost was only one hundred and twenty-five dollars."

"The receipt was for four hundred and twenty-five dollars," Duvane said harshly.

"Yes, it was," Dr. Jefferson promptly admitted. "You see, that's what's so strange about Mr. Rich's last visit. Mr. Rich gave me three hundred dollars to drive Thor to Yonkers after the dog recovered."

"Yonkers?" Camellion's eyebrows rose.

Duvane's face became one big question mark.

"Yes, sir—Yonkers. I told Mr. Rich that I didn't operate an animal delivery service, but he pleaded with me. He said his sister in California was dying of cancer and that he was leaving that very night for Los Angeles. He said he might be in California for as long as a month. I felt sorry for the man. I knew how he loved his dog; and when he practically made me take three hundred dollars, well, I agreed to deliver Thor to the address in Yonkers. Yonkers is only twenty miles from here, and three hundred would more than pay for my time and gas."

Duvane made a loud noise with his lips. "California, hell! The next day Rich was out at Kennedy Airport trying to kill some terrorist. But the terrorist killed him."

The Death Merchant looked at the vet with narrowed eyes. "Did he tell you why he didn't want the dog delivered to his apartment in Queens? You do know his home address was in Queens, Doctor?"

"Of course. He said he was closing his apartment. He said that while he was in California, a friend of his in Yonkers would look after Thor. At the time, the day before yesterday, I didn't think anything about it. But in view of what the papers have said, I now think it's very unusual, which is why I mentioned it."

Camellion said, "Doctor, give us that address in Yonkers—and, Doctor, we don't want you to mention what you have told us to anyone. Understand?"

Dr. Jefferson's eyes widened and he nodded. "Of course. I understand. I'll have Thor's file brought in. The address in Yonker's is in the file. Excuse me." He went to his desk and picked up the telephone.

Since it was too late in the afternoon to set up an operation to investigate Clyde Hayden, Apt. 306, 1481 Tenth

Avenue, Yonkers, the Death Merchant and Duvane, with Fred Thumm behind them in a repainted laundry van marked Steel's Janitorial Service, had no choice but to return to the Chapel of Prayer in Mt. Vernon and make detailed plans for the next morning.

All of the men were on edge, burdened down with tension, for they knew that with every second, Dr. Davis was getting farther and farther away from them, and closer to the Soviet Union.

Stretched out on a black contoured chaise, his hands behind his head, the Death Merchant directed his words at Courtland Grojean, "I could go to Yonkers tonight, by myself, and investigate Hayden.

Actually, Camellion had no such intention. Doing the job alone in uncharted territory, especially at night in a crowded city, would be too risky. The odds would be against him. Late at night he could be stopped by the police, who just might become suspicious and hold him for investigation.

"Oh, no, you're not!" Grojean said firmly, sitting up straight. "We're not going to take any unnecessary chances. I'll tell you something else you're not going to do. You're not going to kidnap any Soviet diplomat at the UN. That's final. So if you're thinking about it, forget it."

"I trust you didn't forget the uniform I requested?" Camellion said.

"It will be here in time for tomorrow," Grojean said mechanically.

Roger Barnkoff began wiping his eyeglasses. "I don't think you're going to find anything on Tenth Avenue that will help us," he said, glancing at the Death Merchant. "So Hayden is a friend of Rich's. So what? He won't know where the Ruskies have stashed Dr. Davis. Even Rich wouldn't have that information, if he were alive. He and Hedman were only triggers."

"You could be right," Camellion said, "but we can't pass up any leads. We have to follow the Yonkers thing through."

"When you get right down to it, I wonder if Dr. Davis is all that important," mused Fred Thumm from across the room where he was making a cup of tea. A man who loved weapons, he wore two Smith & Wesson .357 mag Highway Patrolman revolvers in shoulder holsters. "I mean the concept is something right out of fantasy-land, the idea that a

33

human being can function as a biological transducer and become a brain-body device that will change one form of energy into another."

"Not necessarily," Camellion replied. "The most paranormal thing of all is that I know that I am I, that I can observe *myself*, that I can speculate who I might really be in relation to the universe. When you think seriously about the entire situation of psionics, the only paranormal thing left to understand is the human mind. . . ."

Chapter Four

Like people, neighborhoods change. While Tenth Avenue was not exactly a slum area, the neighborhood was not of the type where one found the best people. At one time, most of Tenth Area had been upper-middle-class, but over the years, starting with World War II, the neighborhood had undergone a social metamorphosis. Minority groups had moved into the area. Businesses had closed, some for good. Others had moved north or to the suburbs. By 1981 most of the sixteen blocks of Tenth Avenue had degenerated into a hodgepodge of cheap businesses; pawnshops, second-hand furniture, appliance and clothing stores, bars, used car lots, greasy spoons, fifth-rate hotels and apartment houses whose owners never saw them and never made repairs.

Wearing the same face, the same disguise, he had worn at Doctor Jefferson's animal hospital, the Death Merchant parked the Monaco in front of a radio and TV repair shop at 1483 Tenth Avenue. A 1978 model, the Dodge needed a paint job and looked as if it were only weeks away from the junkyard. It wasn't. The car was a special operations vehicle with a souped up engine. This type of dilapidated vehicle had been chosen because "newness" in anything would be quickly noticed on Tenth Avenue.

The Death Merchant glanced around. Traffic was normal on Tenth Avenue. At 9:37 in the morning, any people going to work had long since passed, and the people on the streets were not lingering. The temperature had dropped, during the night to almost forty degrees and the sky was heavily overcast. Winter would come early.

Camellion picked up the Repco TEX-10 transceiver from the seat, pulled up the antenna, switched on the walkie-talkie, and called to Merle Duvane and Fred Thumm. By now Duvane should be parking the Chevy step-van—another special operations vehicle—in back of The Ark, the apartment house at 1481 Tenth Avenue. Thumm should be a block away, on Bussard Street, in the Steel's Janitorial Service van.

"Blue Turtle, Red Rose, come in." Camellion spoke into the W-T. "I'm parked and ready to go in. Over."

"This is Blue Turtle." Duvane's low voice floated out of the transceiver. "I've just parked. It won't take me more than five minutes to walk through the alley to Tenth. Over."

"I'm several hundred feet from the mouth of the alley," Camellion said. When I see you come out of the alley, I'll start for The Ark. Acknowledge. Over."

"I got it—out."

Thumm's voice jumped out of the walkie-talkie. "Red Rose here. I'm in position. But it won't be wise for me to stay here over fifteen minutes. This is a main street and the cops might start wondering why I'm parked here."

"Keep your channel open and wait for instructions. Out," the Death Merchant said. He shut off the transceiver, pushed down the antenna and shoved the set into a case on the belt buckled around his brown coveralls, across the back of which, in raised cloth letters, was GOODMAN & SON. EXTERMINATORS.

Camellion went about checking his "exterminating" equipment. On his belt, on the left side, was a long leather pouch, the outside of the pouch was filled with four loops that contained a nozzle each. The nozzles would fit the end of the brass spray tube attached to the hose of a three-gallon capacity tank on the floor in front of the seat. The plastic tank did not contain poison for bedbugs and cockroaches. It did contain two 9mm Wildley auto pistols, each with a silencer attached. The pouch on the Death Merchant's left hip contained a silenced .45 "Thomas" DA autoloader and a remote control detonator that could set off the one pound block of Composition-4 explosive.

The Death Merchant adjusted his dark glasses and the brown peaked uniform cap on his head; then he saw Duvane step from the mouth of the alley that stretched east and west and slowly start to walk south toward The Arms. Camellion picked up the plastic tank and its hose and spray tube, got out of the car and began walking briskly toward the double-doors entrance of the seedy apartment house. As he pushed through one of the doors, he saw that Duvane was slightly over one hundred feet away but was quickening his pace.

The lobby smelled of age and dirt, of frustration and bitter despair. The white and blacked checked tile floor had not been cleaned in months. Just inside the lobby to the left, were the mailboxes with buttons that controlled the intercommunications system to the apartments—but they no longer worked. A large rubber plant was at each end of the long, narrow lobby. Toward the rear of the lobby, to the right, were four self-service elevators.

Camellion stopped by the mailboxes. More than half the names were missing. It didn't matter. Thor's file had supplied "Clyde Hayden's" apartment number—number 306. *All I have to do is go upstairs and see for myself."*

He was halfway down the length of the lobby when the doors of one of the elevators slid open and gave him the first surprise of the morning. Out stepped "Clyde Hayden" and four other men. Two of the men were on either side of him, holding him by his arms that were handcuffed behind his back. The last two men were behind Hayden, whom the Death Merchant recognized as Arnold Quincy, the best friend of the dead Manny Rich. The newspapers had not printed Quincy's picture, but Stephen Melbert had obtained a photograph of Quincy from his contact in the NYPD and had brought it to the safe house.

The Death Merchant felt a surge of disappointment. He had been too late. The police had located Quincy and had grabbed him. Or had they? Carrying the tank and its hose in his left hand, Camellion continued up the length of the lobby, in the direction of Quincy and his four captives. Thin-faced, half-bald and in his forties, Quincy looked terrified—*too frightened! Police do not inspire that kind of fear in professional criminals and Quincy's been in trouble since he was fourteen.*

During those five seconds, as the Death Merchant drew closer to the group, he could see that the four men were simply not police officer types. For one thing, they were dressed too expensively to be flatfeet. For another, their topcoats were of European cut. For a third, Camellion always listened to intuition when it was coming through loud and clear. He was far too experienced not to sense KGB trash when he bumped into it. *These four slobs aren't cops any more than a jackass is a camel!* It wouldn't have made all that much difference to Camellion; he would still have taken Quincy from the four.

He walked right past the men, not even bothering to glance in their direction, nor did they glance toward him. He was only several steps past the two KGB agents when he spun around; at the same time, Merle Duvane swung through the front doors into the lobby. With such speed did the Death Merchant attack that Pytor Blintov and Josef Fendezsko, the two KGB agents in back of Clyde Hayden, never had a chance to defend themselves. Camellion slammed a left-handed *Seiken* fist blow to the back of Blintov's neck, feeling a few of the Russian's top cervical vertebrae crack under the sledge-hammerlike slam.

With a choked cry of pain and surprise, Blintov sagged. He was not a fifth of the way to the black and white checked tile when Camellion chopped Josef Fendezsko across the right side of his beefy neck with a right handed *Shuto* sword-ridge hand, the edge of the "sword" digging deeply into the Russian's pillarlike neck, such as there was of it. So stocky was Fendezsko that his head seemed to rest squarely on his shoulders. Nonetheless, he did have a neck and Camellion's lightning chop slashed into the flesh, the blinding pain staggering Fendezsko, but not cutting off the flow of consciousness. His knees bent on their bony hinges but he did not go down. Instead, with a hoarse bellow of mingled rage and shock, he attempted to turn around. He didn't get far. The Death Merchant smashed him in the neck with a powerful *Seiken* fist. This time, Fendezsko wilted faster than a fragile flower in a desert sun. The lights went out of his brain, and he began to tumble end-over-end down a long corridor into blackness.

Only nine seconds had drifted into the past, but it had been sufficient time for the gasps of Blintov and Fendezsko to alert the handcuffed Clyde Hayden and Nicholas

Mazanadze and Antonin Yudin, the two KGB officers holding the terrified Hayden by the elbows.

A short stream of Russian oaths jumped from Mazanadze's mouth and, reacting instantly, he reared up on the balls of his feet and swung a right-handed SAMBO[1] angular-knuckle blow at the Death Merchant's nose and upper lip. The shorter but larger Antonin Yudin was even faster. Moving closer, Yudin used a left-legged short *Chibbi*[2] kick, directed at Camellion's groin and a left handed *Zovtysky*[3] chop aimed at Camellion's right temple.

A near-hit was the same as a ten-mile miss, and both Russians missed. The Death Merchant ducked his head and jerked it back, the quick movement wrecking Mazanadze's right-arm blow and also causing Antonin Yudin's Zovtysky chop to slice only open air. All in the same motion, the Death Merchant brought up his right leg in a *Marki Gok* block that made Yudin's *Chibbi* kick ineffective.

The two Russians instantly recovered from their surprise and geared themselves for another attack while "Clyde Hayden"/Arnold Quincy made his bid for freedom. He ran to the front of the lobby, intending to push through the double doors and get to Tenth Avenue. He was stopped by a grim-faced Duvane, who practically shoved a silenced Smith & Wesson M-39 auto pistol in his face and snarled, "On the floor, you bastard. Flat on your face. Breathe hard and I'll blow your head off!"

Then . . . no sooner was a trembling Quincy was on his knees, than the lobby doors opened and a young couple in their twenties came in from the street; the man unshaven, a cigarette dangling from his mouth, the woman dressed in showy clothes, smelling of cheap perfume and wearing too much makeup. The cigarette fell from the man's mouth, and the woman, with an expression of shock on her heavily rouged face, raised her hands to her mouth.

"On the floor with Junior, you two," commanded Duvane in his best warning snarl. "Eat the tile and don't move! Don't even wiggle your toes."

Nicholas Mazanadze and Antonin Yudin again came at

---

1. The Russian version of karate. Sambo is a combination of *Tae Kwon Do Hyung, Shito-Ryu* karate, and *Goju-Ryu* karate.
2. The same as a short spin kick.
3. The same as a *Shuto* chop.

the Death Merchant, both moving extremely fast but still too slow to be effective, Mazanadze trying for a left *Zovtysky* chop and a right four-finger *Bozkachurne* stab,[4] Yudin attempting a left-handed Sambo *Kimchuva*[5] as he pulled a .38 Colt "Cobra" revolver from the right pocket of his topcoat.

Camellion twisted, ducked, and retaliated against Mazanadze with a left-legged *Uchi Mawashi Geri* inside roundhouse kick, the bottom of his foot burying itself in the Russian's stomach. Mazanadze had walked right into the grand slam that ruptured his stomach and crushed the main arteries and veins as flat as tissue paper. Instantly, shock sent the pig farmer into unconsciousness, and, dying, he started to fold while Camellion's left hand streaked out and his fingers closed around Yudin's right wrist. Coetaneously, his right hand shot out in a try for a *Yubi Basami* knuckle/fingertip strike against Yudin's throat. But he missed; the Russian jerked to one side. The Russian grabbed Camellion's right wrist with his left hand and, breathing heavily, went for a *Chiv-i-ko* foot strike.[6] aimed at the Death Merchant's pubic region—and missed when Camellion arched back his hips and twisted to the left. Before Yudin could recover his total balance, Camellion attacked, striking the Russian's right leg with a right-footed *Soku*-To edge-of-the-foot blow, the trip-hammer force making the KGB agent stumble sideways to the left. Yudin did not have time to collect his thoughts and regroup his reflexes. Camellion let him have an old-fashioned knee-lift that connected solidly with the pig farmer's testicles. Yudin might as well have been struck by a thunderbolt Agony exploded in the lower part of the Russian's body, switched off his strength and made him as helpless as a baby in the grip of a Goliath. Camellion jerked his right arm free of Yudin's grasp and, hearing one of the elevators descend to the lobby, slammed the Russian with a fast *Seiken* forefist—once, twice, three times. The first caught Yudin under the left lower jaw; the second on the left upper jaw, the third just above the bridge of the nose. The unconscious

---

4. The same as a *Yon Hon Nukite* four-finger spear stab.
5. The same as a reverse knife hand *Yok Sudo*.
6. The same as a *Tae Kwon Do Chungdan Ap Chagi* middle-front-snap kick.

KGB agent started to go down; just as quickly, the Death Merchant grabbed the Colt Cobra from his right hand.

The out-cold Russian hit the floor and lay still. One of the elevators stopped; the doors slid open. A man stepped out, stopped short, and did a double take when he saw what was going on in the lobby. He was an elderly man in his sixties, skinny and bent, whose clothes looked as if they had been around since 1 A.D.—and so did he!

Without a change of expression, Merle Duvane raised his S&W auto pistol and fired. A *ppyyytttt* sound came from the silencer and the elderly man gave a short cry and fell back; a 9 X 19 parabellum slug in his chest.

Duvane sighed—never leave witnesses! Just as calmly, he swung the pistol to the man and the woman on the floor, lowered the muzzle and pulled the trigger twice. Two more *ppyyytttsss* from the silencer, the 9mm hollow-point projectiles tearing into the backs of the man and the woman and making them jump before they relaxed in death.

Arnold Quincy began to tremble uncontrollably. "Oh, G-God! Don't s-shoot!" he whined. "Please don't shoot!"

"I can't!" admitted Duvane. "We need you alive, crumb. You're going with us. On your feet."

By then, the Death Merchant had pulled the silenced .45 DA auto-loader from the pouch on his belt and had moved to the front of the lobby. Arnold Quincy was getting to his feet and Camellion grabbed him by the shoulder.

"Turn around and hold out yours arms as far as possible. I'm going to free you from the handcuffs."

Quick to comply, Quincy turned his back to Camellion. He extended his arms and Camellion placed the muzzle of the silencer against the middle link and squeezed the trigger of the DA pistol. A loud whisper! The cuffs parted. A .45 slug buried itself in the tile.

"Listen you guys," began Quincy in a shivery voice. "I—"

"Shut up." Camellion jerked the man around and pointed to the unconscious Antonin Yudin with the DA pistol. "Pick him up and carry him on your shoulder. We're going out through the rear fire door. . . ."

"But, he's—"

"He had better not be too heavy," Camellion growled. "You either carry him or stay here—with a bullet in your head. Take your choice." As an afterthought, just to be on the safe side, he asked, "You were listed in this fleabag as 'Clyde Hayden,' in 306, weren't you?"

"Y-Yes. . . ."

"Good enough. Pick him up and be damned quick about it. Move!"

Quincy scampered toward the rear of the grimy lobby and, with Camellion watching him and the door to the rear room, while Duvane eyed the lobby doors, began tugging at the unconscious Antonin Yudin. He jerked in fright as Camellion triggered the .45 and put a bullet into the heads of the three other Russians on the floor. The three almost totally silent shots were just the tonic Quincy needed. Without too much effort this time, he picked up Yudin in a dead-man-carry. Breathing heavily under the 200 deadweight load, he staggered to the walnut colored door at the end of the lobby, almost stumbling and falling over the corpse of the old man.

"Are you sure there is a fire door?" Duvane asked Camellion, all the while backing toward the rear, his eyes watching the front doors of the lobby.

"There has to be," Camellion said. "The City of Yonkers housing code states that all hotels, apartment houses, any public building, must have a fire door in the rear."

Camellion came to the door and tried the knob. The door was locked. The Death Merchant moved back five feet, raised the .45 DA pistol and began firing, the silencer hissing. There were six loud rings as the flat-point projectiles tore through the brass housings of the two deadbolt locks, the last bullet opening the steel door a few inches. Camellion shoved the door the rest of the way open with his foot, stepped inside and looked around. The room was a storage area for trucks and other belongings that deadbeat tenants had left in The Ark.

The Death Merchant motioned with the .45. "Let's go, Quincy. Your life's hanging on a thread and your soul's three-fourths of the way to hell already."

Almost panting under the burden of Antonin Yudin but spurred on by the fear of death, Quincy moved through the doorway into the storage room. Merle Duvane was right behind him and was about to close the door when the double doors of the lobby opened and two woman and a man, talking and laughing, walked in. All three stopped abruptly at the sight of the six corpses spread out on the lobby floor.

41

One of the women screamed. Duvane cursed and fired. Three spits from the silencer and the Cosmic Lord of Death gathered the three into his body arms. Nice, neat kills. There was only one flaw: The 9mm projectile that hit the dumpy blonde in the stomach first chewed up her gut, then knocked her back against one of the thick glass doors. Momentum and her weight did the rest—pushed open the door. Out she went, falling on the sidewalk, her legs preventing the door from closing.

"Well, you can't win them all!" Duvane muttered to himself in disgust. He then said to the Death Merchant, who had moved ahead of the weighted-down Quincy to the ordinary fire door in the back wall of the room, "The woman fell on the sidewalk. The cops are sure to be here now."

The Death Merchant put down the plastic tank and its hose and spray rod. "Sure, but they'll take their sweet time," Camellion said, pulling a fresh magazine for the "Thomas" DA pistol from his pocket. "They couldn't care less about the down-and-outers in this section of town. It's unfortunate though that we had to whack out innocent bystanders."

Duvane made a face but did not respond with any countering comments. He watched Camellion move from the door to the barred grimy window, to the right of the fire door, and looked out.

"You won't be able to see the van from here," Duvane said. "I parked it in front of the left-side garage. Anyone out there?"

"No one except a wino. He's either passed out or dead," Camellion said. "Don't kill him unless he wakes up."

The Death Merchant then jammed the DA .45 into his belt and pushed down hard on the horizontal bar of the fire door. The door did not open. He tried again, much harder this time. The hollow metal door creaked open. The stink of garbage drifted in through the door. Camellion picked up the plastic tank and its hose, pulled the DA pistol from his belt and shoved it into the pouch dangling on his hip. Moving through the doorway, he said to Duvane, "Keep that Smith and Wesson under your topcoat. No telling whom we might meet in the alley. If we do meet someone and he sees a weapon, he'll know right away we're up to no good."

Poking at Quincy with the muzzle of the silencer, Duvane chuckled.

"I don't guess we are up to any good from a moral point of view. Of course, morals are anything one wishes to make them." He shoved Quincy once more before hiding the pistol under the front of his coat. "Move it, stupid. You're not all that important to us."

With sweat pouring down his face, Arnie Quincy staggered out the door, only five feet behind the Death Merchant. Duvane stepped outside and pulled the fire door shut behind him.

In spite of Quincy's having to carry the KGB agent, it took only a minute for the three of them to move down the broken concrete sidewalk and get within ten feet of the alley. Camellion moved to the corner of the garage to the left, looked out and saw the Chevy step-van. He also saw the four black dudes—big men in their twenties, all muscle, all larceny, all trash. They had jacked up the right rear wheel and were about to remove it from the axle, three of them looking up and down the alley while the fourth man pulled a lug wrench from underneath his bulky blue leather coat.

Pulling the DA pistol with his right hand, Camellion put his hands behind his back, stepped out from the corner of the garage, smiled at the four surprised black men and said, "You, with the wrench. Put it down and place the hubcap where you found it. The rest of you remove the jack—now!"

The man who had just pulled the wrench from underneath his coat—he had a green scarf wrapped tightly like a turban around his fuzzy head and an earring in his right ear—looked at the Death Merchant in astonishment. He didn't drop the wrench, but he didn't apply it to the first nut on the wheel either. The three other toughs, all decked out like the main attractions in a freak show, grinned at the Death Merchant, then at Quincy carrying the Russian; finally at Duvane who had his hand underneath his coat. Seeing that Camellion was holding the .45 "Thomas" DA behind his back, Duvane knew that the Death Merchant was toying with the four pieces of gutter trash.

Only twelve feet from Camellion, the closest man grinned, showing big teeth as he put his right hand in the slit pocket of his coat. Camellion could read his mind, his every evil thought, from the sly expression on the joker's broad face. *He's thinking that here are three stupid honkies who've been up to something illegal inside The Ark. Three of us and four of them. Why steal only the wheels and tires when they can ace us out, get the keys and steal the whole damn van. Tch! Tch! Tch! The poor halfwit no doubt has a switchblade or a piece of pipe in his back pocket. Ah . . . sic transit gloria mundi. . . .*

"Like you know, man, you done walked out at the wrong time!" the man closest to Camellion said in a voice that was one big sneer. His eyes went to Quincy with his burden of a body. "Whatchall carryin' him fo? Huh, man?"

"We all should call the pigs on dese dudes," laughed one of the other men, the one with the orange hat with a wide brim. "Bet they done kidnap that por man they is carryin'?"

He and the other two men kept moving closer, very slowly, toward Camellion, the moron with the lug wrench holding it the way one would grasp the handle of a hammer.

The big black closest to Camellion dropped all pretense. He pulled a switchblade from his pocket, button-opened the sharp blade and, snarling, "Get the mutherfukkers!" came at Camellion.

He didn't get far, only a few steps. Calmly, the Death Merchant brought up the .45 DA from behind his back and pulled the trigger when the scum-tough was only five feet away. The big bullet hit the useless mistake of humanity in the right center of his chest and brought his charge to an abrupt halt. His eyes were as round as full moons, and his mouth was open and slack as Camellion put a bullet into the stomach of the goon with the lug wrench. Duvane jerked out his Smith & Weston autoloader and shot the third thug twice in the chest. The fourth punk knew he was face to face with his own execution. A man with pride would have sneered and said, *Shoot, you son of a bitch!* But Willie Joe Brown didn't have any self-respect. What he did have was an enormous fear of death!

Sweating more than a Black Muslim who had been caught spying at a KKK rally, Brown stopped, threw up his arms and tried to twist his gorillalike face into a friendly grin.

"Now brothers, we was jus' kiddin'," he whined. "You know, kiddin'. Ain't no need to put me away, you know."

"Sure. I'm kidding too," the Death Merchant said and shot Brown in the stomach and in the chest, the big 240 grain Hornady .45 slugs knocking him off his feet. With one short moan, he fell against the doors of the garage, then lay still.

"What did you say about innocent bystanders?" chided Duvane, who, moving to the side of the van, was taking a ring of keys out of his pocket.

"They weren't innocent, and they weren't bystanders," Camellion said, glancing at Duvane who was unlocking the doors on the left side of the van. He looked down at the four bodies. One of the men was still alive, his right leg jerking every now and then. "They were trash that interferred. The penalty for that is always death."

He stepped over to the dying man, put a .45 slug into the back of the goof's neck, then turned his attention to Arnold Quincy, who was dropping the still unconscious Russian into the back of the van. The moment that the Russian national was sprawled out on the seat on his back, Duvane stepped up behind Quincy, slammed him across the back of the head with the S&W auto pistol and, as the hood began to sag, shoved him through the door onto the floor, then slammed the door.

Duvane walked around to the right side of the van. Camellion, already busy removing the jack from the rear axle, glanced at Duvane as he picked up the large hubcap. "Don't bother to put it on," he said. "Throw it inside and we'll get out of here."

Camellion pulled out the jack, tossed it to one side, then went around to the rear door on the left side of the vehicle. He picked up the tank and hose, opened the door and got in, rolling the KGB agent, who was beginning to groan slightly, onto the body of Quincy. He unzipped his coveralls for the length of a foot, reached into his shirt pocket and pulled out a flat leather-covered case.

Duvane, who had hurried to the driver's side of the van, opened the door, put the hubcap in front of the seat on the passenger side, got in and slammed the door. He had the van moving north in the alley by the time the Death Merchant had given the KGB agent 300 milligrams of secosodiumthimide, a very powerful tranquilizer. Duvane was nearing the end of the alley and preparing to turn to the east as the Death Merchant plunged the needle of the second hypodermic into the right buttock of Arnie Quincy.

"Hear those police sirens?" Duvane sounded worried. "Another thing: we have no way of knowing who might have seen us from the rear windows of the apartment house?"

"True . . . very true." Camellion put the second hypodermic into the case, shoved the case into his pocket and pulled the Repco TEX-10 transceiver from its case. "When the C-4 explodes, it will slow the boys in blue long enough for us to get lost."

Pulling up the antenna, he could see Duvane giving him a quick, puzzled glance in the rearview mirror.

"What C-4 explosion? Where?" Duvane demanded, turning the steering wheel to the right and swinging out onto Blair Blvd.

"There's a one-pound block underneath the rear seat in the Monaco."

Duvane chuckled. "You don't miss a single trick, do you?" There was admiration in his voice. "A pound will scatter that car all over Tenth Avenue and then some."

"That, my friend, is the idea." The Death Merchant switched on the walkie-talkie and contacted Fred Thumm. "Red Rose—make the call to the police. Tell them there's been a big bang in front of The Ark. Give the information and the address only twice; then hang up. I don't even want the fuzz to suspect that the call was made from a portable phone inside a moving vehicle. Confirm. Over."

"Confirmed," replied Thumm. "But I haven't heard any firecrackers yet. Over."

"You will. Out."

Camellion replaced the W-T in its case, reached into the pouch, pulled out the remote control detonating device, opened the cover and pushed the switch from OFF to ON. Immediately, a small red light began to glow. Camellion pressed the green button below the light.

The van by then was almost two and a half blocks from the Monaco parked on Tenth Avenue in front of SAM'S TV & RADIO REPAIR; yet the explosion, a monstrous WWEE-ROOORUUUUMMMMMM!, sounded much closer. Camellion and Duvane could only imagine the damage the C-4 had done, the scores of windows that had been shattered by the concussion, and the way traffic for the next hour would be snarled for blocks around.

The Death Merchant leaned back and put his cerebral

cortex on overtime. Not only had he and Duvane acquired "Clyde Hayden," who had turned out to be Arnold Quincy, just as the Death Merchant had expected, but they had also nabbed a man who almost had to be a KGB kill-specialist—a *Mokryye Dela* assassin of the KGB's First Chief Directorate. *Only now the other three "wet affair" boys are stiff in the marketplace and we have the fourth.*

The pieces of the puzzle were slowly falling into place in the Death Merchant's mind. The KGB, too, had learned of Arnold Quincy, Manny Rich's bosom buddy, had learned that he was missing. It followed that the KGB, fearing that Rich might have confided something of vital importance to Quincy, wanted the two-bit hood dead. The four Soviet intelligence officers had not terminated Quincy in his apartment because they wanted to take their time questioning him—*accordingly, they must have planned to take him to New York. But how did they find him? Who tipped them off?*

"Listen, Giffwangle," began Duvane, "we didn't expect to grab an ivan—if he is one of the Main Enemy. He's one helluva catch. Why not drive to the Main Safe House in New York instead of going back to the Chapel? It would save a lot of time."

Camellion said, "Duvane, did I ever tell you about the little red corpuscle who was swimming in the bloodstream of a horse?"

"No, but what's that—"

"This little corpuscle was always in a hurry. One day he decided to play hooky from the school of red corpuscles, so he told the teacher he had a headache. Well, this was a mistake. As he swam down the main artery, using the Australian crawl, he came to a fork in the stream—it was high tide."

"Damn, will you listen to me? If we go to New York—"

"The little corpuscle took the fork on the starboard side. He proceeded to swim lazily down the new stream when suddenly disaster struck. The little red corpuscle was swallowed by a huge virus. The virus' name was Cyrus."

"What the hell does that silly tale have to do with going to the safe house in New York?" Duvane finally managed to get in.

"It's the moral of the story that counts. Never change streams in the middle of a horse!"

"I'll be damned!"

"So was the red corpuscle who was swallowed by Cyrus. The point is, we're not going to make the same mistake. Our prizes are too valuable. We're going back to the Chapel of Prayer."

"Have it your way," Duvane said disagreeably. "But I'm telling you, the Chapel S-F doesn't have the facilities to maintain enemy subjects. Taking two of them back there is asking for trouble."

"Suppose you let me worry about that. You just drive and obey all the traffic laws like a good, decent citizen. . . ."

Chapter Five

THE TENTH AVENUE MASSACRE! That was the headline some of the evening papers in the area used to refer to the murders that had taken place in the lobby of The Ark and to the rear of the apartment house. Nine Caucasians and four blacks had been "brutally gunned down, in what is one of the most horrible slaughters ever to occur in the United States." Newspapers across the nation (especially those owned and controlled by those who wouldn't know a BB gun from a cannon), ran long editorials calling for "gun control to rid the nation of a soaring crime rate that is already out of control."

The "work of terrorists," said the newspapers and TV commentators.

Six people, including three police officers, had been injured when the C-4 in the Monaco had exploded—three cops who had just arrived at the hotel, in response to a call from Sam Reggio, the owner of SAM'S TV & RADIO REPAIR; Sam Reggio who had been slashed across the face by a piece of flying glass, when concussion blew in his front window; and two passersby who had been on the sidewalk, in front of The Ark. Concussion had knocked them to the sidewalk and had broken one man's arm.

The thirteen murdered victims, including the three KGB gunmen, had been identified. At the time, when the first papers were on the street, the police did not suspect that the identification of the three was false, and Camellion couldn't prove that the three corpses and one of his prisoners were members of Soviet Intelligence. He couldn't because the two men he and Duvane had captured were in no condition to be put through hostile interrogation.

The soundproof attic was the main part of the safe house at the Chapel of Prayer. There wasn't any holding room for enemy prisoners. Nor would Courtland Grojean permit the Russian and Arnold Quincy to be brought to the attic, even though both men were so heavily drugged they were more asleep than awake.

Grojean even managed to lose his temper when Camellion tried to persuade him to permit the two men to be brought to the attic.

"Enemy agents have never seen the inside of this station and they never will!" raged Grojean, who no longer looked as if he belonged in an English drawing room. "That cheap hood and that atheist son of a bitch from the Soviet Union are going to stay drugged in the casket storage room—and that's final!"

The Death Merchant (much to the embarrassment of the other men) was equally as adamant. "I don't know why they shouldn't be brought up here," he said, unruffled by Grojean's outburst. "Other enemy agents have been inside other safe houses all over the U.S., and Quincy and the ivan will never be in a position to tell the outside world anything."

"I'll tell you why!" Standing and waving his arms, Grojean practically snarled the words. "Because I'm the Boss and you're working for me! Because if I don't OK your cash payment for each mission, you don't get paid—that's why!"

Since money was always the bottom line with the Death Merchant, he could hardly refute Grojean's argument. He couldn't and he didn't. For the remainder of the day and far into the evening, Arnold Quincy and the man presumed to be a KGB operative remained in the mortuary's casket storage room in the basement, their arms handcuffed behind their backs, Roger Barnkoff and Wilbert Donovan guarding them.

There was a limit to the use of tranquilizing drugs on the two subjects for two reasons: (1) The CIA was totally ignorant of the medical histories of the two men. Too many milligrams of Thorazine, Secosodiumthimide, mephenoxalone, or any of the other powerful soporifics could cause cardiogenic shock; and under no circumstances could the two be taken to a hospital. Dead men could not reveal anything, nor would there be time to fly Quincy and the Russian to the CIA's special hospital in Virginia. (2) Massive doses of tranquilizers would keep the two subjects in such a deep-tranquil state, such a half-asleep state, that questioning them with any accuracy would be next to impossible. The CIA could not afford to take the time, to wait several days for "zombies" to become normal. Accordingly, the Secosodiumthimide was allowed to wear off. By nine-thirty that night, Quincy and the Russian had almost regained full consciousness and full attention span.

Quincy was visibly frightened, his eyes moving around like marbles in his head, resting for a time on Donovan and Barnkoff, both of whom sat across from him and the Russian, then moving on to the huge crates filled with caskets. In contrast, the KGB agent sat and glared like a chained, defiant tiger, unlike Quincy, making no attempt to engage Donovan and Barnkoff in conversation.

"At least you could tell me where we are and who you are?" Quincy whined, doing his best to obtain information. "At least you could tell me that!"

As part of the psychological conditioning process. Donovan and Barnkoff remained silent, merely looking at Quincy and the KGB officer in a detached, disinterested way, their eyes shifting only when they happened to see a mouse scampering across the floor, occasionally across the top of one of the crated caskets. Mice plagued not only the storage room but the entire basement, regardless of the numerous traps that had been set.

Only once did the Russion show any emotion, one of fear, when a mouse happened to lose his way by the wall, run across the space and scamper over his right foot. The ivan jumped so hard on the chair that he almost tipped it over backward.

"Can't you damned CIA people keep mice out of the houses you control!" he shouted in almost perfect English.

arts of South China. He rushed Quincy with such speed that the terror-stricken man didn't have time to duck. Donovan's right arm streaked out, the knife-edge of his hand connecting solidly with Quincy's left temple. The hood let out a quick low "Uhhh!" and fell sideways, tripping over the chair and starting to go down. Donovan quickly thrust out his left foot and placed the instep under Quincy's right cheek to keep the man's head from striking the hard tiled floor.

"Nervous fella, wasn't he?" commented Taimesser. "Imagine! Thinking that we were going to do him in." He bent down, pulled up Quincy's right sleeve and felt for the pulse of the cephalic vein.

Roger Barnkoff faked a snicker. "What could you expect. When you tell a bum like that he's going for a ride, he presumes it means you're going to kill him."

"I see what you mean." Having found the vein and inserted the needle, Taimesser pushed down on the plunger of the hypodermic, sending four CCs[1] of vesorene into Quincy's bloodstream. Made from the venom of the Bald-faced hornet, the drug would keep Quincy and the Russian agent in a very deep slumber for three to four hours, without any side effects upon awakening.

All this time, the Russian had sat impassively, a hard, fixed expression on his face, his eyes staring straight ahead as if the other men in the room were invisible. His eyes didn't waver even when Luke Drayer handed the second hypodermic to Basil Taimesser, who walked to the back of the KGB agent's chair and jerked up his right shirtsleeve.

"You're being sensible, Ivan," Taimesser said heartily. He felt for the pulse of the vein. "After all, you can't fight the inevitable."

"He knows we're with the Agency," Roger Barnkoff said, staring coldly at the enemy agent. "And he knows we're not going to terminate him." He grinned mockingly at the Russian, who was a thickset, beefy-faced individual with iron control, a trained agent who would not let his emotions color the facts of reality, no matter how brutal those facts might be. Not once had his expression revealed the pain that—generated by Camellion's knee-lift in the lobby of The Ark—was still a torment in his testicles.

"I don't suppose you'd care to tell us your real name,

---

1. One cubic centimeter (cc) is roughly 15 drops of fluid.

Quickly then, realizing what he had said—that he had deduced his captives were CIA—he clamped his mouth shut and reverted back to his former stony-faced self.

Arnold Quincy's eyes almost bulged and his lower lip began to twitch as he stared at Donovan and Barnkoff as though they were aliens from another planet. "Is it true? Are you—are you the CIA?"

Donovan and Barnkoff continued to play their part of being brothers to the sphinx. . . .

Eleven thirty-four P.M. Luke Drayer and Basil Taimesser, the latter a CIA Case Officer from the Russian Desk, walked into the storage room, Taimesser carrying an attaché case.

The Russian's expression didn't change. If anything, it became more grim and determined. Not so with Arnold Quincy. He became more frightened, his eyes following the stocky Taimesser who placed the attaché case on one of the crated caskets, then opened it and took out two hypodermics. He handed one to Drayer, then held the one in his hand with the needle pointed upward, and pushed slightly on the plunger to make sure that the yellow liquid was going through the end of the needle.

"What is that stuff?" demanded Arnold Quincy fearfully. He drew back on his chair, as if trying to push through the wooden back. "What are you going to do?"

"You and the boy wonder from Russia are going for a ride," Taimesser said, all the while pushing slowly on the plunger and watching a few drops of the fluid ooze out of the end of the needle.

"You're going to kill me!" Quincy yelled hoarsely, getting up from the plain wooden chair, to which he was handcuffed. When he was halfway erect, the chain-links of the manacles pulled against the horizontal slat in the middle of the back, and the chair was jerked from the floor.

Startled, Luke Drayer and Basil Taimesser stepped back. Donovan and Barnkoff moved forward. Afraid that Quincy might kick at the hypodermic in his hand, Taimesser said harshly to Donovan and Barnkoff, "Shut him up—fast!"

The slim Donovan, who didn't weigh more than 150 pounds, didn't look very strong—and he wasn't. He was, however, an expert in *Chuka Shaolin,* one of the martial

Russian?" Barnkoff said good-naturedly. "You might as well. Sooner or later, you'll tell us. Or wish to God you had!"

"Why not. My name is Virgil Paterson. I'm from Peoria, Illinois," the Russian said in good "American" English. "Why ask me? You guys have my billfold. You know my name."

"Sure we do." Barnkoff's voice was pleasantly calm, but his eyes were angry. "And I'm Ronnie Reagan. I live in the White House. The man shooting the sleepy bye-bye in your arm is George Bush." He glanced at Luke Drayer. "And he's Alexander Ha—"

Barnkoff stopped speaking, knowing that the Russian could not hear him. The vesorene had taken effect immediately and the Soviet agent's head had dropped in unconsciousness.

"I suppose they're going to New York via the casket route?" Donovan said, looking after Luke Drayer who was hurrying from the room.

"Yes, in two caskets," Taimesser said. Having put the empty hypodermics into the attaché case, he closed the lid and snapped the catches shut. He stood up. "The hearse will take them to the funeral home in Brooklyn. Tomorrow morning, they'll go to the safe house in Amityville."

"In the motorhome?" asked Barnkoff.

"Yeah. I know. It's risky, but they'll be stashed in the 'body storage' compartment underneath the beds. They won't smother any more in the motorhome than they will in the caskets. There'll be plenty of airholes." Taimesser looked from Barnkoff to Donovan. "Which of you has the keys to the cuffs?"

Ten minutes more and Taimesser and Barnkoff were lifting the unconscious Arnold Quincy into the casket that Drayer had wheeled into the room on its stand. The casket was one of the $12,000 bronze models with plush genuine silk lining, all white and blue.

"It's difficult to see how they won't smother inside with the lid down," Barnkoff said pensively. He let Quincy's shoulder slip from his hands onto the padded interior of the burial box.

"You're some technician!" laughed Barnkoff. He pushed down on Quincy's legs, shoving them down into the casket. "There are three dozen airholes in the bottom. The casket's specially built. When the lid is closed, even when it's locked, it only looks like its snug against the rest of the casket. But there's almost half an inch of air space all around the lid, even if you can't see it. It's all a matter of clever construction."

Grinning, Will Donovan looked down at the sleeping Arnold Quincy.

"By God, doesn't he look like he's dead?" He reached into the casket, pulled up the man's arms and folded his hands on his chest. "There! That's more like it. Might as well do it right."

"Watch it. I'm going to close the lid." After Donovan moved to one side, Taimesser carefully let down the lid and fastened the latches.

Barnkoff wiped his face with a handkerchief and leaned against one of the crated caskets. "I guess what's his name?—Giffwangle—is going to the safe house with the two subjects? I certainly hope so. He gives me the creeps."

Donovan nodded understandingly and took a toothpick from his sweater jacket. "I don't know about you men, but when I'm around him I keep feeling guilty and I'll be damned if I know why."

"I don't know him that well," Taimesser said. "I've only spent an hour or so in Giffwangle's company. But from what Jacob Hall told me about him, he must be a real oddball. Hall said he went downstairs this afternoon to do 'breathing exercises.' Whoever heard of such a thing— 'breathing exercises!' "

Donovan took the toothpick from his mouth. "I have. Giffwangle's a master karateist. What he's doing is using *kata*[2] to magnify the powers of his mind and body via breath control, usually with what is called the *sanchin*. He's supercharging himself."

Barnkoff cast a dubious eye at Donovan. "Oh, that's it! 'Supercharging' himself, huh! I don't know about that, but I think something is damned weird about a man who seldom eats a full meal before eleven at night and sleeps only an hour or two. And the way he and Duvane terminated all these people! Yet the other day, Giffwangle was calling

2. A set pattern of movements in which the practitioner defends himself against a series of imaginary opponents. These exercises develop timing, focus, balance, coordination, and imagination. *Sanchin* is a breathing exercise of 20 movements; it teaches one to tense the body instantaneously and to control breathing during intense combat.

whale and seal hunters 'sadistic trash.' You know what I think?"

Taimesser made a cautious observation, one that carried a warning. "Just don't let The Fox hear you making those kind of remarks. The boys in New York told me that Giffwangle is the Old Man's best troubleshooter. Anyhow, that's their opinion." He lowered his voice. "Gabetts, at the Long Island station, said Grojean only uses Giffwangle for top jobs—'impossible missions' one might say."

Donovan nodded and his attention turned to Barnkoff. "What were you going to say, Roger?"

Barnkoff thought for a moment. "I was going to say that I think Giffwangle is really—" He gestured with one hand. "Never mind. It's not that important."

Donovan glanced at Taimesser, then toward the door. "Here comes Luke with another casket. Let's get the Russian ready."

Amityville, Long Island. A community of ten thousand people, Amityville is a small, quiet town, so peaceful and tranquil that it's difficult to believe that Queens is less than 20 miles to the west. During the season, when summerhouse renters are in town, Amityville perks up somewhat; otherwise . . . nothing ever happens in the sleepy little town.

A mile and a half north of Amityville, just off Route 41 that branches off Amityville Road—the "main street" of the town—is the Flechter Rest Home (licensed by the State of New York) where executives from various companies and corporations could recover from mental breakdowns induced by constant business pressures.

Housed in a sixty-three-room stone mansion, there was a gentle dignity about the rest home, a peacefulness that made people passing on Route 41 almost wish that they were behind the white high chainlink fence surrounding the home. The mansion had been built by a real estate millionaire who lost his fortune during the Depression. As a result, the mammoth house had been empty and desolate for years until the U.S. Government purchased the property in 1941 and used it to monitor Nazi braodcasts from Europe. In 1958, the Government sold the property to Kinner, Cash & Fuchs, a real estate firm in Buffalo, New York. Kinner, Cash & Fuchs then unloaded the estate on

Winfred Laurence Flechter, a psychiatrist with a practice in New York City. Dr. Flechter remodeled the old Hancock property and opened a rest home.

It was the Central Intelligence Agency that supplied Dr. Fletcher with the money, not only to buy the property but to remodel it.

The rest home, which had never admitted, or administered to, any executive from the business world, had been established for three reasons: to bring back to normalcy those case officers who, in the covert division, could no longer take the pressure and were on the verge of a nervous breakdown[3]. In this sense, the Flechter Rest Home was a genuine rest home.

Of equal importance was the fact that the rest home was also one of the main operational safe houses in the eastern United States. Only several dozen men in the Agency knew that the rest home was the main testing laboratory in that part of the country for CIA experiments in mind control, in the Agency's constant search for a "Manchurian Candidate."

In CIA files the rest home was coded *Apple Cart D-3KK*.

Getting Arnold Quincy to talk was less than easy. All the two CIA interrogators had to do was handcuff Quincy to a chair and tell him that they were going to use him for a target in a little game of Russian roulette.

Standing in front of the gangster, Cliff Reid shoved a single .44 magnum cartridge into the cylinder of a Ruger "Redhawk" revolver, spun the cylinder and handed the powerful weapon to Norman Self, the second interrogator who stood to the right of Quincy.

Self put the muzzle of the Redhawk behind the trembling Quincy's right ear. "Well, you have four chances in five of not having your brains scrambled, or one chance in five of dying," he said and pulled the trigger.

The hammer jumped forward, the firing pin hitting an empty chamber. *Click!* Quincy let out an animal sound of

---

3. Alcoholism, suicide, mental breakdown, and divorce are very high in the Agency's covert section, but not necessarily because of the danger. Members of the CS are hard-driving, hard-living individuals who must be constantly on guard.

fear, his chest rising and falling rapidly. Logic dictated that if they killed him—how would he be able to tell them anything? Yet he had seen Reid put a cartridge in the cylinder. He had seen him spin the cylinder, swing in the cylinder and hand the weapon to Self. Quincy's peripheral vision had enabled him to see that the second man had not switched weapons or taken the cartridge from the cylinder. He had no way of knowing that while the .44 cartridge looked real, it was only a dummy. Only God could have made it explode. . . .

"It's time you tell us what we want to know," Cliff Reid said politely, "or we play the game until you do. Should you die in the process . . . tough. . . ."

Much to Reid and Self's surprise, Quincy blubbered, "A-Anything! I'll t-tell you anything you w-want to know."

Richard Camellion and Courtland Grojean, who had been watching and listening to the proceedings through a two-way mirror and a speaker in the next room, came into the small interrogation chamber. Quickly, more pieces of the puzzle began to fall into place.

In a quivery voice, Quincy explained that he, too, had had an opportunity to go with Manny Rich to Kennedy International; that, originally, Rich had been contacted for the "special job as backup" and paid fifteen thousand dollars, this money to be split between himself and a second man—any trusted friend he might care to bring along.

Contacted? By whom? By Valdamir Kosminkovov, a staff member of Tass, at the United Nations. Rich had met Kosminkovov in a bowling alley and had known him for several months.

The Death Merchant said in a sinister voice, "Then you and Rich knew that the airport job involved killing. Is that correct?"

Quincy confessed that he had backed away from the offer because he and Rich realized that since weapons were involved, someone might be murdered, even though Kosminkovov had assured Rich that "you and your friend will only be on the backup team to the main force. Quincy didn't know what the "main force" was or what it was supposed to do. "All I know is that I backed down," he whined. Manny—he was different. He didn't mind killing. He tried to talk me into goin', but I wouldn't. That's why he got that shitass Hedmann."

Did Quincy know anything else about the airport assignment? No. He did not. That was it. Anything else about the airport, he knew only by reading the papers.

However, there was more, much more, to the strange tale. Manny Rich, who liked to think he could outwit fate, had foreseen that difficulty might arise from the airport job; that it was possible that he might have to hide out for a time. To further complicate an already complicated and potentially dangerous situation, he had been forced to take his pet dog to a vet. Accordingly, he had had Arnold Quincy rent an apartment in Yonkers. Not only would he be able to hide out at the apartment—if it came to that— but Thor could be delivered to Quincy at The Arms. But Manny Rich had made a mistake in more ways than one. For one thing, he had not counted on the Death Merchant's executing him at the airport. For another, he had forgotten the money hunger of Arnold Quincy.

Shamefacedly, Quincy then confessed that, after he had read of Rich's death, he had telephoned the Soviet Consulate in New York City and had demanded $25,000 in "small, unmarked bills" to keep silent about Valdamir Kosminkovov. The woman answering the phone had hung up on him.

Quincy had then managed to reach Kosminkovov by phone at the U.N. Building and had again demanded $25,000. The Russian agreed to pay the sum—"Where shall I meet you with the money?"

Quincy had chosen the *Saito*, a Japanese restaurant at 305 East 46th Street, just north of the U.N. Building in New York City. "I wasn't going to meet that son of a bitch in any lonely spot," Quincy told Camellion, Grojean, and the two CIA men.

Valdamir Kosminkovov had arrived on time at the *Saito* and had turned over the money to Quincy, placing a Samsonite attaché case under the table. Quincy had taken the attaché case and had left the restaurant.

Feeling that he was being very clever and cautious, Quincy had returned to Yonkers by taking a very circuitous route, one so round-about that it had taken him six hours to get to Yonkers. Afraid to park on Sixth Avenue at 12:30 A.M., he had driven to an all-night parking garage. From there he had taken a taxi to a first-class hotel in downtown Yonkers.

At eight the next morning, Quincy had left the hotel and had returned to the parking garage via cab. In his own car, he had then driven to Sixth Avenue, hurrying into The Ark with his right hand wrapped around the butt of a snub-nosed .38 Colt revolver.

Once he was safe in his apartment on the third floor, he had immediately gone to the bathroom and had taken the $25,000—in packets of five, ten, and twenty dollar bills—and stuffed it between the old-fashioned tub and the wall, shoving the stacks of bills through a small, square opening in the wall, just above the rim of the tub. He had then taken the square of white tile and reglued it to the wall.

The attaché case? It appeared to be brand new. Why throw it away? Quincy had placed it in the bedroom closet.

He had been relaxing over whiskey and coffee and congratulating himself on a job well done when someone had knocked loudly on the door. Apprehensively, he had hurried to the chained, double-dead-bolt-locked door and looked through the viewer, at the same time calling out, "Who is it?" The viewer revealed a heavyset man in a gray overcoat.

"Millitron. Frank Millitron," the man said. "I'm the insurance inspector for this building. I'm inspecting all the apartments. May I come in, please."

"Look, I'm busy!"

"Yeah? Well so am I, Mac, and I ain't got all day to fool around. Until I inspect every apartment, the policy on this building can't be renewed. I'm not going to stand here and argue with you. I'll just tell the manager you wouldn't let me in for five minutes."

Very nervously Quincy explained to Camellion and the others that, at the time, the last thing he wanted was trouble with the manager of The Ark—"So I unlocked the door and let him in."

Only "Frank Millitron" had not been an insurance inspector. No sooner had Quincy opened the door than three other men—they had been by the hallway, out of range of the viewer—had shoved their way in behind the Russian who had posed as "Frank Millitron" and who instantly shoved a 9mm Beretta pistol, with a silencer, under Quincy's nose.

Another man, carrying what appeared to be a brown attaché case, opened it, took a meter device with a long cord from his topcoat pocket, pushed the plug at the end of the cord into a receptacle in the panel contained in the larger section of the attaché case, then pushed upward on a toggle switch. A beeping sound began coming from the case, the sound growing louder as the man walked slowly then quickened his steps toward the bedroom.

Arnold Quincy's heart—and hopes—fell all the way to the basement. He knew then that Valdamir Kosminkovov had given him an attaché case equipped with a recovery device—with a hidden transmitter!

"I ain't no dummy," Quincy said bitterly to the Death Merchant, Grojean and the two agency "hostile" interrogators. "In the Jap eating joint, I had thought of a bug. The first thing I did, once I was in my car, was to take out all the stacks of bills and search for a bug. The case was as empty as a vice cop's head. Jeez! Was I stupid!"

"You certainly were," Clifford Reid said in a clipped voice. "In this age of miniaturization, it's not at all difficult to 'bug' an attaché case. The device was contained in the lid or in the bottom or the sides of the larger section. You were a fool, Quincy."

The "fool" continued his recital of mistakes. After one Russian had found the attaché case in the bedroom closet and returned to the living room, the man with the Beretta had said to Quincy, "Where is the money, Mr. Quincy? Don't lie, don't stall for time. Tell us right now or I'll put a bullet through your kneecaps."

Quincy told him.

"Take us to the bathroom," the Russian said, motioning with the Beretta.

Quincy removed the money from the wall and the Russians marched Quincy back to the living room and shoved him to the couch. One of the Soviet agents looked at his watch. Several minutes passed. Then there was a knock on the door. One of the four men opened the door and admitted a man and a woman. The woman quickly stuffed the $25,000 into her large shoulder bag and the man picked up the bugged attaché case. The man and the woman then left the apartment. The four Russians waited another ten minutes. "I figured they wanted to give the man and the woman with the money plenty of time to leave," Quincy said. The four Russians then told Quincy that they wanted him to tell what he had done to the Soviet Consul General in New York, the man with the Beretta warning, "If you try to call out for help, or run, I'll kill you."

They had marched him out of the apartment to one of the elevators.

"We were in the lobby, headed for the street, when this exterminator guy—he was carrying a tank—and his partner came along and killed three of the guys and those other people. I damn near broke my back carrying that other Russian. He was a big son of a bitch."

Quincy looked from the Death Merchant to Courtland Grojean. "I don't know anything else. I've told you all I know. Tell me. What are you going to do with me?"

Camellion's face remained void of expression. He was no longer wearing the "face" he had worn in the lobby of The Ark and in *Apple Cart D-3KK* and was speaking in his normal voice. Quincy had not recognized him.

Courtland Grojean patted Quincy on the shoulder. "Don't worry about it, son. We'll release you in time."

Sure . . . to a cemetery! thought Camellion.

Clifford Reid and Norman Self didn't get to first base with the Russian KGB intelligence officer. He wouldn't even give his name. Neither did Jeff "Red" Binson and Paul Gibber, two other I-experts more experienced than Reid and Self. Binson and Gibber even tried Narcohypnosis, using Thyzokipine, a derivative of scopolamine, and Thorazine. Failure! Such failure that the Russian could not even be submitted to the SHSS[4] and the HGSHA[5] tests.

There could only be one answer for such a bankrupt effort: The Russian agent had been preconditioned by hypnosis to withstand Narcohypnotic probes by enemy agents, his resistance proving that he was considered a highly valuable agent by the KGB.

Under the circumstances, only one course of action was available—engage in extreme hostile interrogation. The four Agency officers stripped the Russian naked, strapped him in "The Highchair" (which resembled a dentist's chair) and went to work on his gums and genitals with electric shock. For an entire day, they sent charge after charge of electricity into the Russian's body. Often he would faint from pain and exhaustion. They would revive him and start all over again—and they didn't make one iota of progress. The KGB agent would not talk.

They tried Anectine (succinylcholine). The Russian was

---

4. The Stanford Hypnotic Susceptibility Scale.
5. The Harvard Group Scale of Hypnotic Susceptibility.

strapped down and injected with the drug. First the Russian felt a growing numbness in his fingers, a paralysis that very quickly reached his arms and legs. Yet, much to the consternation of Reid, Self, Binson, and Gibber, the Russian did not seem afraid—not even when the dead numbness reached his chest and his diaphram seemed to stop pumping air. It appeared as though he couldn't breathe—but where was the horror of suffocation that was supposed to grip his mind?

A sad-faced individual with a lot of freckles on his cheeks, hands and arms, Red Binson sighed, turned his eyes from the window in Dr. Flechter's private office and said to Camellion, Grojean, and Dr. Winfred Flechter, "He simply will not talk. We don't even know his name; and he's in such a state of exhaustion that if we continue, his heart might stop. Then what would we have?"

Norman Self shifted uncomfortably in his chair. "I could have strangled that damned ivan this morning. After we tried the Anectine on him, he actually managed to laugh at us. He said that we wouldn't dare let him suffocate, that it was all a bluff. He sneered and said that we needed him alive. The hell of it was he was right."

"Winnie, what do you suggest?" Grojean, sitting in a deep armchair, asked the psychiatrist. "This enemy agent must be made to talk."

"In my opinion, we will never make him talk by using methods of hostile interrogation," Paul Gibber said. Bald and wearing thick-lensed glasses, he made the Death Merchant think of Igor, Dr. Frankenstein's laboratory assistant—*all he needs is a twisted neck and a hump on his back*.

Short and heavy with red splotches on his cheeks, Dr. Flechter leaned over the report on his desk. For several minutes he did not speak. Carefully then, he took off his glasses and rubbed the indentations the nose rests had made on his long, bony nose.

"We cannot continue to induce physical pain in the subject," he explained almost solemnly. "Pain has caused his blood pressure to rise dangerously high and a sinus arrhythmia had made itself known in his heart. There have been atrial contractions that are intense." Dr. Flechter cleared his throat and put on his rimless glasses. "I can't give a definite answer. I can't suggest a method, at this point, by which the subject can be forced to talk. It seems he knows our methods and is not afraid. That's placing us at an extreme disadvantage. The man is obviously a fanatic. Such types are the most difficult. They would rather die than cooperate."

The light of a partial idea glowed in the Death Merchant's mind. He knew that the answer was there, but at the moment he couldn't pull it fully into his consciousness.

"Doctor, isn't that a complete report on the Russian?" he said. "Doesn't it give his every word and action since he was taken into custody?"

"To be sure—yes," Dr. Flechter said. "The medical report is twice as long as what he said and did. With the exception of eating and going to the bathroom, he hasn't done anything. He has said even less."

"We can't even get his name out of him," grumbled Paul Gibber.

"May I see the report, Doctor?" Camellion asked. Getting up, he walked to the front of the desk and accepted the sheets of paper that Doctor Flechter handed him.

"A tape recorder was going constantly in the casket storage room," Courtland Grojean looked speculatively at the Death Merchant, who was sitting back down. "What do you have in mind, Giffwangle?"

"I don't know yet. That's what's bugging me." Camellion scanned the pages. He wasn't interested in the Russian's medical condition—*It was something he said! But what?*

Camellion finally found it. Three different times the Russian had complained bitterly! The only time he had spoken full sentences!

Ah—so the slob is afraid of mice! Maybe he is, or maybe he just doesn't like them. Could that be the weakness we need?

Camellion got up, walked back to the desk and handed Dr. Flechter the report; he then turned and looked at a puzzled Courtland Grojean.

"Mr. Grojean, where can we obtain three dozen alley rats?"

"Rats?" Grojean stared in wonderment at the Death Merchant. "Are you serious?"

"I said rats! *Rattus norvegicus!* The big Norway rat. Of course I'm serious!"

* * *

CIA men made a solid wooden cage from two by fours, three feet high and the length of a casket. The bottom was of unpainted pine boards, while both ends, the sides and the top were composed of double strength chicken wire. In the top of the lid they had also cut an eight inch square hole that could be covered with another piece of chicken wire.

On the third day of his "vacation" at the rest home in Amityville, the Ivan was led stark naked into the interrogation room of the basement. A chain, the kind used on convicts, was fastened around his waist and his hands cuffed to the chain.

The four interrogators, with Grojean, Camellion and Merle Duvane, watching, lifted the Russian off his feet and placed him horizontally into the cage whose lid Camellion had swung open. Once the Russian was flat on his back, the Death Merchant closed and secured the lid by its hasp and turned to Red Binson. "Get the rats."

All this time he was watching the Russian in the man-sized chicken coop. At the mention of "rats," he saw the man's eyes widen in fear and the color drain from his cheeks—*I was right! He IS afraid of rodents!*

In a short time, Binson and Cliff Reid returned to the room, carrying between them a wire cage filled with a black, twisting mass of squealing, clawing rodents, some the size of a small cat.

Camellion noted with satisfaction how the Ivan twinged and pulled his body against the floor of the cage as Reid and Binson approached with the rats. . . .

"The ancient Chinese made good use of rats with spies and traitors," Courtland Grojean said pleasantly, carefully taking a tiny piece of lint from his tweed sports coat. "They would first draw blood on the cheeks of the condemned, then put a cage filled with rats around his head. I'm told it took days for the victim to die, in horrible agony all the while."

"Naturally," the Death Merchant said conversationally. "The rats would only eat when hungry." He motioned to Binson and Reid. "Up here on top, men."

With some slight effort, Reid and Binson lifted the cage of rats onto the top of the cage in which the Soviet Agent was entombed, positioning the cage so that several inches of the edge of one side were over the square hole.

Close by, Norman Self and Paul Gibber stood with thin, yard-long cattle prods, they too watching the Ivan whose face was contorting in deep fear. Both men would have bet that the enemy agent was skirting right up to the abyss of blind panic, the kind that gives way to uncontrollable hysteria.

"Now, my Russian comrade, fun time is over. We're going to get some answers," the Death Merchant said amicably, turning to the Russian. "We want your name and every single bit of information you have about Dr. Wayne Davis, his secretary, and the two CIA men who got off the airplane at Kennedy International."

The Russian did not speak.

Camellion shrugged. "Have it your way. If you want to be eaten alive by rats, so be it!"

The bottom of the rat cage was a metal tray. Camellion unfastened the latch and gently pulled the knob toward him so that the tray in the bottom opened a few inches. Three rats, thinking they had found a means of escape, squirmed through the narrow opening, fell through the hole in the lid of the larger cage and landed on the abdomen of the Russian, who screamed and went wild within the cage. He twisted his body from side to side, kicked with his bare feet against the end of the cage and jerked his wrists against the chain around his waist.

"GET THEM OFF ME!" he yelled. "GET THOSE RATS OFF ME!"

His frantic movements only frightened the rats more, all three of which ran back and forth over his body, squealing, seeking an escape route. The Ivan's left leg almost mashed one rat that, at the time, was between his thigh and the bottom of the cage. Feeling threatened, the rodent defended itself. It darted up the Russian's right leg and bit him viciously on the penis, the bite causing the KGB agent to shriek in pain and terror. He screamed again when another rat bit him on the ear and the third rat scampered over his hairy chest.

By now the Russian was thrashing about with such vigor that the large cage imprisoning him was rocking from side to side, with such force that Reid and Binson had to hold it while Camellion and Grojean held the cage of rats in place. Finally, Camellion motioned to Self and Gibber who thrust the thin cattle prods through the chicken wire and soon shocked the three terrified rats into unconsciousness.

The Death Merchant stared at the KGB agent whose penis was bleeding. The man's eyes were as round as saucers, his lips heavy with spittle.

"I'll ask you one more time," Camellion said in Russian, without any trace of an accent. "Then you'll get a full dozen of the little monsters dropped on you. Get this through your head, Ruskie. You're valuable to us only if you cooperate, only if you talk, only if you tell us what we want to know. Otherwise, you're just another lousy commie who will take a long time in dying and as painfully as possible. I'll personally see to that. Now, what is your name?"

"Get those rats away and I'll tell you what you want to know," the Russian said. "But get the rats away."

"You'll tell us right now, or you'll get a dozen rats right now. I'll give you to the count of one. *ONE!*"

"My name is Antonin Yudin!" screamed the Russian.

The Death Merchant leaned back in the chair and stared reflectively out the window of the second story office. Out on the grounds a brisk wind was playing with leaves falling from maples and sycamores, tumbling them by the hundreds across the yard.

Camellion studied the window whose glass was multishot capacity transparent armor, although it appeared to be only thick glass. The multishot capacity meant that the glass could absorb several bullets within inches of each other and still hold up. Camellion admired first-rate security. He admired the mansion that was Doctor Flechter's sanitarium. Every window in the building was made of transparent armor, every door, while it appeared to be wooden, was constructed of solid steel.

The Death Merchant didn't like what Antonin Yudin had confessed to him and Grojean and the others. The KGB had first learned of Dr. Davis and his Alpha One Psionic Unit from loose talk by employees of the Pforzheimer Science Foundation. Three months later, the KGB had managed to actually *bribe* one of the directors of the Foundation, paying the man $100,000 to tell the Russians what he knew about the Alpha One Unit. And he had told them everything.

Who had the KGB bribed? Who was the man who had sold out to the Soviet Union, or could it have been a woman? Three of the directors were female. Antonin Yu-

din didn't know the name of the traitor—and a half-do\
Norway rats dropped in on him did not, could not, make him change his story. He didn't know because the bribe had been engineered by the KGB's *Special Service II*. the Counterintelligence Service of the First Chief Directorate. Yudin, as well as the agents the Death Merchant had killed in the lobby of The Ark and in the parking lot of Kennedy International, had been members of *Department-V* (in the First Chief Directorate), the Executive Action Department, or, in KGB parlance, the "wet affairs" division— blood "wet affairs." *Mokryye Dela* assassins. . . . Yudin confessed that he and the other "wet affairs" agents were members of an *Osobyi Otdel* (special section) unit, one of the best in the KGB.

The Soviet Union wanted the secret of Alpha One for one reason—the military potential of the device. *The Alpha One Unit, among other things, was the ultimate assassination weapon*. With Alpha One, the operator could induce stroke in, or "explode," the brain of any target anywhere in the world. A president, a king, a dictator, any man of power could be killed with Alpha One. Distance would not be a barrier. The target might be 500 feet underground in a room whose walls, floor and ceiling were 15-feet thick concrete reinforced with steel and lead. It wouldn't make any difference. Alpha One would still snuff out his life.

The Soviet Union intended to possess Alpha One at all costs. The KGB had been so desperate that, at Kennedy International, it had resorted to a very dangerous plan. A half-dozen KGB *Mokryye Dela* agents had marched boldly into the office of Airport Security and had presented their forged FBI credentials to the startled chief of airport security. It was all very hush-hush, they explained to him. Specifically, they, as agents of the Federal Bureau of Investigation, were there to take Dr. Davis and his party into custody. It was a matter of national security. Would the Chief of Airport Security lend a half dozen of his men to assist in the arrest?

It had been that ridiculously simple. American Airlines Flight 64 had landed. Dr. Wayne Davis, his secretary, and the two Agency men had walked out of the gate and had instantly been surrounded by a dozen men. They had been handcuffed, led away, and driven from the airport in three cars— into oblivion!

Courtland Grojean had asked Antonin Yudin: "How did your people know that someone would be meeting Davis?"

Yudin had seemed surprised that Grojean should ask such a question.

Number One: The Agent-in-Place within the Foundation—Mr. X!—had given the information to the KGB, Yudin said.

Number Two: Even so, said Yudin, it was only logical, on the KGB's part, to assume that someone would be meeting Dr. Davis and his party. The KGB had prepared for it, which is why they had enlisted the aid of airport guards. If Camellion had not had car trouble and had arrived on time, he too would have been taken into custody.

"I was the one who was supposed to meet Dr. Davis," the Death Merchant said savagely. "Now suppose you tell me how your comrades spotted me in the main concourse? Not even the traitor in the Foundation knew who I was, what I looked like, or how I would be dressed!"

Antonin Yudin could not supply the answer. He did say that the KGB had prepared for any eventuality, up to a point; hence the backup force of four in the airport's parking lot—Manlin Rich, Victor Hedmann, and the two KGB agents, the man and the woman.

Once more the inevitable answer made itself felt: Either Dr. Davis, his secretary, or one of the CIA men had to have told that they were being met by a man who would wait near the United Airlines ticket counter. They would not have volunteered that information. How then had the KGB gotten one of them, or all of them, to talk so fast—within 15 minutes after they were captured.

Another question that demanded an answer is why the KGB "wet affairs" people should have even bothered to lay a trap for Camellion? Why risk it? They had already taken Dr. Davis "into custody." Why go to the trouble to assassinate a single CIA man?

Where is Doctor Davis now? Camellion had asked Yudin. *What is the escape route?*

It had been on the schedule to fly Dr. Davis and his secretary to a farm in northern Maine the same day he was kidnaped. The name of the farm? Its location? Yudin had forgotten.

Five minutes and a dozen rats later, a screaming Antonin Yudin regained his memory. It was the Reed Farm on Route 159, a few miles west of the little town of Patten. Two days later, Dr. Davis and his secretary would be flown to St. John's, Newfoundland, where they and their captors would remain for three days, while waiting for a large fishing boat that would take them to Resolution Island, which lay between the Labrador Sea and the Hudson Strait at the tip of Baffin Island. The vessel would proceed north, very slowly, until word had been received from the *Eugene Origen,* a Soviet submarine, that Russian commandoes from the sub had captured the personnel of the Canadian weather station on the desolate island.

Camellion and Grojean believed the Soviet agent, but they had to be positive; they had to be certain.

"Yudin—you're a liar!" snapped Grojean.

"He's a stinking liar, a lying piece of Soviet filth!" screamed the Death Merchant, pretending to be enraged. To prove it, he dropped a dozen rats onto the horrified Yudin, yelling the question at the man, demanding to know why the KGB should go to all the trouble to take Dr. Davis and his secretary all the way to Resolution Island—more than 1,200 miles north of St. John's, Newfoundland—when they could rendezvous with the *Eugene Origen* almost anywhere in the Atlantic or in the Labrador Sea?

"Why?—damn you." screamed the Death Merchant.

It took half an hour to shock the rats into insensibility and to treat the more than a dozen rat bites on Yudin's body, plus another ten minutes to jerk the Russian's nervous system back from the whirlpool of hysteria. The KGB agent begged to be let out of the cage, but the Death Merchant refused—*No! Not until you tell us everything!*

Yudin—by now convinced that Camellion and the others would let the rats eat him alive—was only too happy to oblige. He explained that his people needed Resolution Island to test one of the Soviet's own "black boxes," a psionic L-Wave Disrupter. The test would consist of blacking out the city of Ottawa, the capital of Canada, and, for several days, to increase the murder and suicide rates of the city by interfering with the L-Waves of the city's inhabitants. Toward this end, the Russians had obtained a photograph of the powerplant that supplied electricity to Ottawa and a large picture postcard of the city.

Yudin explained that the two photographs were necessary, a vital must. They would be dropped into the "well" of the L-Wave Disrupter, as part of the process to obtain the desired results. Yudin's explanation evoked stares of astonishment from most of the men, but loud guffaws from Merle Duvane.

Grojean glared angrily at the CIA troubleshooter. "I take it you're amused?" he said dictatorially. His stare was twin bayonets that stabbed holes in Duvane, who wasn't the least bit awed by, or afraid of, his boss.

"You'd better believe it!" Duvane paused, overcome by giggling. Finally he managed to get out, "I think the Russians are as nutty as Dr. Davis and the rest of the believers in psionics. They all belong in a black hole of crazies. So you can blackout a city by dropping a photograph of that city into a machine, turning some dials, putting on a headband and 'concentrating'. Hogwash!"

"Merle, you're not a scientist!" Grojean said snappishly. "I would advise you not to criticize things you don't understand."

Duvane refused to budge from his opinion. "Maybe so. But I still know that black is black and white is white. I still know that some things are impossible. You don't black out cities with photographs!"

Camellion offered, "I think Thomas Hardy was on the right track when he wrote, 'While much is too strange to be believed, nothing is too strange to have happened.'"

Duvane let Camellion have a reproachful look. "Bullshit! Hardy was a writer, and writer's always have their heads in number nine clouds. I've yet to see a writer who's got enough sense to come in out of a thunderstorm."

With a trace of a smile, the Death Merchant turned his attention to Antonin Yudin—*The trouble with Duvane is that he's too dogmatic. He works on the premise that if he can't conceive it, it can't exist.*

He grinned broadly at the frightened Russian. "All right, my little Comrade. Where in St. John's have your KGB buddies holed up with Wayne Davis and Ursula Czerweny—and don't give me a line about not remembering! You're covered with so many rat bites right now that you'll be lucky if you don't die of rabies."

"I need a doctor," Yudin moaned, his body quivering.

"You'll need an undertaker if you don't answer my question!"

"They're at a f-fish oil refinery. Jebson's Refinery. That's all I know. But it won't do you any good to go to St.

John's. It's been six days since we grabbed Dr. Davis. Anytime now, Colonel Dolgov and the two captives will be leaving by boat for Resolution Island. Colonel Dolgov would kill your precious Dr. Davis before he'd turn him over to you Americans. . . ."

The Death Merchant turned in the swivel chair from the window when Courtland Grojean and Jacob Hall came into the office, noting the worried expression on the faces of the CIA covert section chief and the head of the ONI's New York office.

"Barret said he will meet us at Pepperell Air Force Base," Grojean said wearily. "I didn't give him the details. I only said it was a matter of national importance that concerned both our countries, Even with a scrambler, I didn't want to say too much over a telephone." He sank into a short-backed office chair and glanced in annoyance at Hall, who had gone to the portable walnut bar and was making an Alexander. A nondrinker, Grojean frowned upon those who did, especially when they were on duty. He conveniently ignored the fact that intelligence people never kept regular hours, that, more or less, they were always on duty.

"Did the Center have anything on Colonel Dolgov?" Camellion inquired.

"He's a new name to us." Grojean sounded bitter. "It doesn't matter what his background might be. He has to be good or he wouldn't be handling this caper. And I think he'll kill Davis and the woman if we and the Canadians trap him on the high seas."

"For the same reason, neither we nor the Canadians can drop paratroopers on Resolution Island, or have the navy go in," Camellion said.

Hall called from the bar. "Court, there's no crème de cacao here. "Would you know where there is a bottle?"

"Drink what's there," Grojean spit out. He turned and looked murderously at Hall, then turned back to Camellion. "The Canadians won't go for it—and you are suggesting that we let the Soviet Black Berets overpower the weather station and take the island, are you not?"

"We have to." Camellion's tone was firm. "Dolgov is on the boat. He won't land on the island until he gets word from the sub that the weather station had been secured;

and it's unlikely that we could mount any kind of attack to grab Davis while he's a prisoner on the fishing boat. Dolgov and his men would kill him and the woman before we could reach them."

"You mean, if Davis is even on a boat!" Hall, glass in hand, sat down next to Grojean and crossed his legs. "We can be certain that the two CIA men are dead, even if Yudin did say he wasn't sure of their fate. He only said that to protect himself. Your two men were excess baggage, Grojean. It's almost certain the Ruskies terminated them."

"You do have a point," Camellion responded to Hall. "The KGB knows we didn't kill Yudin, or his corpse would have been found in the lobby. They have to assume we have him and that he's spilled everything he knows."

"Yes, everything but the name of the vessel Davis will be on," Hall said, continuing to play the role of Devil's Advocate. "The KGB must work on the premise that Yudin has talked. Simple security demands that they resort to an alternate plan. Let's face it. The KGB isn't stupid. Those boys have had some amazing successes."

"They have had more failures!" Grojean said through clenched teeth. "We're ahead in Africa—at least the southern portion of the Dark Continent—and way out in front in the Near East."

"It isn't always possible to change plans at the last moment," Camellion pointed out to Jake Hall. "And the KGBers are taking a lot of damn fool chances. The stunt they pulled at Kennedy International proves as much— which reminds me!" He caught Grojean's eye. "I've been meaning to ask you: Why did American Airlines Flight 64 from Chicago land at Kennedy International? Flights that come to New York from within the U.S. always land at La Guardia Airport."

"You know how it is with the airlines in large cities," Grojean said. "One airport will take the extra traffic of another. Chicago for example. You don't always put down at O'Hare. Now and then you land at Chicago Midway."

Camellion's wisp of a smile was shrewd. "Sure. . . . and you had a crystal ball and knew in advance that Flight 64 would touch down at Kennedy International. Bunk! You might as well try to convince me that a doughnut is a pregnant Cheerio. Never play fox with a weasel, Grojean. You pulled wires and had Flight 64 diverted to Kennedy."

"HA HA! The Fox has been caught in the henhouse!" Hall said with a lilt to his voice.

"I had the flight diverted to Kennedy for reasons of security," admitted Grojean without batting an eye, as if being caught in an attempted falsehood was the most normal and natural thing in the world. "For Dr. Davis's security—and yours, Giffwangle. However, because of that arrangement we do have a slight problem."

The farsighted Camellion was way out in front of the CIA's clandestine section's boss. "I deduced that's how the Danish was dashed to the pavement. I take it that no one at the Pforzheimer Science Foundation was aware that Flight 64 was going to be switched from La Guardia to Kennedy—which leaves only your people. And yours, Hall."

Hall's heavy lidded eyes grew sharp and his glass paused halfway between the arm of his chair and his mouth. "You're out of line, Giffwiggle. The—"

"*'Giffwangle!'*" (Camellion felt like laughing at the sound of the name.)

"Whatever! You're still out of line—and I don't give a damn if you are one of Grojean's top spooks. The ONI's agents must pass a poly test once a month. Don't give me any garbage about how they can deliberately mess up a graph. A subject can flex his sphincters until it rains hail in hell the size of snowballs and make the graph look like a series of Mount Everests; but the operator will know he's up to something, that he's deliberately confusing the polygraph. With a man who is telling the truth and has nothing to hide, the graph will be almost as even as a pane of glass—and you know it."

"It's the same with my people," Grojean said prudently, locking his fingers together. "It adds up to this: my employees and Hall's agents didn't reveal anything. Yet somehow the KGB knew the plane would land at Kennedy. There has to be a logical explanation."

"You didn't ask Yudin about it?" Camellion said, thinking of Thor, Manny Rich's German shepherd. "At least you didn't while I was present."

"First things had to come first," explained Grojean, clearing his throat. "At this moment, Binson, Reid, and the others are checking out Yudin's story with him hooked up to a poly. During the questioning the boys will spring it on him out of thin air—how did the KGB know that Flight

64 was diverted to Kennedy International. We'll get the results of the test—and possibly the answer—before we land at Pepperell."

"I'm against it," Hall stated stubbornly. "We should call the President, explain the situation to him and have him call the Prime Minister in Ottawa."

"Don't be ridiculous," chided the Death Merchant. "By the time we explained the situation fully to the President, the KGB would have Davis in Moscow!"

"I'm not so sure about that," hedged Hall, color rising in his cheeks. "I feel that giving a full report to the President beats playing 'Gangbusters!' "

Grojean smiled at Hall—secretly pleased at the way the Death Merchant had insulted him. "Well Hall, if you don't have anymore remarkable rhinestones of wisdom for us, I suggest we make final plans. We take off from Long Island MacArthur Airport in two and a half hours."

"My people are ready." Hall finished his drink with one final gulp. "I just hope to God that the KGB left someone at Jebson's Refinery who can give us the name of that boat—if there is a vessel!"

Grojean, who has stood up and was carefully straightening his coat, did not comment. Neither did the Death Merchant, who was wondering who would now take care of Thor, Manny Rich's pet, now that Arnold Quincy was no longer around.

Quincy's corpse will no doubt be dumped in the Atlantic before sunrise. It only proves that midgets should not try to race with giants. . . .

Chapter Six

St. John's, Newfoundland. 24.30 hours. Ideal weather for the Death Merchant. Without a moon, the night was as dark as the heart of an Arab trader; the drizzling rain—so slight it was only a heavy mist—as cold as butane fluid when it touched one's face.

Camellion had never been to St. John's, one of the oldest and most easterly cities in North America; yet he knew a lot about the capital and largest city of Newfoundland, Canada. In the days of the old sailing ships, before the era of air attack, St. John's was in a strategic, well-protected position from the ocean. Located at the eastern end of the Avalon Peninsula, St. John's stood on the steep western slope of an excellent land-locked harbor that opened suddenly into the Atlantic. The entrance, known as the Narrows, was guarded by Signal Hill and by the South Side hills, and was about 1,400 feet wide, narrowing to 600 feet between Pancake and Chain rocks. A permanent settlement since the early seventeenth century, St. John's had begun as, and still was, a fishing port.

The Death Merchant also knew that the city of 90,000 dominated the economic and cultural life of the province. St. John's was Newfoundland's leading retail, wholesale, and service center and was the focus of transportation. It was a major ocean port and the base for the provincial fishing fleet. It was also the eastern terminal for the Canadian National Railway, the Trans-Canada Highway, and several national airlines; and it was a city that thrived with industry—shipbuilding, fish processing and fish-oil refining, tanning, and the manufacture of hardware, clothing, paint, furniture and marine engines.

St. John's also had, four and a half miles to the northwest, Pepperell Air Force Base, the first U.S. military installation outside of the continental United States. It was at Pepperell Air Force Base that Gordon Barret, the Director of the Canadian Intelligence Directorate, and his two men, and Admiral Ceil Webb, of the Royal Canadian Navy, met Courtland Grojean and the nine men with the American spymaster.

The Canadians were waiting on the tarmac for the Americans when the DCH-4 landed at Pepperell. The two intelligence chiefs greeted each other solemnly, after which they and their men piled into jeeps, which took them to one of the white buildings. Once they were in the building's large briefing room with American Air Force security men posted outside the outer door, Grojean and Roger Barnkoff explained the situation to the Canadians, the four men listening with grim fascination.

"It's utterly fantastic!" Barret said bleakly after Grojean and Barnkoff had finished giving the essentials. A chunky incisively intelligent man, Barret, slightly younger than Grojean, was an intellectual who quickly grasped the seriousness of the plot confronting him and his American counterpart.

He stared intensely at Grojean and Barnkoff. "Are you positive that Soviet scientists intend to black out Ottawa with their—what did you call their sinister machine?"

"An L-Wave Disrupter," said Barnkoff.

"We're sure." Sitting at the end of the long folding table, Grojean hunched himself forward. "We got the results of the polygraph test half an hour before we landed. Antonin Yudin told the truth. The Ruskies mean business."

"How can they interfere with the L-Waves of the Ottawans?" queried James Burke-Whit, one of the Canadian intelligence men. "In fact, what are these L-Waves? Are they related to the human aura?"

Roger Barnkoff quickly shook his head. "No relation at all to the aura. L-Waves are not electromagnetic in nature. To quantum physicists, Life-Waves involve that intangible force that makes a thing what it is. We're human beings because of L-Waves. A rock is a rock and a star a star because of L-Waves."

"One might say that L-Waves are direct thoughts from God," added Wilbert Donovan, who had a mystical turn of mind.

Charles Fond, another Canadian intelligence officer, began tapping the Sandalwood top of the conference table with the fingers of his left hand. "On the surface, I'd say that to knock out a power development station with a so-called 'Black Box' was impossible," he said in a deep baritone, "and to cause the murder and the suicide rate to rise—ridiculous!"

Grojean frowned at Fond. Gordon Barret, who didn't like his men talking out of turn and making snap judgments, looked disapprovingly at Fond, who was tall, needle-thin and had once been a basketball player of championship potential.

Barret and Grojean stared hard at Admiral Webb, who said, "It's my feeling that you Americans are trying to make a typhoon in a teapot." He glanced in amusement from Grojean to Barret. "In my opinion, this psionic business is science-fiction. No doubt, the Soviets are trying to pull something off against both our countries. But it's all probably a gambit operation."

"Admiral Webb, you are making a rash conclusion without having all the facts," Grojean said curtly, masking his anger at what he considered Admiral Webb's stupidity. "I'm not at liberty to tell you how we know, but I tell all of you—psionics works. I don't know how the Soviet L-Wave Disrupter works. I do know that Dr. Davis' Alpha One is a success. We tested it."

Webb smiled condescendingly and flicked ash from his cigar. "Or your people have interpreted the tests as being successful," he intoned. "Why even the name 'psionics' is misleading."

"Misleading?" Grojean's smile was barely discernible. "Perhaps, but only to those who have not taken the time to learn the facts. I lump those ingoramuses with the fools who believe in the myth of the 'Soviet Superman.' Those same uninformed nervous nellies are quick to point to the drug problems we are having with our troops, but they ignore the problem of the Soviets with their men—alcoholism! The highest rate in the world. Another thing is that few outsiders realize how the people of the satellite nations hate the Russians."

"There are also serious problems in the Soviet officer corps," pointed out Fred Thumm, looking at Admiral Webb. "For example, maps in the Soviet army are classified. Officers seldom work with them and the Russian GI never sees one. The company-grand officers are seldom brought into the planning process, and there's the problem of driver training. Eighty to ninety percent of Soviet enlisted men don't know how to drive. So they spend a lot of their time in truck parks wheeling around and around, under officer supervision, just learning."

"Yes, and the Soviet Union is well aware of its weaknesses," Jacob Hall said. "They know they're not strong enough to attack NATO."

Merle Duvane snorted. "That's obvious. The fact that the Russian pigs haven't attacked proves that!"

"We are ahead of the Soviet Union in other areas," Courtland Grojean announced. "We are 10 to 20 years ahead of those cultural primitives in microelectrics and constantly increasing our lead. We are three or four generations ahead in precision-guided weapons systems, and 10 to 20 years ahead in surveillance techniques. We're at least five years ahead in computerization in general, and steadily increasing our lead in war gaming, antisub warfare, signal processing, and early warning systems. We're another generation out in front in antitank and antiair missiles and are at work in several areas that the Soviets have hardly touched." He paused, cleared his throat and looked at the tip of the unlit Barclay cigarette in one hand. "Unfortunately, the Soviets are ahead of us in the field of psionics. At least they were until Dr. Davis invented his Alpha One unit."

"Admiral Webb," began Roger Barnkoff, "it would be evident to anyone that psionics is simply a name for the link between mind and matter. We have the theory of how psionics works, even if we can't commit that theory to mathematical formula. In all ultrasimplification, the mind of the operator 'leads' the energy of the emmanations—radiation, cosmic force, prana, Universal Mind—call it anything you want—along the path to the destination he desires. If the energy patterns of the earth are likened to a worldwide network of interconnected rivers and the waters in those rivers symbolize the particular frequency of each object, then the operator with his mind modulates those waters into waves and ripples, sending them along individual routes to their ultimate destination—forgive me, but I'm fond of analogies."

Admiral Webb drew a deep regenerative breath. "I'm not impressed. I hardly think the 'mind' of any operator can destroy a city's electrical source, much less take lives with murder and suicide." He sat back on the folding chair, folded his arms and set his jaws. "I think you Americans should spend your time on more rewarding enterprises. Crime control for example. Your streets are full of guns, full of crime."

Richard Camellion, who had been listening all this time, slumped in a chair, suddenly became alive.

"The streets are also full of scum and trash, Admiral. I suppose your solution would be to confiscate all weapons? Is that what you are implying, sir?"

Webb turned his head to the Death Merchant, for a moment his eyes devouring the tall, lean figure clad entirely in black.

"I would," he said, his expression and demeanor suggesting he expected a rebuttal. "For some years now, guns have been illegal in Canada and crime in our major cities has dropped."[1]

"I doubt that," Camellion said easily. "It's been over five years since Washington D.C. subjected people to the inanity of 'gun control.' In that time, despite a decrease in population, murder has increased 18 percent, robbery 24 percent and aggravated assault by 46 percent. The message is clear. The handgun ban is an asset to the criminal and a liability to the law-abiding citizen. Of course, citizens with common sense ignore the law. Since the halfwits in government won't protect them and the police can't, they have to protect themselves. You see, Admiral, you don't know what you're talking about!"

Not used to such bluntness, Amiral Webb drew back in angry surprise, not really knowing how to reply. Grojean smiled. Gordon Barret toyed with a cup of coffee, his nervous fingers busier than Fred Thumm's.

"You talk like a man who's had his head screwed on backwards, Admiral!" said Merle Duvane, who was even more blunt than Camellion. "You should join forces with Senator Edward Kennedy, Senator Moynihan, and the rest of the fools who were elected by even bigger fools. They're always screaming for gun control, when they take time out from trying to get Prime Minister Thatcher to grant political status to IRA trash."

"Now see here!" started a red-faced Webb. "I don't have to sit—"

The Death Merchant cut him off as though he didn't exist.

"Yeah, and isn't it strange how 'King Edward the First,' Moynihan and all the other bleeding heart liberals conveniently ignore how the brave freedom fighters blow up innocent women and children with bombs."

"Hold it!" Luke Drayer said crisply. "Admiral Webb has a point." He focused his attention on Camellion. "And don't give me that hogwash about a 'well-regulated militia.' If you're not a member of the National Guard, you don't have a constitutional right to keep and bear arms."

"Another idiot heard from," Duvane said to no one in particular.

"You're confused. Patrick Henry wasn't," Camellion said drily. "He said, 'Who are the militia? They consist of

---

[1]. There has been no change in the crime rate in Canada.

the whole people.' I suggest you read the Militia Act of 1792. It defined militia as 'every free, white, able-bodied male.' So you see, dummy, you and I are the militia and have a constitutional right to keep and bear arms."

Grojean, seeing the raging expressions on the tight faces of Webb and Drayer, realized that it was time for him to intervene. He knew that Drayer was no match for Camellion and Duvane in any verbal battle. Camellion alone would have slaughtered him and Admiral Webb as well. There was also Gordon Barret. The chief of Canadian intelligence was embarrassed for Admiral Webb.

"Gentlemen, gentlemen! Let's get back to the business at hand," Grojean said in a firm, rather loud, voice. He glanced at Barret. "Don't you agree, Mr. Barret?"

"To be sure," consented Barret, relieved. "The control of firearms in the United States doesn't have anything to do with the situation confronting us, the danger facing both our nations."

"Exactly," agreed Grojean. "By now, Colonel Dolgov and his men have Dr. Davis and Ursula Czerweny on the fishing boat and are headed for Resolution Island."

"It will be a simple matter for navy patrol boats to intercept the vessel, once we have her name," offered James Burke-Whit. An oddly attractive man, even though he was angular and stooped, he was completely bald and had very black, very bushy eyebrows.

"I'll have to have more definitive information before I send any vessels on some wild goose chase," Admiral Webb said stiffly, almost defensively. "I've given you my opinion of this psionics nonsense."

"Admiral, you will do as you are ordered!" Gordon Barret's voice came out like an unexpected shot. "You'll do what the Prime Minister orders you to do. If he says go to the North Pole in a row boat, you'll do it."

"We can't use the Canadian Navy," the Death Merchant said. "The KGB boy we captured maintains that Colonel Dolgov and his cutthroats will terminate Dr. Davis and the woman should we try to close in. We have to have Davis alive."

Barret, hesitating, studied the Death Merchant, confusion in his eyes. Grojean was in command, but this lean man, dressed in black, also spoke with authority.

Seeing the confounded expression on his Canadian counterpart's face, Grojean said quickly, "Mr. Giffwangle is the Chief Coordinator of this operation. In the field, he's an expert and I trust his judgment completely."

"I see." Barret looked at Camellion for a long moment, then shifted his attention back to Grojean. "Since you don't intend to stop the fishing boat on the Atlantic, what is your intention—to follow the vessel all the way to Resolution and attempt a rescue at the last moment—on the island?"

Courtland Grojean moved a finger slowly along the right side of his mustache. "Yes, but only after Dolgov and his men have taken over control of the weather station. It's our only halfway chance to get Dr. Davis out alive. Colonel Dolgov won't set foot on the island until he receives word from the Soviet submarine that the island has been secured."

Charles Fond pulled a long face. "It could be a no-win situation for the men at the weather station. The KGB will probably kill them."

Barret appraised Grojean with cool eyes, speculation and implication flowing all over his face. Finally he said, "And you expect me to go to the Prime Minister and ask him to risk the lives of the personnel at the station. That's what you're doing. You know that."

"Yes, I do. I'm asking you—I'm asking the Canadian Prime Minister—to risk the lives of a dozen men against. . . ." Grojean's voice trailed off and he sighed deeply. "Should the Russians get Dr. Davis to the Soviet Union and force him to reveal the secret of Alpha One—"

"They'll drag the secret out of him; you can bet on it," cut in Stephen Melbert. "Any man can be made to talk."

"Alpha One could give the Russians a weapon more valuable than a million hydrogen bombs. You must also realize, Mr. Barret, that by waiting until the Russians are on Resolution, we increase our chances of grabbing the Soviet psionic L-Wave Disrupter."

"The lives of twelve against possible millions!" Barret said in a brittle voice.

"You know the old cliché," Grojean said. " 'Either we hang together or we hang separately!' Your security is our security."

"Has the CIA Deputy Director talked to your President?" asked Barret. "I will need more than your word to convince Prime Minister Trudeau."

Grojean nodded. "The President has all the facts and knows the seriousness of the situation. He will give them in detail to the Prime Minister. Should Trudeau then refuse, then we will have done all we can do."

"In the meantime, we can investigate the fish oil refinery," suggested Richard Camellion. "If we don't get very lucky and find out the name of the boat, we'll be like ten cows in a five cow pasture."

Intervened James Burke-Whit rigorously. "We can't use American Air Force security people. It's against Canadian law."

"Manpower is no problem," Barret said in a relaxed tone. "We can use St. John's Metropolitan Police. In fact, I've had them standing by, ever since I talked to you on the radio." He turned and looked at the clock on the wall. "It's one-forty-four. By the time we contact the police and get to the refinery, it will be close to four o'clock."

The Death Merchant pushed back his chair and stood up. "I suggest we get organized. At this point, the fish oil refinery is the key to the success of the operation."

"Assuming you do obtain the name of the vessel, what will be required for the voyage to Resolution Island?" Barret inquired of Grojean, who looked at Camellion.

"A small, fast vessel, something on the order of an ASR, a submarine rescue vessel," Camellion said, "plus cold weather gear. Also antisubmarine ballistic missiles and a couple of dozen Canadian commandos—the best you have."

"That's a tall order," Barret said. "Anything else?"

"What everyone in our high-risk business needs—luck. Lots of luck. . . ."

Chapter Seven

"Are we going to stay out here in the rain all night or move in on the office?" hissed Merle Duvane, who was on his haunches next to the Death Merchant. To the right of Camellion was Luke Drayer, a short .45 Safari Arms Enforcer autoloader in his right hand. The three men were in front of a truck parked a hundred feet southeast of the office of the Jebson Fish Oil Refinery.

Luke Drayer mumbled, "There's no point in rushing in until we know what we're doing, right, Giffwangle?"

"We'll do it shortly," whispered the Death Merchant. "It's the lights on the second floor of the office that concern me. It's not right."

"It is unless you expect who ever's up there to sit in the fuckin' dark!" Duvane said laconically. He scratched his cheek with the muzzle of the silencer attached to the 9mm Super Star pistol.

"The lights are like an invitation," explained Camellion. He continued to stare at the pale yellow glow behind the shaded windows. "The KGB must operate on the supposition that we grabbed Yudin; therefore, the people at the refinery must have been warned. They should be expecting trouble. Yet the lights are on. It's illogical."

"So what else is new?" Duvane watched Camellion with sharp attention. "We'll never find out anything out here."

"It's also irrational that I'm here in Canada," mused Drayer. "My wife thinks I'm in France. That's the trouble with this business: you even have to fib to your own family."

"I don't have that problem." Duvane sounded grateful. "I've always thought of marriage like a dull meal, with the desert served at the beginning. I tried it once; I almost died of boredom."

Drayer didn't answer. Neither did the Death Merchant. Quite a few things were illogical in Camellion's estimation. Back at Apple Cart D-3KK, Courtland Grojean had implied—*By his silence!*—that the President of the United States was being kept in the dark about Operation Basilisk—*Yet only hours ago he told Barret that "the President has all the facts and knows the seriousness of the situation." Grojean is playing both ends against the middle. That is one of his weaknesses: he's too cautious.*

There was the leak about Flight 64. Mr. G. doesn't seem at all concerned about who it was that had tipped off the KGB. Nor did he seem worried about the identity of the traitor in the Pforzheimer Science Foundation. Totally illogical. Grojean was not only a perfectionist but a worrier. For him not to be concerned about untied knots was against his nature—*Unless he suspects Amschel Roth of selling out.*

Amschel Roth had been—and still is—a member of the famous House of Roth, the famous banking family that had operated in the Sudatenland for several hundred years. Herr Adolf Hitler had changed all that. He had bankrupted the family's fortunes. Most of the Roths had died in the various Nazi death camps. However, several were still alive. One of the fortunate members of the clan, Amschel had come to the United States in 1971 and had been hired by the Pfrozheimer Science Foundation as a financial consultant. Only he did little "consulting." The CIA was only interested in using his name.

But now is not the time to dwell on these paradoxes.

Feeling the cold drizzle on his face, Camellion studied the refinery. Right smack on the south central shore of St. John's Harbor, less than 30 miles west of St. John's Bay, the Jebson refinery was composed of two long buildings, each built of gray-white quarry stone, the northeast end of the shorter building attached to the southwest end of the larger—both in length and width—structure. The office—the destination of Camellion, Duvane and Drayer—was at the east end of the larger building. In this larger building fish were cleaned, then boiled in the rendering process to extract the oil (mostly glycerides) that was used to make soap, vitamin pills, and other commercial products. The boiler that supplied the steam was in the west end of that building, the long dock attached to its northeast side. The loading dock, where the fish oil barrels were loaded into trucks, jutted from the south side of the smaller and shorter structure.

The Death Merchant saw that only four small bulbs burned over the loading dock. Otherwise, the entire area was as dark as the inside of a mackerel's gut. Camellion made up his mind. Something was wrong—*And it's not in Denmark.* But what?

Camellion pulled a Yaesú FT 207R handie-talkie from its case on his belt underneath his wool cape-style jacket, switched it on, pressed the button for the 143 MHz channel and contacted Charles Fond, who was the acting Canadian coordinator for the strike force moving against the fish oil refinery.

"Fond, is everyone in place—over?"

"A dozen of the police are scattered among the trees

west of the short building," replied Fond, his voice tinny over the walkie-talkie. "Half of them will enter the smaller building; the other half will go along the northwest side, then come down along the northeast side of the main building. We'll move in from the south. There are two police speedboats a third of a mile out in the harbor, in case anyone tries to escape by water. What's the delay? You were supposed to give the word five minutes ago. Over."

"Close the ring. Move in," Camellion said. "We'll take the office. Give me word that you've got it. Over."

"Confirmed and out."

"Well, that's that," Duvane announced, watching the Death Merchant put away the walkie-talkie. "We can pick the lock of that office door in sixty seconds flat. Damn it! This body-danger shield itches."

"It must be a case of nerves," Drayer said. "Mine doesn't itch. These bulletproof deals are made by CCS Communications Control[1] and that outfit is the biggest and the best in the business. I've worn their vests for years and they don't itch."

"You sound like you're a salesman for them!" chided Duvane. He glanced up at the pitch-black sky and muttered under his breath because he couldn't see anything.

The Death Merchant pulled a .22 High Standard "Victor" auto-pistol from underneath his coat. The top-of-the-line production gun produced by High Standard, the Victor was intended for use by the advanced competitive shooter, its features including a full-length ventilated rib, which held both front and rear sights, removable barrel weights (which Camellion had removed) and trigger adjustments for weight of pull and overtravel. With a five and a half inch barrel, the Victor weighed 47 ounces. To the muzzle of the barrel of this Victor was attached a noise suppressor.

Camellion was not going to engage in any "advanced competitive shooting." He had chosen the High Standards because they were deadly effective at close range. It was for this reason that most assassination teams[2] preferred weapons of .22 or .25 caliber, although experts among experts, such as Camellion, preferred heavier calibers, such

1. In quality of equipment, CCS Communications Control, Inc. is the Rolls Royce of the security world. World Headquarters are at 633 Third Avenue, New York, N.Y. 10017.

2. The Mossad prefers a Beretta .22 fitted with West German cartridges.

as 9mm pieces. In this area, the High Power Browning and Walthers were favorites.

"We're not going in through the office door," the Death Merchant said, pulling back the slide of the .22 Victor, then pushing on the safety. "There's something funny going on in there and we're not going to do the expected."

Merle Duvane didn't argue. "How then?"

"Did you notice the glow of lights from the north, from the other side of the main building?" offered Luke Drayer.

"We'll angle in to the southeast corner of the office, go up the east side and go in through a window on the north side, or maybe through one of the windows in the main building itself," Camellion told Duvane. "The lights are from the pier," he said to Drayer. "But there should be boxes and crates on the wharf. We can keep to the shadows when we go inside through a window."

"Let's stop yakkin' about it and do it," Duvane said, annoyed. "We'll be damned lucky if we don't come down with the crud from this rain."

The three left the truck yard and, spreading out and keeping as low as possible, began darting in a crisscross to the southeast corner of the two story office, their booted feet crunching against the wet asphalt that was part of the area where the trucks were parked.

Within several minutes they reached the corner of the office and started to move along the east side, all three stopping in alarm when the chattering of a submachine-gun shattered the stillness of the early morning.

"THAT tears it!" snarled Duvane. "The sons of bitches are wise to us. I knew this was going too easy."

"It sounds like the firing's coming from the south end of the storage building," Duvane said angrily to Camellion and Duvane. "Whoever it is must have spotted the police to the south."

"No doubt," Duvane said. "There's a light by the southwest corner of the storage section." He tapped the Death Merchant on the shoulder. "Okay, wiggle-waggle—what now?"

"Simple. We continue on schedule," Camellion said, and pulled the second .22 High Standard from the special holster on his belt. "Luke, you watch the windows on the second floor."

With all the stealth of a big cat on the hunt, he moved

along the east wall to the northeast corner, looked cautiously around the edge, then drew back, hardly believing what he had seen. Jackpot!

He turned and whispered gleefully to Duvane and Drayer, "Take a look. It's winning night at Vegas!" Then he stepped to one side.

Duvane and Drayer moved to the corner and looked around the edge.

"By God! This must be the Night of the Big Santa!" exclaimed Duvane, his gaze traveling up the wooden planking of the 150-foot long pier that, from the north side of the building to the edge of the water, stretched 40 feet. Another 10 feet was directly over the water.

By the dim light cast from the shaded single 60 watt bulb, mounted on a post in the middle of the pier, Duvane and Drayer could see a group of people hurrying toward the edge of the dock, a few of the women carrying small suitcases, some of the men holding either machine-guns or assault rifles—impossible to tell which in the dim light.

Duvane and Drayer—and Camellion, who had gotten down on his knees and was looking through Drayer's legs—didn't need a crystal ball (or a "Black Box") to know that the group was headed to the edge of the pier where a sleek Blue Star cabin cruiser was bobbing gently in the dark water. All the people had to do was climb down the wooden ladder, cross the narrow pier at almost water level and get on board.

"They're not even halfway there yet," Camellion said, several notes of victory in his voice. He stood up and switched off the safeties of the .22 High Standard autopistols. "But be careful. They won't give up without a fight. We'll wait until we reach those crates twenty feet in front of us. They'll give us cover."

"Okay—GO!" Drayer said.

They were three-fourths of the way to the refrigerator-sized crates (each of which contained eight small empty barrels) when their plan dissolved like smoke before the wind. To the northeast, a few hundred feet out in the harbor, several spotlights suddenly knifed the blackness with their shafts of dazzling white. One of the police boats had floated in close and had spotted the would-be escapees on the pier.

A voice came loudly over an electric bullhorn from the

police vessel, "You people there! Stay where you are! We're the police!"

Just as the Death Merchant and the two other men reached the crates and got down, another voice shouted from the west end of the pier, "Hands up, all of you, or we'll open fire!" This voice did not come through a bullhorn.

"We have them cold," Drayer said with satisfaction and started to raise himself from behind the crate, preparatory to stepping out into the open. The Death Merchant grabbed him by the shoulder and roughly jerked him down.

"Idiot! You want to get yourself killed?" Camellion said huskily. "The police don't know who you are. We're supposed to have gone into the office—remember?"

Duvane giggled. "Yeah, you dumb paper-pusher. If those trigger happy cops at the end—"

The screaming roar of weapons cut him off. Instead of surrendering, the enemy had elected to fight; some of them firing at the police as they turned and ran back across the pier toward the building, the others firing at the two spotlights on the police boat.

For the moment, Camellion, Drayer, and Duvane, crouched by the southeast side of three crates of empty fish oil barrels, were safe. The police to the west couldn't see them. Neither could the police in the boat. Where to go next?

The Death Merchant looked at the side of the main building, thirty feet away, to his left. All the overhead-folding doors were down and locked, except for those a hundred feet to the west, toward which the enemy was running. There were windows every thirty feet or so—the old fashioned rope, pulley-and-weight kind, that could be raised. The closest window to the Death Merchant and Duvane and Drayer was directly across from the crates and slightly behind them, to the east.

Camellion caught Duvane and Drayer's eyes and motioned toward the window. "It's our only chance," he said. "If that boat pulls in any closer, we might get raked with slugs."

"It's probably locked." Drayer almost shouted to make himself heard above the roaring of automatic weapons. "And if the police to the west see us? . . ."

"Shoot out the glass," suggested Duvane. "With all the

firing going on, neither the cops nor the Canadians will hear the falling glass."

"But how do we get through the window?" demanded Drayer. "It will take at least several minutes for us to crawl through . . . well, a minute anyhow. The cops could ace all three of us in less than ten seconds."

The Death Merchant supplied the answer. "We'll wait until the Canadians are inside. The police will knock out windows up front. After everyone's inside, we'll make our move."

"This time tell sad-butt Fond where we are," Duvane said heavily.

The Death Merchant raised one of the .22 High Standard silenced target pistols. . . .

The police at the west end of the dock and in the boat on St. John's Harbor returned the fire of the Candaians who would dart toward the building, stop, fire, then resume their dash for momentary safety. Riddled, three of the police lay sprawled on the ground.

The police were also getting results. One of the Canadians cried out loudly, spun halfway around and crashed to the dock. Then another man cried out, dropped his 9mm Star sub-gun and toppled forward to the dock. A third Canadian screamed as several 9-millimeter Sterling MG projectiles practically ripped his right hand from his wrist. He staggered but kept going. One of the women with a suitcase didn't. A bullet caught her in the right hip. Another one stabbed into her right rib cage. With a short, high scream, she fell to the dock, quivered a moment, then lay still.

Having shot out the glass of the window, including the shards at the bottom of the frame, the Death Merchant shoved a full magazine of .22 Long Rifle cartridges into the High Standard pistol he had used. Now, he and the two intelligence operatives waited. To their right, the bright beams from the spotlights continued to sweep over the dock, now and then one of the shafts of light touching the north side of the crate against which Luke Drayer was making himself small.

At length, Camellion and the other two men heard glass breaking to the west. Good. The St. John's police were moving in. The Death Merchant looked around the edge of the crate protecting him. He couldn't see any of the Canadian enemy, except for the corpses of the two men and the woman lying on the dock. Toward the end of the building, he could see a knot of men, some of them crawling through a window.

"Get set," he said. He waited until the last of the police officers was inside the building, then whispered, "Let's go."

Camellion turned and raced across the short space to the window he had shot out. A .22 High Standard pistol in each hand, he was swinging his left leg over the sill by the time Merle Duvane and Luke Drayer reached the window. In almost no time at all, all three were inside the dark building and down and listening beside a stainless steel cooking vat. While there were sounds of gunfire from the shorter building, the inside of the main building was very still, the only sound a low *ger-uug-ger-uug-ger-uug* of a pump in the southeast corner.

The Death Merchant took out the walkie-talkie, contacted Charles Fond and, in a low voice, told him of their new position, that an approach had not been made through the office building, but that they had come in from the dock side, and that they should "Contact the police and let them know where we are. Tell them that the Canadians are between us and them. Give me confirmation—over."

"You have it," Fond's voice came back. "I'll contact Inspector Wickson then I and my group will move forward—out."

Shoving the Yaesu transceiver into its case, the Death Merchant glanced at Duvane and Drayer. In the very dim light he could barely see the two men; yet he could see enough. A .45 SA Enforcer in each hand, Drayer looked worried, his big face forlorn. As for Duvane, he looked the way he always looked—angry at the world.

Drayer's voice was as edgy as his expression was restive. "I estimate that the targets are maybe seventy to eighty feet ahead of us. Since they have automatic weapons, we're going to have a devil of a time getting even one prisoner. How do you want to do it, Giffwangle?"

Camellion, checking his backup firepower, a Smith & Wesson .41 magnum revolver, whispered, "We'll swing toward the center. The police know we're here. The Canadians don't. The police will drive them straight to us."

"Suppose none of them want to surrender?"

"We'll have to play it by ear; it's the best we can do."

"What we need is some light," Merle said. He had taken an Ingram MAC-11 submachine gun from underneath his suede coat and was inserting a magazine of .380 shells into the deadly little weapon, which was not equipped with a noise suppressor. "We can't be more than twenty feet from the back wall. Let's look for the switchbox and shed some light on the situation."

With the stink of fish strong in their nostrils, they crept toward the wall that was between the office and the main floor, or section, of the fish oil plant. As the minutes passed, their eyes became accustomed to the darkness; even so, their sight extended to only a few feet around them. Consolation in that the vision of the enemy—and of the police as well—would be as equally limited? Indeed not. For there was a danger in mutually limited vision, the danger of the enemy bumping into them and both sides firing at point blank range—the danger of mutual annihilation.

Five feet apart, the Death Merchant in the lead, the three men reached the wall and began to creep to the left, looking for the switchbox. There wasn't any. The surprise came when they were almost to the center of the wall. The lights came on in the shaded bulbs overhead. The police, at the opposite end of the building, had found the master switch.

Blinking against the sudden glare, the three men tossed themselves prone to the floor and, listening intently, took stock of their position. They deduced at once that they were in the cleaning section of the plant. There were long, porcelain-topped tables on which rested knives and other cleaning instruments. After the fish were cleaned—heads hacked off and organs removed—they were placed on large metal trays, resting on skate wheel conveyors, and taken to the washers toward the center of the floor. From the washers the fish were conveyed to the steam heated cookers. The next step was the oil extracting machines located in the west end, not far from the enclosed boiler that furnished steam for the cookers.

The Death Merchant was not happy about the setup in the east end—*In some places there is too much cover. In other spots, not enough. Fudge! A white blind honkey in South Chicago would have a better chance!*

He motioned to Drayer and Duvane, indicating that they should squirm ahead and take positions behind metal drums filled with fish heads and intestines. *Only a vitamin plant could stink more!*[3] Along with the other two, he began to belly-crawl on the dirty concrete floor, hating the stink, hating the Russians, hating the murderous human race, but loving the line of work he had chosen. His was a job in which he constantly had to cross swords with the unknown and the unpredictable.

A few moments before he and the other two men reached the garbage drums, gunfire exploded once more, the inconsonant racket shattering the tension-filled quietude. There was the middle-pitched snarling of Heckler & Koch MP line submachine guns, mingled with the higher snarling of the Sterling MGs the St. John's police were using, the firing punctuated by the screaming of ricochets.

"Well now, that double-twists the tail off the turtle!" Duvane whispered grimly. "The targets are not more than fifty to sixty feet in front of us. A dozen or more of them! Three of us! And them with chatterboxes. Makes a guy wanna write his will, doesn't it?"

Luke Drayer also proved he had battle-wise experience by saying calmly to Camellion, "We have here a situation in which the odds are eighty percent against us. I suggest we retreat to the office."

"I suggest we even the odds. You two keep a sharp lookout," Camellion whispered back. On his knees beside a hydraulic drum lifter supporting a large cargo plate with two open barrels filled with fishheads, he reached into the left pocket of his jacket and took out a flat, metal blue box, opened it and removed the Seltex speaker. The device was only two inches wide in diameter and an inch thick—an inch and one-third including the "bump" filled with the miniaturized transmitter. He placed the speaker on top of the drum lifter's right side flat bar brace, then returned the blue box to his pocket, picked up the two High Standard autopistols and whispered in a loud voice to Duvane and Drayer, "Let's move to the right, to the sides of that first cooker."

"Well—hell!" muttered Duvane. "We could have done this a while ago—or stayed where we were." But he didn't

---

3. Some vitamins are made from rotting animal organs. The "rotting" is, of course, carefully controlled.

argue. He began to crawl. So did Camellion and Drayer, all three moving along the grimy floor caked with blood and hardened bits of the insides of fish. They squirmed between drums filled with fishheads and intestines, went underneath several skate wheel conveyors and all the while kept their eyes toward the west. The enemy could appear at any moment.

Three-fourths of the way to the other side, the Death Merchant, spotting nine drums resting on three no-tilt factory platform trucks, got an idea. One of the trucks was parked with its front facing south, the three drums on the bed facing the west. The two other trucks were placed in such a manner that their sides were to the south.

Camellion called a halt and whispered, "I'm going to wait here behind these drums. You two go on to the first cooker. Shoot to kill. I'll cripple several of the slobs if I can."

Drayer and Duvane crawled on. The Death Merchant snuggled behind the "walls" of nine metal drums. To the west the firing continued, but with some difference: the firing of the Canadians to the west was steadily getting closer to Camellion.

Out again came the blue box. The Death Merchant opened it and removed the Seltex microphone with its built-in AVE-C.[4] Patiently he waited. Patiently he watched. He soon spotted the first two of the enemy, frantic-faced men who looked trapped and desperate in spite of the H&K MP5 machine guns they carried. Stumbling, at times almost on their hands and knees, the two men, both in their early thirties, finally got down behind some garbage barrels ten feet or so east of the positions that Camellion and his two companions had occupied.

Presently, three more men appeared, coming from around a hydraulic jack crane, the one in a thick brown turtleneck sweater holding his left arm, blood dripping from his left hand. Falling all over the place, they got down with the other two men and waited for the police to put in an appearance.

4. *Automatic volume expansion circuit.* This is an audio-frequency circuit that automatically increases the volume range by making loud portions louder and weak ones weaker. This is done to make radio reception more like the actual program because the volume range of programs is generally compressed at the point of broadcast.

A woman appeared. Gray-haired, dressed in a navy pant suit and a tan shearling jacket, she carried a man's overnite case. She was followed by a Mutt & Jeff pair of cruds. One man, without a coat, had a gaudy shirt so colorful it reminded the Death Merchant of wallpaper in a fag's bedroom. He carried a .357 Llama Comanche revolver in his left hand.

The taller boob—*He looks as oily as a corporate head and as scared as an Arab at a Barmitzvah!*—decked out in a Tartan plaid jacket carried a Ruger carbine chambered for the .44 magnum cartridge. Furthermore, the woman and the two men were moving straight toward a now concerned Camellion, who knew he had to act before he was face to face with the woman and the two creeps with her. Even if the trio went around the barrels, the odds were that one of the approaching enemy would see him. Much worse, several enemy weapons were still firing to the west, in the hands of men the Death Merchant could not see. One was definitely a chatterbox. The other sounded like an assault rifle.

I don't have much choice! In another half a minute that broad will be close enough for me to tickle her tits! Camellion switched on the small microphone, put the instrument close to his mouth and said, "You're surrounded!" Amplified by the mike and by the volume compressor circuit in the 2½" Seltex speaker, his order came out of the speaker almost as a low shout, a commanding cry that completely frightened the five men behind the barrels to Camellion's right and terrorized the woman and the two men, now only six to nine feet in front of the Death Merchant.

The explosion, a thunderous crash so close that it rattled empty trays on tables, sent more waves of panic rolling through the Canadians—and it didn't do anything for the nerves of Merle Duvane and Luke Drayer, both of whom realized their act was about to begin. And it startled the well being of one Richard Camellion, who leaned around one of the barrels, raised the silenced High Standard pistols and expertly began squeezing the triggers, firing with a deadly accuracy, making his hundreds of hours of practice pay off.

The woman screamed like a tom cat stuck with a pitchfork when a .22 Long Rifle bullet shattered her right knee cap and another hunk of .22 lead stabbed her in the left shoulder, the high velocity slug streaking through the deltoid muscle and breaking the scapula. Knocked first one way and then another, Nadine Pouchett acted, for a mini-moment, as if she didn't know which way to fall. But fall she did. The overnite case fell from her hand as she went down, falling to the left, striking the concrete on her right hip only a second after Camellion had put two .22 projectiles into the chest of the crum with the fag wallpaper shirt, and placed a bullet into the left kneecap of the stringbean with the Ruger carbine. The .357 Llama revolver slipped from the fingers of the tall corpse who was toppling to the right, an expression of horror fixed on his wedge-shaped face. He had almost reached the floor, just five feet behind the woman who was squirming and moaning, when the silencers on the High Standards went *bazitttttt* and two .22 Long Rifle slugs hit stringbean who was crashing to the right, one striking his left forearm and lodging in the brachioradialis muscle, the second, in the right upper arm, coming to rest in the biceps. Screaming, stringbean fainted and collapsed to the floor.

No sooner had the Death Merchant fired the last shot than he pulled back and threw himself down behind the six filled drums facing the south. He was just in time, the five men behind the other barrels—thirty feet away, spotting him sooner than he had expected.

Three of the men cut loose with an MP5 SD1 music box, a British 9mm EM2 sub-gun and an Israeli 5.56mm Galil assault rifle, the firing a tornado of savage sound. Scores of hydraulically swaged round-nosed projectiles bored through the rounded metal sides of the three barrels in the outer row, the powerful slugs ripping through the fishheads and intestines and tearing out the other sides into the metal of the other three drums. But now the power of the projectiles was on the wane and they came to rest halfway through the barrels, lodged in the stinking mass of fish entrails.

Huddled like a giant fetus by the inner sides of the barrels, the Death Merchant holstered one High Standard and pulled the big Smith & Wesson .41 magnum. For the time being, there wasn't anything he could do but wait for lag time on the part of the enemy and hope that Duvane and Drayer were only half as good as they were cracked up to be.

The CIA man and the ONI agent were even better.

Merle Duvane had already spotted Dennis Mense and

Lowren Pettiford, the last two Canadians to the west, the two that the Death Merchant had heard but had not been able to see. Fortunately for Camellion, Duvane and Drayer had obeyed only half his order. While Duvane had taken a position by the west side of the first tall cooker, Drayer had not. Drayer had felt that for him to take a position on the east side of the cooker would put him in too close a proximity to Duvane. One horizontal enemy burst might ace them both out. Accordingly, Drayer had crawled across the floor, moving east until he came to a counterweight lift truck that was only eight feet from the east wall. He had gotten behind the lift truck and waited. Now he acted. Looking out, he saw that he was only 50 feet to the northeast of the men firing at Camellion. Experience quickly warned him that he would have only a few seconds to whack out the three before one had time to turn a chatter box in his direction. Grant Heary, the fourth, was down among the drums, both his 9mm Browning auto and his Finnish Valmet rifle[5] empty. He had shoved a magazine into the Hi-Power Browning and had pulled back the slide, but the weapon had jammed. Troy Labruyere, the fifth man, was in agony from a bullet in his arm and unable to fire. Heary was trying to extract the jammed cartridge in the firing chamber when lag time caught up with the three men who were firing. It was the jammed Browning that saved Heary's life, for the instant that the three stopped throwing projectiles at Camellion, Luke Drayer brought up his twin Safari Arms Enforcers, aimed with both eyes open—partly by instinct, partly by experience—then pulled the triggers, the first two flatnosed .45 bullets hitting the targets within a hundredth of a second of each other.

"UGG!" Dropping the Galil assault rifle, one man was flung back by the impact of the bullet in the right side of his chest. Half a blink! The man with the British EM2 jerked and fell to the left, a .45 projectile having gone into his body below the breast bone and blown apart his spine. He was dead before he even started to sag. Confused, the third man hesitated, unable to comprehend for the moment what was happening. He gave up trying when the Death Merchant's .41 magnum slug and Drayer's .45 bullet put two large holes in his chest and sent him stumbling back

---

5. The Finnish semi-automatic version of the Russian AK-47. The weapon uses a 7.62 X 39mm cartridge.

against one of the other men who had fallen, as well as against Heary and Labruyere, the latter of whom had passed out.

Due to his position behind the counterweight lift truck, Luke Drayer did not see Lowren Pettiford who had been ducking and dodging to the east with Dennis Mense. But the Death Merchant spotted Pettiford, then Mense, at the same time, Merle Duvane caught sight of first Mense then Pettiford.

With a low laugh, Duvane raised the MAC-11 and fired simultaneously with the Death Merchant. A stream of .380 projectiles popped all over the massive Denny Mense, the hail of swaged lead tearing off itty-bitty pieces of his shirt jacket as they stabbed into his flesh and took away forever his hopes and his dreams, his cares and his worries. Duvane didn't swing the vicious little MAC-11 SMG to Pettiford. He didn't have to. He saw what Camellion's .41 magnum slug was doing to Pettiford's head. The man's cranium exploded into a bloody mess of shattered bone, flying blood, and fragmented brain matter. Almost headless, his neck spurting a fountain of thick red, Pettiford toppled to the floor, his Czech M-58 assault rifle falling beside him.

Heh, heh, heh. . . . Duvane, who derived great satisfaction from killing swine, pulled back by the side of the washer, got down and waited. Drayer dropped behind the lift truck. *Listen! Don't make a sound. Wait.* . . .

The Death Merchant was doing the same thing—listening and waiting—knowing that he who rushes in a fire-fight often ends up with cemetery grass for a cover.

There wasn't any firing, the stillness acquiring an extra measure of intenseness without the roaring of SMGs and A-Rs. He became instantly angry with himself when he jumped slightly from the buzzing of the walkie-talkie on his belt. He pulled out the transceiver and switched it on. The caller was Inspector Claude Wickson of the St. John's Police.

"Mr. Giffwangle? Over."

"You're talking to him—over."

"All the wanted men are in your area. We heard the firing. Did you get them all?"

The Death Merchant explained that a man and a woman were wounded but not in immediate danger of dying—"They're not in any condition to offer resistance. Don't worry about them."—and that, to his knowledge, there were only two men left in fighting condition. "Behind some drums not far from me. I'll toss some slugs their way to draw fire. That will give you an idea of their location when you come this way. Is that okay with you, Inspector? Over."

"Jolly good. We'll do it that way—out."

Camellion switched off the walkie-talkie. *Jolly good? Maybe I should have said "Smashing, old bean?"* He shoved the transceiver into its case, leaned around one of the barrels, raised the .41 magnum revolver and triggered off four rounds, the loud BOOMS of the big weapon echoing up and down the long building.

Taking his cue from the Death Merchant, Luke Drayer also sent six slugs into the cans. The enemy would not be able to hear the SA Enforcers, but they wouldn't escape hearing the *WANGGGGSSSS* of the projectiles cutting through the metal.

Grant Heary—all alone among the dead, except for Troy Labruyere who was unconscious—was neither crazy brave nor a fool. To continue fighting would be ridiculous. They'd kill him. His hands shaking, he threw the still jammed Hi-Power Browning and the empty Valmet rifle over the cans and shouted at the top of his lungs, *"I QUIT! I SURRENDER! DON'T FIRE!"*

The police force had taken casualties. Three of the St. John's policemen had died on the dock. Two had been killed inside the main building and one seriously wounded with a bullet in his right thigh. Four more policemen— three uniforms and one plain clothes dick—had died instantly from the explosion in the office, by the dynamite that had been triggered when the police had forced open the door.

"How did you know the office was wired?" Duvane, cocking his head at an angle, looked quizically at the Death Merchant.

"I didn't know. It was only a hunch," Camellion said. "If a hunch is constant and strong enough, I listen to it." He turned and walked toward Charles Fond, who was talking to Jacob Hall, Fred Thumm, and Inspector Wickson, all four watching ambulance workers place dead bodies onto stretchers.

Paramedics were giving emergency treatment to Nadine

Pouchett, Troy Labruyere, and Stanley Edelbrock whom Camellion had shot in both arms. All three were on stretchers and were about to be carried from the building into ambulances.

Grant Heary, his arms handcuffed behind his back, stood frozen-faced and fearful, a police officer on either side of him.

"Mr. Fond, tell the medics and the police to leave the building and leave the four prisoners behind."

Inspector Wickson, perplexed over Camellion's brutal request—or had it been an order—frowned at the Death Merchant.

A large-boned man who was prematurely gray, Fond hesitated, a shadow of doubt veiling his face. He had never been confronted with such a decision-making situation and was unsure of what course of action to follow.

The Death Merchant, deducing the Canadian intelligence officer's thoughts from the dubious expression on his face, helped Fond to make up his mind.

"Nine policeman are dead and one is seriously wounded," Camellion reminded him in a low serious voice, "and Time is the biggest thief in town. We must have the name of the vessel."

"Time is what we don't have!" Merle Duvane interrupted, staring at Charles Fond whom he considered a namby-pamby yes-man. "And your boss and our boss aren't here. Big brains like them can't afford to be shot at; they might get scratched."

"We must have the name of the ship," Camellion said again, only more firmly.

Fond made up his mind. "You're right, Giffwangle. We're going to have to stretch time as it is." His eyes shifted to an amazed Inspector Wickson. "Inspector, you and your men please leave the building and wait outside, and give orders to the ambulance people and the paramedics to leave. On our way back to town, we'll get together on what information you're to release to the press. All of you and the ambulance men will have to sign a loyalty oath about what happened here tonight." He raised his hand when he saw anger forming on the lined rugged face of the police official. "Wait! This is an intelligence affair and involves the security of Canada. Now, what did you want to say?"

"We'll wait outside," the Inspector said nervously. He

moved off to gather his men and to tell the ambulance people to vacate the building. One paramedic refused so adamantly that Wickson brought him over to Fond and "Mr. Giffwangle."

A short man with red hair and an aggressive manner, the paramedic glared first at Fond, then at Camellion. "I don't know what is going on here," he flared, "but I can't leave that man over there." Half-turning, he pointed at Troy Labruyere who, strapped to a stretcher, was barely conscious. "He's lost a lot of blood and needs a transfusion. He must be taken to the hospital immediately. All of the wounded need medical attention. Do you understand that?"

"Fella, you're butting into things that don't concern you," Camellion said evenly. "I suggest you leave."

Fond held up a hand. "I'll handle this, if you don't mind." He reached into his pocket, pulled out a leather card case, opened it and thrust it under the startled face of the paramedic whose eyes widened when he saw the words *Office of Intelligence, Government of Canada* at the top of the blue card.

Fond said, "Now leave the building unless you want to spend the next five years in Wentworth-Col."[6]

The paramedic didn't hesitate. He turned and hurried from the building with the other men.

Luke Drayer and James Burke-Whit had taken Grant Heary in tow and, on the Death Merchant's orders, jerked him by the arms over to where the three wounded captives were lying on stretchers.

Camellion pulled a High Standard auto-pistol, ignored the frightened Heary and said pleasantly to Fond, "What's the maximum penalty for espionage in Canada?"

"Death," Fond replied. "All of them will probably be executed."

The Death Merchant nodded, turned to a terrified Heary and smiled. "In that case, if this piece of trash and the others die in the next ten minutes, it won't make any difference. You, walking corpse, what's the name on your birth certificate?"

"Grant Heary." The doomed man tried to keep his voice steady.

---

6. The nickname for Canada's "Alcatraz"—located 17 miles northwest of Ottawa.

"Well, Grant Heary, if you feel that I'm only kidding or merely trying to frighten you—wrong you are!"

Calmly, the Death Merchant turned halfway, pointed the High Standard at Troy Labruyere and gently squeezed the trigger—once, twice. The noise suppressor whispered. Two black-edged holes appeared in the center of Labruyere's forehead. His body shuddered, then lay very still.

Camellion turned the muzzle of the silencer on the High Standard .22 target pistol toward Heary, who would have sagged to the floor on rubber legs if Luke Drayer and Burke-Whit had not been supporting him.

"It's remarkable how easily a man can die," Camellion said cheerfully. "On the other hand, a man can die slowly and very painfully. I'm told that when a man is shot in the gut it's like having a redhot poker stuck in your insides."

Smoking a cigarette, Jacob Hall helped to intensify the fright of Heary, saying with a sneer. "This son of a bitch isn't going to talk. Shoot him in the naval and get it over with."

"I want the name of the vessel the Russians are using to go to Resolution Island." Camellion glared at the man and shoved the muzzle forcefully into his stomach. "I want the name—right now!"

"The *Night Hawk*," blubbered Heary. . . .

Chapter Eight

The weather report did not fill Richard Camellion and the other people on board the *Amphitrite* with confidence. The sleek PC submarine chaser was 182.7 nautical miles[1] northwest of Newfoundland when the bridge received confirmation of the previous day's weather survey: a warm

---

1. 6,080.20 feet in the U.S., as against 5,280 feet in a statute mile.

front was moving in from the east, from across the Atlantic.

"That's not good for us," Captain Philip Veach said. He explained that the report meant fog, lots of fog, ". . . and quite possibly choppy seas of 22 to 27 speed, with wind at BSF[2] of 6 to 7."

There was the consolation that the *Amphitrite* was a first class vessel, fitted with the most modern of gear. With a displacement of 282 tons, the vessel had a length of 175 feet, a beam of 24.6 feet, a speed of 34 knots and a complement of 76 men. Powered by an all-diesel propulsion system, the U.S.-made sub-chaser had a dipping sonar encased in a large housing at its stern and was fitted with an ADAWS2 Action Data Automation System connected to the inertial navigation system, various radar receivers and weapons sensors, plotting surface and subsurface movements in the vessel's vicinity. Better yet, the ADAWS2 A-D-A-S could control any fire on all systems automatically.

Amphitrite had been made to fight, to attack. There were four ASW torpedo tubes, and two 80mm guns in the forecastle. On the upper deck were four 400mm guns, four 30mm Gatling guns and two depth charge racks; also the rocket launchers with their ASROCs. Each ASROC was a rocket-assisted antisubmarine ballistic missile carrying as payload an MK 44 Model 0 high-speed acoustic homing torpedo. The length of ASROC was 15 feet, the firing weight 1,000 pounds, the range from 1 to 6.4 nautical miles.

There wasn't any lack of agreement that *Amphitrite* was more than capable of defending herself against any submarine, including a Soviet Typhoon class submarine, the largest ballistic missile submarine in the world[3] and that she could easily catch up to and overtake *Night Hawk*, the enemy vessel, which was a steel-hulled, medium-sized fishing boat that was owned by Lawson Jebson who, according to Grant Heary, was on board *Night Hawk* and acting as the skipper of the vessel.

2. Beaufort Scale Force.
3. As large as a WW II aircraft carrier and equipped with 20 launch tubes for multiple-warhead ICBMs with a range of 4,000 miles. The Soviets now have over 300 subs and are still building. The USSR outnumbers the U.S. 20 to 1 in diesel subs; 3.5 to 1 in attack subs; 2.2 to 1 in ballistic missile subs. But bigger . . . and more numbers . . . do not necessarily mean better.

Although Night Hawk was only half the size of the *Amphitrite* and was diesel-powered, the fishing boat could make only 28 to 30 knots. Grant Heary had said that *Night Hawk* had sailed from the Saint John's Quidi Vidi Harbor at 21.00 hours. The *Amphitrite* had left St. John's Harbor 31 hours later. In theory, the *Amphitrite* could overtake *Night Hawk*—if she wanted to. . . .

But was *Night Hawk* even there? The Americans and the Canadians had to have proof that *Night Hawk* was on the high seas, headed toward Resolution Island, or had the KGB decided not to take any chances, now that it had Doctor Davis? Had Moscow Center ordered Colonel Aleksei Dolgov to head straight out into the Atlantic to rendezvous with *Eugene Origen,* the Soviet submarine? The *Amphitrite* could not afford to chase a fishing boat that wasn't there. Absolute proof was necessary. How? Even if *Night Hawk* was boring its way north, there were other vessels in the North Atlantic, other fishing boats, freighters, etc.

"We need a 'Black Radio' plane," Courtland Grojean said. This craft was a North American Rockwell OV-10, an all-weather, night electronic countermeasures aerial relay platform. With extended wingspan and silenced engines, and carrying supersecret laser illuminators of the neodymium-aluminum garnet type developed by Martin-Marietta's avionics division at Orlando, Florida, and so-called Lear-Siegler coordinate converters, this airplane was a true "airborne dirty tricks platform."

There were only three of these PAVE NAIL (code named) aircraft, and none were available, so Grojean radioed after the *Amphitrite* had been 14 hours at sea.

A Lockheed U-2A was flown from March Air Force Base in California to Pepperell Air Force Base in Newfoundland. If any aircraft could find *Night Hawk*, the U-2A could. A high-altitude photo reconnaissance, multireconnaissance and special reconnaissance aircraft, the U-2A had the very latest in ESM (electronic surveillance measures) and optical and IR (infrared) photography. The airplane could fly 850 mph at a service ceiling of 70,000 feet. It's range was 4,000 miles.

It was said in various circles that the U-2A, with its camera that had very large aperture lenses and very long focal lengths and modern film emulsions that were "fine-grained"[4] could read the numbers on a license plate at 60,000 feet. It couldn't.[5] It could read the numbers on a license plate at 48,000 feet. . . .

Piloted by Colonel Frank J. Godwin, the U-2A found the *Night Hawk* on the third search probe. Using laser illuminators that "saw" through the thickest fog and cloud cover, Godwin had photographed the name on the *Night Hawk's* portside bow. At the time, Godwin had been at an altitude of only 1,409 feet and seven air miles, or 42,532 feet[6] west of *Night Hawk*, which at the time had been 189 nautical miles due east of Cartwright, a settlement on the lower east coast of that part of Newfoundland that was on the Canadian mainland. That placed the enemy vessel roughtly at 850 miles southeast of Resolution Island. Since the U-2A's engines were silent, it was doubtful if the lookouts on *Night Hawk* had been even aware that the plane was in the area.

"Unless there is electronic listening gear on board," Richard Camellion said to the other men at the regular morning meeting, the third day at sea.

"I doubt it," Jacob Hall observed, slowly rubbing the end of his nose. "Such equipment is complicated and very bulky. I don't think the KGB would have had the time to obtain and install such sophisticated gear."

"The KGB probably didn't even think of such equipment," Sammy (Smoky) Bair intoned in his deep voice. "When the KGB planned the operation, the bosses in Moscow weren't counting on failure. They didn't frame their moves on the basis that Americans or Canadians would be looking for the escape vessel or trailing it."

"I'll buy that," Wilbert Donovan said. "What happened is that we caught the Ruskies with their pants down.

"And their shorts as well," Merle Duvane added with a grin that was a sneer. "Now they've got a tiger by the tail and can't let go of it."

"Yes, I'd say so," agreed Bair, who was a top agent in Canadian intelligence and Gordon Barret's representative

---

4. Means to stand enormous enlargement without losing definition.

5. But the Lockheeds SR-71 can! This craft can fly at an altitude higher than 80,000 at an excess speed of 2,000 M.PHH. Mach-3, 3 times the speed of sound. But the "Blackbird" is big and very loud. As of 1980, there were 37 in service.

6. An air mile is 6,076 feet.

small boats. A large vessel has to anchor a mile and a half out. What I am saying is—"

"We do have oceanographic relief maps of the area around the two islands of Resolution," cut in Sam Bair. "As I recall, a vessel would have to lay out a mile or so anywhere around the islands, except for that small section south of the weather base."

"That's right," Wiptonfield said with enthusiasm. "The Russian submarine will no doubt use that small harbor. She can stay a mile and a half out and send in power boats. A mile and a half is as close to Resolution as the *Eugene Origen* can get."

"So how does that help us get to the weather station?" asked Charles Fond in a tight voice.

The Death Merchant said, "Let's get out the maps."

The hours passed into another night and then into another day, a day shrouded in deep fog. The *Amphitrite* moved into the cold blue water of the lower reaches of the Labrador Sea. Earlier, the Canadian sub-chaser had passed an occasional freighter, several times a private yacht; but now, having left the regular shipping lanes, *Amphitrite* had the vast lane of water all to herself. There was only the water and the low lead-gray sky.

By 17.00 hours, of the fourth night out from St. John's, the rain came and an icy northwesterly began blowing at force 3. By 20.00 hours the rain intensified, and a damp cold gripped the vessel, the *Amphitrite* glistening all the way to her foretop under a silvery sheen of moisture.

Because it was the *Eugene Origen* that the American and the Canadian force feared, the dipping sonar was monitored around the clock, as well as the RAN-10 S radar on the main mast. If the Soviet submarine got within 6.8 nautical miles of *Amphitrite*, the anxious people on board the Canadian vessel would know it.

The Dardo Firing System had been activated and was ready. This system had been developed for short range defense against various type missile targets, including sea skimmers, divers, and aircraft. The guns/radar combination locked the guns onto the target and the proximity ammunition gave a wide fragmentation area, which destroyed the homing or navigation equipment of incoming missiles, including missiles fired from a submarine. Should a submarine get within range of the DFS system, the computers would calculate the position of the U-boat and automatically fire two of the antisubmarine ASROC missiles.

Captain Beach had slowed to 26 knots, but not because of the foul weather. The Lockheed U-2A, flying at 40,000 feet, had used its sensitive equipment to keep track of *Night Hawk*. The enemy ship was only 43.7 nautical miles ahead of *Amphitrite*. Either *Amphitrite* had to cut speed or she would overtake *Night Hawk* at a point 26.8 miles southeast of Resolution Island.

"Unless something happens, like *Night Hawk's* changing course, she'll reach Resolution in fifty-four hours, at about six A.M.," Captain Beach said. "As far as our getting there and the paratroopers sneaking ashore, it's a question of how long the Russians will be on the island."

Standing behind the helmsman, Major Moan glanced at the Death Merchant who was looking out to port through one of the bridge windows, staring into the wet and windy night.

"Giffwangle"—Moan spoke loudly—"it seems to me that if *Night Hawk* is going to reach the island in fifty-four hours, the Russian commandos from the sub will have to get into action in a very short while."

Merle Duvane, also on the Bridge Deck, had just taken a drink of *Canadian Club* from a small silver-colored flask. Capping the flask, he studied the Canadian commando officer through eyes that looked half-closed. "Hell Major, we all know the Russians in the submarine have to have the island under control before the KGB on board *Night Hawk* will come ashore with Dr. Davis. So what?"

The Death Merchant turned from the window, leaned against a hand railing and folded his arms. It came to him that Major Moan must be six-feet four-inches tall.

"What's your point, Major?"

"I'm wondering if we'll have the room to maneuver past the Soviet sub to the north side of the big island. Even if we do, will we have the time after we anchor to get to the station? That's one hell of a long swim!"

"Captain Beach says we will have the space," the Death Merchant said. "Tell him, sir."

A rugged man with a weather-cured, broad face and a short but thick brown beard, Beach turned to Major Moan and spoke rapidly in a no-nonsense voice. "The Soviet skipper will have to keep at a minimum of a mile and a half from the south shore. No doubt he will stay out even farther—I should say about three miles out, where the depth is almost 200 fathoms. At twelves hundred feet, the skipper of the Soviet submarine would have plenty of room to maneuver, in case of trouble."

"The hell with the commie pig-boat," Moan said between teeth grinding in impatience. "Can you get us to the 'back' of the island without the Russians picking us up on their radar and sonar? That's what concerns me."

"It shouldn't," Beach said. "Our vessel will turn west at Cape Chidley. We'll go forty miles into Hudson Strait, then turn north and move until we're parallel with the north coast of the larger island. We'll go due east and anchor several miles off shore. Such a three-angled course will put us beyond the submarine's sonar and radar."

Commented Major Moan in a skeptical voice, "Presuming that the *Eugene Origen* is three miles from the south shore. Suppose it isn't?"

"Major, there aren't any absolutes or guarantees," the Death Merchant said. "There is always a risk. Being too cautious can get you killed."

"I didn't ask for advice on tactics. Do we have the time?" Moan said gruffly. "I'm not about to toss my men into a no-win situation."

"We have the time. The captured KGB agent told us that his comrades would be on the island three days. All things considered, we should have almost an entire day to spare. To those of us who go west, that extra day won't make a bit of difference."

Major Moan's hard eyes crawled reflectively over Camellion. The Canadian officer had always felt vaguely uncomfortable around the American, this quiet man who always moved like a jungle cat on the hunt and talked so calmly about life and death.

It wasn't exactly that Moan disliked Camellion. It was impossible to have an aversion to an individual you didn't know. A man must give his opinions about the ordinary subjects of life—women, politics, the economy, whatever—in order for you to form any judgments. Giffwangle was different. He never revealed his views on anything, except the business at hand. Damn it. It wasn't natural. But Giffwangle wasn't natural. Neither were some of his habits. He never became excited. He never lost his temper. He had owl's blood, never coming alive until after the sun had set.

Many years earlier, Moan had changed his name from the original German of *Moannbarger*. His parents had spoken German at home, and to Moan it was a second language. Automatically, especially when he was under a load of stress, he thought in the German language. *Ya*, that's what the steel-hard American with the strange blue eyes was—*Der Todes-engel*. The Angel of Death! Wherever he went, Death followed. But somehow, suspected Moan, Camellion would never be one to hear the dark chimes at midnight. . . .

Shaking himself free of his despondent thoughts, Moan said harshly, "I'm concerned with only the time factor, Mr. Giffwangle, and with the safety of my men."

"A commendable trait," said Camellion. "I'm also determined to keep casualties to a minimum."

"You must admit that so far American intelligence has not had much success with the Russians on this operation," Moan said with a straight face. "The KGB has always been several steps ahead of you. There wasn't one single clue in the house in Maine the Americans raided. That doesn't matter now. We know where Dr. Davis is."

"You have it, Major. All is not lost, in spite of your pessimism," Camellion said, gently admonishing Moan. "We know the location of the target. All we have to do is bash the bullseye at the right time. With a bit of coordination, the choosing of the right time, a dash of knowhow and a sprinkling of luck, we'll do it."

Major Moan was trying to formulate a comment when Merle Duvane gave a low laugh and said good-naturedly, "Yeah, that's all we have to do. Hell, you might as well tell us that Betelgeuse is an instant space drink made from insects or that a Cyborg is a bionic tennis partner." He paused, then concluded expansively, "What the hell! I've been on deals where the cards were more stacked in favor of the enemy—but I'm still here."

Camellion, Captain Beach, and Sam Bair smiled. Major Moan was annoyed, as evidence by his scowling expression.

"When is the next report from the U-plane due?" he demanded, thrusting out his jaw.

"In another forty hours," Camellion said with exaggerated politeness. "That will place *Night Hawk* fourteen hours south of Resolution. When she gets that close, it isn't likely that she'll change course, not after coming all this way."

Captain Beach said thoughtfully, "You can't discount the possibility that the enemy ship will link up with the Soviet submarine at the last moment. The *Night Hawk's* passage north could be some kind of diversionary tactic."

Major Moan quickly agreed. "The *Eugene Origen* must know we're here?"

Merle Duvane snorted. "If that pile of Russian nuts and bolts does, she didn't find out by getting within sonar range of us."

"You're right about that," admitted Moan. He took out a pack of Canadian Queen cigarettes. "I suppose if worse comes to worse, the Russians could try to sink us with a missile."

"I doubt it," Camellion said. "The Soviet Union doesn't want an international incident any more than we do. Why seismographs at listening even in Europe would pick up a missile blast in these waters. Enough of the world is down on the Soviet Bear. The old gangsters in the Kremlin aren't after more hate from the world community."

Duvane pushed out his lower lip with his tongue. "I'd feel a lot better if we were permitted to use our ASROCs. World opinion doesn't mean much when you're nothing but atoms floating around."

"We do have permission to use our antisub missiles," Camellion said. "If we're attacked by the sub's missiles."

"Let's hope it doesn't come to that," Duvane said with a large sigh. He zipped up his heavy parka. "You can argue the pros and cons if you want. I'm going to the galley and get some more of the oyster stew we had for dinner." He pulled up the fur-lined hood, then added cheerfully, "Who knows? It could be my last meal."

Winking at Major Moan, Duvane headed for the door.

Tension increased as the hours passed, as the *Amphitrite* neared Cape Chidley. Somewhere about 04.00 hours of the next morning the weather worsened. The sea rose, and low dark rain clouds, driven by a steady Force-6 wind from astern, ran with the vessel like sheltering curtains. Visibility became almost zero, and it was all Captain Beach could do to keep the vessel boring ahead at 26 knots. The men got little sleep. By 09.00 hours the wind slackened and visibility increased to 35 kilometers. The sea remained rough, Amphitrite's bow dipping deeply into the water, spray at times almost reaching the enclosed bridge before vanishing in the wind.

At 10.41 hours the Radio Room received a coded message from Courtland Grojean who was making Ottawa his present base of operations and was staying at the home of Gordon Barret. The first part of the message was for the American and Canadian intelligence people. The news was not good, even though the tragedy would not affect what had to be done on Resolution Island.

Bryan Lee Walsch and Raya Walsch, Dr. Davis's lab assistants, had been found murdered in Hancock, Wisconsin. A professional job. Two .25 bullets in the back of the head.

What had the Walschs known that had necessitated their being murdered by KGB agents?

The second part of the message was a For-Your-Eyes-Only type—and only for the Death Merchant. Camellion decoded the message which read:

Peacock.
The Peoples Democratic Republic of Yemen.

Camellion tore the message he had decoded into small bits and pieces and flushed them down a toilet. He almost gritted his teeth in frustration—*I don't like the desert and I like sand crabs and their Moslem crackpotism even less. This mission hasn't even gotten off to a good start and Grojean is bumping his gums about the Near East. Damn! What else can happen?*

The Death Merchant found out—four hours later in the afternoon. At 15.30 hours, the sonar operators at the consoles flashed a warning throughout the ship—*seven underwater craft*—*very small vessels*—*were approaching Amphitrite from her starboard bow!*

Chapter Nine

The Death Merchant, Sam Bair, Major Moan and some of the other intelligence officers stared at the cathode ray tube, watching the "pips" on the horizontal calibrated distance scale. Seven pips! Seven Soviet swimmer delivery vehicles, all spread out in a semicircle, with the vehicle at each end of the line being several hundred feet to the side and the rear of the lead SDV.

"How far away from us are they?" Camellion inquired of the chief sonar operator who was adjusting the heterodyne amplifier and the horizontal sweep.

"How soon will you be able to pick them up as images on the sonoptography scope?"[1] Sam Bair asked the chief operator.

"They're about eight miles away and traveling at maybe 2 or 3 knots, about 15 fathoms down," the chief sonar operator replied. "It will be another ten minutes before we can pick them up in the S-Scope."

Bair, standing to one side of the Design Assign Console-2, stared balefully at the tube, watching and listening to the seven pips. "It's obvious who they are, where they came from, and what they intend to do. They're either going to plant mines against our hull or try to board us—or both."

"It's also obvious that the KGB people in charge are damned desperate, or they wouldn't be trying this suicide scheme," Merle Duvane said. "Hell, they've got to know there isn't any way they could sneak up on us with those baby subs, so—"

---

1. The use of sound waves to obtain a 3-D image of an object. No lenses are required. In essence, a two stage process in which the diffraction pattern of an object irradiated by sound waves is biased by a coherent sound wave and recorded. The resultant pattern is like a hologram.

"Swimmer Delivery Vehicles," corrected the Death Merchant.

"Same difference!" snapped Duvane. "They're still underwater."

"We can knock them out with depth charges," suggested Major Moan. He looked first at Sam Bair, then at Richard Camellion. "Four or five big bangs and that will be the end of the Soviet commandos. Concussion will shut off their lights very effectively."

"Probably." Camellion nodded. "But if only one vehicle got through and some of its men planted only one mine against our hull, we'd be in for the worse kind of trouble."

Duvane snickered. "It's too cold out there to go floating around in lifeboats."

The Death Merchant's face was calm and relaxed. "There's more to it than a mine exploding against our hull. The last I heard, the Soviets have SDV models that are impervious to concussion." He stared straight at Moan. "The only sure way is to go down into the water and meet them. Whack out those SDVs and kill the crews with shock rods and USTs. If we kill them now, we'll not only lessen the Soviet numbers on land, but we'll seriously lower the morale of the rest of the Soviet force"—*Moan is going to give me an argument!*

Sam Bair's voice was tight and hard. "Cyrus, you and your boys have had underwater training, haven't you?"

"You're right, Giffwangle," Major Moan said. "I can speak—"

So I was wrong about him!—

—"for my men and I know they'd rather have first contact with the enemy here than meet the full Soviet force on Resolution Island. I have them on alert. We can be suited and in the water in ten minutes."

"The sooner the better." Camellion started for the bulkhead door at the end of the sonar compartment. He stopped at the bulkhead and glanced back at Major Moan. "The quicker you and your men get into the water, the better chance you'll have."

"Yes, I'm thinking along the same lines," Moan said. He brushed past Camellion and left the Sonar Compartment. The Death Merchant stepped over the bottom rim of the oval opening, Bair asking him, "What about us and the crew? The Russians can use magnetic ladders to come on board. We've got to protect the Bridge and the Engine

Room. We're lucky in that we have more than enough men."

"We'll distribute the crew—and ourselves—around the vital points upstairs," the Death Merchant said. "The instant you see a pig farmer—shoot."

They started down the corridor of the third deck, hurrying toward the Armament Room. The klaxon was still screaming a warning, telling every man on board that the enemy was approaching. Bulkhead doors were double-checked, weapons distributed.

Duvane asked Camellion, "Listen, how many Russians do you think are in each sub—okay, each SDV? If there's only two or three in each little sub, there won't be enough of the sons of bitches to come aboard."

The Death Merchant began a slow run, Duvane and the others keeping up with him.

"The largest SDV the Russians have is the ELMO-7," explained Camellion. "It carries seven. If those SDVs are ELMOS, we're in trouble."

He stopped by a telephone on the wall. "Go ahead," he ordered the other men. "I want to talk to Captain Beach."

Captain Beach and his officers on the Bridge began to steer *Amphitrite* in a large circle, the sub-chaser having made half a circle by the time Major Moan and his 36 commandos jumped from a portside cargo opening into the water. Each man was in an Arctic type deep-dive dry suit with a closed circuit breathing system, armed with two knives, an eight-foot long shock prod and an underwater shot tube. Although the water was freezing, Moan and his force would be in no danger, the dry suits and the two layers of special woolen underwear the men wore being electrically heated by duel solenoid packs. Should one pack malfunction, the second pack would automatically activate to keep the suit warm.

The well-trained crew was ready. In the Engine Room, the Chief Engineer and his men—sweatbands around their foreheads, a slice of lemon in the right corner of their mouths—checked the powerful diesels. They were ready to execute any order from the bridge, from *Full Speed Ahead* to *Full Speed Astern*.

Other members of the crew, with either a warrant officer or a petty officer in charge, were stationed at strategic positions around the vessel. Five men were on the open bridge, armed with Canadian M-C1 submachine guns, dressed in heavy, warm clothes, including thermal face masks, for the temperature—this including the wind chill factor—was 4.6 degrees above zero. Five more of the crew were on the Captain's Control Bridge, armed to the teeth with 9mm Browning pistols and 7.62mm FN C1 automatic rifles. Other guards were in the Radio Room, in Engineering, and on the second deck, just below the hatches. More guards were stationed on the top deck of the superstructure, around the four 400mm guns, the four antiaircraft Gatling guns and the ASROC missiles; three men in the forecastle turret that housed the two 80mm guns. James Burke-Whit and Basil Taimesser were with these three. In the stern, four crewmen and Will Donovan and Luke Drayer had set up two .30-06 Canadian Mark II Bren guns on bipods in the warping winch housing.

The Death Merchant, Merle Duvane and Sam Bair had taken positions portside in Engineering on the Upper Deck. Roger Barnkoff, Fred Thumm, and Charles Fond were on the starboard side. Jacob Hall was on the Captain's Bridge. He would handle the AN/PQC-1 communications[2] from Major Moan and transmit reports to Camellion, in effect throughout the ship. Each group of men had a transceiver open and locked on a channel. When Hall transmitted to Camellion from the Captain's Bridge, he reported to the entire vessel.

They waited. Camellion had given orders to Captain Beach to stop the vessel the instant he received word from Major Moan that the Soviet frogmen were close by. "We'll make it easy for Moan," Camellion said. "And we'll save time. Either the Soviet commandoes will get through or they won't. The quicker we smear the pig farmers, the sooner we can get under way."

A clever and efficient officer, Major Cyrus Moan believed in making use of the enemy's mistakes. The Soviet SDVs were coming in at 15 fathoms, or 90 feet below the

2. Better known as UTEL. This is a device designed to permit a diver to communicate with a ship, a sub, or another diver. Not only can the diver receive transmissions, but he can transmit his own voice via a "lung microphone" imbedded in his full face mask. On the surface he can transmit with a surface mike.

surface of the sea. Major Moan and his commandoes dove down to 110 feet and swam several hundred feet away from the *Amphitrite*. There, treading water rhythmically, they waited, their helmet lights turned off.

The Soviet pilots of the SDVs had switched off the bow lights of the ELMO7s, but lack of illumination did not bother Moan and his waiting "Hell Eaters." Water is a great conductor of sound and in a very short time, Moan and his men heard the faint humming of the SDVs' electric batteries, a humming that grew steadily louder in the water above them.

"We can hear them," Moan said, his words carrying not only to the commandos but to Jacob Hall at the receiver on the Bridge. "I estimate they're several hundred feet east of our position. We are between them and the vessel."

Moan waited until the humming became louder, until the humming was a full volume and slightly ahead of him and his men—between them and the *Amphitrite*. He gave the order—*Go up and do it. Don't turn on your helmet lights until you're on them.*

With quick, expert motions, Moan and his men swam upward, to the rear of the Soviet SDVs. They were less than ten feet behind the ELMO-7s when they turned on their helmet lights and started to close in, seven of the commandos swimming to one side of the small propellers and duel rudders, the rest of the Hell Eaters swimming for positions that would put them to the left or the right and slightly above the Soviet swimmer delivery vehicles. The Soviet frogmen sat single file in each craft, enclosed underneath a hard plastic housing that could be opened either in sections or flung off in one complete unit. The canopies were another serious mistake on the part of the Russians.

Colonel Lavrenty Kossior, the commander of the Soviet *Morskaia Pekhota,* or "Naval Infantry," had surmised that the *Canadiansch* vessel would detect him and his men on sonar and attempt to expedite the annoyance as speedily as possible, with depth charges. The enclosed canopies would offer protection from concussion. The boats—each resembling a kind of oversized pregnant torpedo—would take a pounding, but the men would survive. Kossior had discounted the possibility that the enemy would send down divers. Too late, Colonel Kossior and his men realized that to attack with the housings in place had been an extremely serious mistake.

By the time the alarmed pilots in each SDV pressed the button to release the entire canopy of each craft, three of Major Moan's Hell-Eaters had succeeded in planting magnetic Marcus mines against the stern sides of three of the ELMO-7s.

Each M-Mine, while three times the size of an ordinary hand grenade, had only three-fourths of a grenade's power. The large size was due to the 3" armor plate on the outside of the mine's casing, this thickness preventing the blast from moving outward. All the force was, therefore, directed in one direction, inward through the thin metal skin of the SDV, inward toward the batteries. In effect, each explosion of each Marcus Mine was similar to a blast from a double-barrelled shotgun.

The three Hell-Eaters had slapped on the M-Mines and turned the firing knobs all the way to the left, setting the mines to explode in 18 seconds. Explode they did, with muffled booms. At the same time, the canopies in all the seven SDVs shot upward. The Russian frogmen began to defend themselves. While some, parrying with their shock prods, held off the attacking Hell-Eaters, others freed themselves from their seat belts and pushed themselves from the vehicles, whose pilots were using evasive tactics, taking the ELMOs not only downward but rolling them over in an effort to help the occupants dislodge themselves and to protect them from the Canadians. The exceptions were the three SDVs against whose hulls the M-Mines had exploded. With their batteries and one of their aft trim tanks wrecked, the ELMOs had stopped moving and were slowly sinking into the pitch black depths. The twenty-one frogmen had left the three vehicles and had turned to the Hell-Eaters to prevent them from following the four other Soviet ELMOs that now turned slightly to starboard and, moving upward, headed for the *Amphitrite*. The Soviet effort was not entirely successful. On orders from Major Moan, Lieutenant Buster Altengid and thirteen commandos started swimming after the ELMOs.

Behind them the water churned furiously from the frantic maneuvering of the eighteen Russians, clad in gray dry suits, and the efforts of Major Moan and the other twenty-two Canadians, outfitted in black suits. On each side, men dove, rolled over, or swam upward to avoid the shock prod of adversaries, at the same time trying to use their own weapons.

A Russian tried to wriggle away from Major Moan, twisting his body to one side like a giant eel. But his luck had run out; so had the sands of his life. The tip of Moan's shock rod barely touched the instep of Stephen Bigitt's left foot and Moan pressed the button, sending 20,000 volts of electricity through the Russian's body. Bigitt's body went rigid, then limp. The shock rod slipped from his fingers and, with his head and torso pointing downward, he began to sink.

"MAJOR! STARBOARD AND BELOW YOU, AT FOUR-THIRTY!" Moan heard the frantic voice of Sergeant August Voges come in through the speaker in his helmet. He immediately rolled to port on his back, in time to avoid a shock prod poke by a gray-suited Slavic slob coming up underneath him; and the thought flashed across his mind that he and his men were, in some ways, similar to air crews under fire, in that he and his commandoes used the same kind of warning system, calling out to each other the way pilots would. Only the medium of the battlefield was different—water instead of air. But the dying was the same. It was always quick, violent, and expected.

The Russian diver shot upward past Moan, rolled to starboard, executed a very fast loop, came out of it on his stomach and jabbed outward with his shock stick. But Major Moan had done the unexpected. Instead of diving or swimming upward, he had swum straight at the Russian, calculating that he would be able to catch the man off guard. He had been correct. Before the Soviet frogman could pull back his prod from the miss and attempt another jab, Moan blocked the enemy's shock stick with his own electric prod and, kicking himself forward, slashed out with the razor sharp knife in his right hand, the blade slicing through the Russian's suit on the right outer thigh, opening a six-inch long cut in the rubberized material. Ice cold water began pouring in the Russian's suit. The man was doomed. Feeling the water, he went into a panic, and that's all Moan needed. With one quick thrust, he pushed the knife into the man's abdomen, pulled it out and detected a figure coming in from above and to port.

Emelyan Oppokov had lost his electric prod, but he was a very powerful swimmer and was positive in his own mind that he would be able to slice open the enemy's suit with his knife. He was very fast, but so was Moan, who twisted around, let the shock rod fall from his fingers, grabbed

Oppokov's right wrist with his left hand and attempted an undercut with the knife in his right hand, his efforts frustrated when Oppokov grabbed his right wrist. A Mexican standoff! Furiously the two men struggled, each looking for some kind of opening, each waiting for the other man to weaken; and each man waited for one of his comrades to come to his assistance.

Over and over they rolled in the water, somersaulting through the blackness, the beams of their helmet lights crisis-crossing and forming weird, ever-changing patterns of light that blended in with the other stabbing shafts of brightness from the helmets of Russians and Canadians doing their best to kill each other. The water churned. Men gasped within their helmets and blood flowed. The lives of both the Americans and the Russians depended on more than killing skill. Their lives hung on the balance of pure chance, of sheer luck.

Cyrus Moan got lucky. As he and Oppokov rolled over and over, Moan decided on a bold gamble. He rolled violently backward, taking the Russian with him and managing to bring his right leg up between his own body and Oppokov's. He twisted his right arm with all the strength at his command and was gratified when he felt the fingers of the Russian's left hand slip from his wrist. In that tiny shave of a second, Moan brought up both legs to the level of the Russian's chest. With a tremendous effort, he pushed against the Soviet frogman with his right foot while hooking the instep of his other foot underneath the right side air hose running from the tanks on the man's back to the mouthpiece of his helmet. Oppokov shot away from Moan, his airhose catching against the top of Moan's left foot. Something had to give as Moan jerked savagely with his left foot. Something did—the hose coupling pulled away from the valve-check and gasket ring of the mouthpiece assembly and, with air bubbling from its end, began thrashing back and forth and up and down in the water like a ringed snake. Water poured through the Russian's mouthpiece as he kicked his legs and moved his arms helplessly. He was on the very edge of the springboard of life and was about to jump into the vast, endless pool of death, and there wasn't anything he could do about it.

There wasn't anything the other Russians and Canadians could do when their time ran out. A Soviet frogman touched Arnie Drumm on his helmet and the Canadian commando from Moose Jaw, Saskatchewan, was instantly unconscious from 17,000 volts of electricity. His body would sink until the pressure crushed all life from his body. In this part of the Labrador Sea, the depth was 430 fathoms—2,580 feet.

The Soviet frogmen were having even less luck than the Canadians. Five Soviet "naval infantrymen" died within several minutes of the initial clash between the two groups, either from the shock rods of the Canadians or their underwater shot tubes.

The Canadian shot tubes were four feet long and held five shotgun shells, each shell a bullet-sabot set, meaning that each shell shot a single large projectile that weighed 280 grains and delivered a muzzle velocity of about 1700 fps. The result in muzzle energy was 1800 foot-pounds. No man could survive being shot by a sabot-projectile. The Russians couldn't either.

Billy Cutte jackknifed in the water and tried to duck a Russian's shock prod; he only barely succeeded. He then brought up his UST as the Soviet diver, carried forward by his own momentum, came toward him. The Russian attempted to roll over to port to escape the deadly muzzle of Cutte's Underwater Shot Tube, but his forward momentum was too powerful. He twisted over on his back and frantically tried to wriggle away. A little more and he would have made it, but his luck was all bad. He had turned over when Cutte kicked himself to the right, jammed the muzzle of the UST against the small of his back and pulled the trigger in front of the handle. A muffled boom and a Sabot projectile stabbed into the Russian, tearing his spine into parts and boring all the way into his intestines. Instantly he went limp, dropped his shock stick and began to sink, air coming through the rip in his suit, churning the water red with blood.

Then Cutte jerked and went limp, knocked into unconsciousness by the shock rod of Pytor Roskovsky, who then jackknifed like a large fish and dove almost straight down to escape Oran Killian who was coming at him from starboard. Roskovsky had made the biggest and the last mistake of his twenty-six years of life. He had dove right into the path of Oliver Woll who was swimming upward, straight toward him. Like two knights of the Middle Ages, the Russian and the Canadian came at each other, the water their steeds, shock rods their lances.

Roskovsky stabbed outward with his rod—and missed. Woll used his own shock stick to knock the Russian's to one side. Before Roskovsky could recoup and try again, Woll jammed him in the left shoulder and pressed the button. Roskovsky might as well have been banged on the head with a lightning bolt. He slumped, and started to sink.

The four other Soviet ELMO-7s—with Lieutenant Buster Altengid and thirteen commandos swimming after them—were only 108 feet from the starboard side of the *Amphitrite* when their pilots released a cloud of what looked like black ink from the rear of each swimmer delivery vehicle. The Hell-Eaters were only seventy-five feet to the rear of the four ELMOs and closing in fast when the spreading Inia-ink-blackness in the water engulfed them, a blackness their helmet lights could not penetrate.

As angry as a bull in a tall briar patch, Lieutenant Altengid used the UTEL in his suit to contact Major Moan, who had just saved the life of Albert Rickenberg by killing a Russian with his shock rod.

"The ivans have pulled a fast one," snarled Altengid. "They're released a cloud of something in the water. It's blacker than ink. All four SDVs are almost to the ship. Better warn our people."

"How big is this black 'cloud?'" inquired Moan.

"It's hard to say. It's spreading rapidly. If it goes all the way to the surface, you'd have it rough up there. But I can't imagine it going downward past our depth level."

"Okay. Try swimming underneath it. That's all you can do," Moan said. He then switched over to the *Amphitrite* and reported what was happening to Jacob Hall in the captain's bridge.

"Damn it! The hull had better hold if they have mines!" Hall replied forlornly. "Do what you can, Major."

Moan switched back to the divers. "All of you heard What Altengid said. You bastards swim like you've got propellers in your butts. If those Russian turds have large type limpets, we can all say good-bye to home."

In a vile, vindictive mood, Colonel Lavrenty Kossior calmly gave orders over his own UTEL system (set two meters below the UTEL being used by Moan) to the pilots of the three other Soviet ELMO-7s.

"Sergo, take the stern. Andrew, to the portside. Lazar, portside bow. We'll take center starboard. Use your 'sky ladders' and board."

Sitting directly behind Gevin Mekhlis, the pilot of the SDV in which he was strapped, Kossior spoke evenly to the pilot, "Gevin, take us straight in, then surface. We'll use the *stev-oskitisshi* ("Sky Ladder") to get on board."

"Comrade Colonel. We should have brought mines," said Martin Losvok, his voice low and heavy with gloom. "We'll never accomplish the mission by boarding."

"We've been through that," Kossior said angrily. "I've told you—all of you—that when the *Origen* left the Motherland, no one expected this mess. All the submarine carries is small Z-mines used for gunnery practice. They would never penetrate the double hull of that damned subchaser. Our only chance is to get to the engine room and cripple her with explosives. There is no other way."

Alexandr Biron, the last frogman in the SDV, observed sadly, "Comrade Colonel, there are only twenty-eight of us in these four boats. You have not been able to contact the others; we know they are dead."

"*Da*, they are dead," Kossior said with characteristic bluntness.

Martin Losvok said, "They will be expecting us to board and will have positioned men accordingly. We can't possibly succeed, Comrade."

"We have our orders from Moscow," Kossior said without any hesitation. "Those of us who die will be honored in the Motherland and remembered as heroes."

Biron made a noise of disgust. "What good is being a hero when you're dead and in the ground?"

"No good at all," Kossior admitted. "But it's better to be a dead hero than a live coward standing before a firing squad, or worse, a prisoner in one of the Gulags[3]." He switched on the full UTEL so that his voice would be carried to the *Morskaia Pekhota* in the other three ELMO-7s. "Don't you agree, Comrade Josef Marsevesky?"

First Class Private Josef Marsevesky in Number 3 SDV did not reply. Colonel Kossior knew the reason for Marse-

---

3. The Russian nickname for work camps.

vesky's silence: because the now surprised Marsevesky had deduced why Kossior had made the totally unexpected remark. Marsevesky now knew that Kossior knew that he was a secret officer of the hated *Napravleniye,* the Political Security Service[4] of the KGB. Josef Marsevesky was a damned spy, his job to report on the political reliability of the comrades in his unit.

Colonel Kossior, smiling grimly to himself, switched back the UTEL to only the men in his own ELMO-7. He was positive that all of them would soon be dead. There was only one consolation. Josef Marsevesky would die with them.

"Comrade Colonel, why should Josef agree?" The question came from Paul Levomov, a demolition expert. "What did you mean?"

"Marsevesky is *Napravleniye,*" Kossior said, pressing his lips firmly together when he heard the exclamations of surprise.

"You are sure?" Martin Losvok said in a strangled kind of voice.

"I'm positive."

None of the men spoke. There wasn't anything to say. It was more than obvious to the men that Colonel Kossior would not have made the open remark to Josef Marsevesky if he had expected any of them to come out alive. The men were doomed. With typical Russian stoicism, the men accepted the dismal fact.

"Comrade Colonel Kossior, we are only fifteen meters from the Canadian vessel," Gevin Mekhlis said, his voice slightly nervous.

"Keep the light off and don't surface until we touch the hull."

"Comrade Colonel, do we keep our air tanks on after we surface?" Levomov asked.

"Leave them in the craft," Kossior said. "Once we surface, we must make every second count. We'll carry nothing but weapons, grenades, and explosives. We have a job to do and I intend to see that it gets done."

The pressure of the water become more intense as the ELMO-7 closed in on the *Amphitrite.* The seconds clicked

---

4. One of the more important branches of the KGB. Within the *Napravleniye* are 15 major units, called Directions. It is Direction 10 that spies on the armed forces.

by on the tachometer in the panel lighted by a soft green light. Mekhlis shut off the 3.2 HP electric motor, then placed both hands on the trim tank levers, his eyes on the ball of the distance indicator. The distance narrowed . . . 2.1 meters . . . 12 meters . . . 0.9 meters . . . 0.3 meters. There was a dull clanking sound as the nose of the SDV touched the hull of the *Amphitrite.*

Mekhlis pulled back the levers. The valves of the four trim tanks opened, the swift rush of compressed air expelling the water through the side vent valves. Now the compressed air in the tanks made them buoyancy chambers and the swimmer delivery vehicle began to rise to the surface of the Labrador Sea as another ELMO-7, still submerged, turned and headed for the stern of the *Amphitrite.* The other two Soviet SDVs dove and slowly moved under the hull of the submarine chaser. They would go to center port and bow port of the *Amphitrite.*

Colonel Kossior's ELMO-7 jumped to the surface. All at once there was light and the rough, almost stormy movement of waves, the water splashing and breaking over the seven Russians and the top of the 26.4 foot long vehicle.

Kossior and the other six Russians worked quickly and expertly. Off came the air tanks. Out came the three grenade launchers, Dragunov submachine guns, grenades and the bulky *stev-oskitisshi,* the "Sky Ladder," that resembled a rectangular barrel four feet high, eighteen inches across, horizontally, and seven inches wide. Inside the "barrel" was a folded/packed steel mesh ladder that could be shot to the side of a vessel by means of charges in the bottom casing, the end of the ladder securing itself to the steel hull by means of four electromagnets on the top cable, the top "rung" of the ladder.

"Forget the grenade launchers," Kossior said. "We're too close. We'll flip grenades over the side by hand, once we're high enough on the ladder."

With Mekhlis, Colonel Kossior held the tube of the *stev-oskitisshi.* Levomov pulled the cord that ignited the charges in the device. There were two big bangs, like large firecrackers going off, and the mass of packed steel cable shot out of the large tube and unfolded in flight like some weird spider web. The magnets clanked loudly against the upper hull, only a few feet below the deck railing, and held.

"Good luck men," Colonel Kossior said. He first tested the cable ladder to make sure it was secure. Then he began to climb. The other men followed, but not with enthusiasm. . . .

In the Engineering Department on the Upper Deck, the Death Merchant, via Jacob Hall, received another report from Major Moan. Moan had lost six men during the short underwater battle with the Soviet *Morskaia Pekhota*, but, with the exception of the twenty-eight Russians in the four ELMO-7s, the Hell-Eaters had annihilated the Russian attack force.

Camellion wasn't at all happy—*It takes only one pig farmer to plant one or two mines against the hull. So be it. Some of the ELMOS got through. As the ancient Romans would say, "Aequo pulsat pede!"*[5]

The Death Merchant relayed orders to Captain Beach and his officers on the bridge—"Start the engines. The turning propellers will keep the damned pig farmers away from the rudder."

And to the men throughout the *Amphitrite:* "Keep all doors tightly closed, especially the cargo doors. Hold your positions."

Came the report from Group 6 on Deck 4 in Stores, the voice of Petty Officer Fleming filled with tension, "We just heard something clank against the center starboard hull. It sounded like metal."

"It's either one of the Russian boats or a mine," Camellion said. "Get the hell out and make sure the bulkhead door is closed! Move—before you get blown out of there."

"This is one fine mess," grumbled Merle Duvane who was by one of the portside portholes. "We have to stand here and wait. No telling what the vodka-drinking trash are up to."

"Oh, yes, we know. They're either planting mines or preparing to come aboard," commented Roger Barnkoff from the starboard side of Engineering.

Also on the starboard side, Fred Thumm cocked his head to one side.

"Did any of you hear that?"

"You're hearing things," Charles Ford, on the same side of the cabin as Thumm, said.

Suddenly there were two loud POPS like firecrackers in

5. "Pale Death knocks with equal foot."

the distance, then two fairly loud CLANKS against the hull of the vessel from the starboard side.

"Hearing things, am I?" Thumm said triumphantly. "Those idiots are going to try to board us. I'll give them an 'N' for nerve, if nothing else. They're either double-stupid or crazy-brave!"

"You heard a magnetic-hold chain-ladder taking hold," the Death Merchant said. "Get ready. First, they'll use grenades."

Standing by the starboard bulkhead door that was open a foot, Camellion reached out, wrapped his fingers around the handle, pulled shut the oval-shaped door and spun the lock-wheel.

However, the first exploding grenade did not come from either port or starboard. It came from the stern. Five explosions in all. One right after the other. Grenades, judging from the sounds. Camellion and the other men knew that Soviet commandos were about to board the vessel from the stern.

They were only half right. Sergo Kipiv, the pilot of the ELMO-7 that had moved to the stern of the *Amphitrite*, had guided the SDV thirty feet directly behind the rounded stern so that the grenade launchers could be used. Gennardi Kashva and Valentin Silin had then lobbed five RKG-3M antitank grenades across the stern onto the deck.

BLAMMMMMMM! The first grenade exploded only eleven feet in front of the warping winch housing protecting four crewmen, Will Donovan and Luke Drayer, all six of whom were deafened by the explosion.

The Soviet RKG-3M antitank grenade is a very powerful weapon, its 567g (1¼ lb) HE charge able to penetrate 165mm of armor!

The second RKG landed and exploded almost in front of the housing. The third, fifteen feet to starboad. The fourth, ten feet to port. The fifth, on the edge of the roof of the warping winch housing, the edge facing the bow.

It was the concussion from the explosion of the second RKG that picked up the two Mark II Bren light machine guns and sent them smashing into three of the crewmen, killing one man instantly by caving in his forehead. The fourth crewman and Donovan and Drayer threw themselves flat on the floor and put their hands over their heads.

The explosion of the last grenade on the edge of the roof

turned the interior of the housing into a shambles and killed another crew member and Luke Drayer. Metal plates from the roof stabbed like giant shrapnel into Drayer's back, shattering his spine and cutting the cord. He screamed once, then was dead. Bobby Youngston, the crewman, was killed by pieces of flying metal that smashed the back of his head into bloody pulp.

No sooner had the fifth grenade demolished the roof than Kipiv steered the ELMO-7 to the rounded stern of the *Amphitrite* and two commandos shot up the stev-oskitisshi.

The three crewmen and James Burke-Whit and Basil Taimesser in the forecastle turret were luckier than the shattered group on the stern Lazar Chubar, the pilot of the ELMO that had gone to the port bow, had taken his SDV against the hull of the vessel, thus preventing the other frogmen in the craft from using launchers to toss the powerful RKG grenades.

Andrew Gamarnik also took his ELMO-7 straight up to the hull, afraid that if he surfaced any distance from the Canadian vessel, topside gunners would open fire. Hence the six other men in his craft could not use their launchers.

Hanging on the "sky ladder," only four feet below the deck railing, Lavrenty Kossior lobbed four RGD-5 antipersonnel grenades over the railing, but the 110 grams of TNT in each grenade did little damage, other than turn a lot of decking into large splinters and make Camellion and the others in Engineering feel that they were inside a steel drum on whose sides someone was pounding with a large hammer.

"Only one man can climb up at a time," grinned the Death Merchant. "We'll pick them off one by one."

He opened the bulkhead door, leaned around it and watched and waited. He could always duck back behind the bulkhead door the instant he saw another grenade sailing up from the side of the vessel.

From above, from the turret of the Foreward Fire-Control Station, he heard two NATO CI 7.62mm heavy machine guns firing. If he had been able to see above and around corners, he would have seen 7.62mm projectiles boring into Sergo Kipiv and three other Soviet commandos who had climbed up on the smoking roof of the warping winch housing. The stream of slugs not only ripped the

the black sack. But the Cosmic Lord of Death gets them all in the end, including all the self-righteous hypocrites and the gawd-shoutin' Billy Grahams. They all turn to dust and are blown into nothingness by the winds of time."

Finished with pouring a shot of whiskey into his coffee, Duvane cast a baleful eye at the Death Merchant. "Uh-huh, and sooner or later Old Man Bones is going to get us. I'd prefer it was later, but I have a feeling that if we make a mistake within the next few days, it will be sooner."

Sam Bair's face was still and attentive, his eyes extra sly. "The Soviets won't take kindly to what happened this afternoon. They sent their best and we beat the hell out of them. I can't conceive what they can do about it, other than resort to missiles or else meet the *Night Hawk* on the open sea, then take off Dr. Davis and the KGB people and head for home."

Camellion moved the oily rag back and forth over the gleaming stainless steel of the Auto Mag. "They won't use missiles," he said confidently without looking up from his monotonous task. "They don't want the world to know anymore than we do. The Soviet sub is on a Black Mission, and the KGB aboard her, and the old sons of bitches in Moscow know it's the same with us. No, my friends, the pig farmers won't resort to nuclear weapons."

"That seems logical, or they wouldn't have sent the frogmen against us," Duvane said slowly as if analyzing each word. "They would have tried to blow us out of the water with a missile."

Sam Bair smiled without amusement and his voice was tinged with just a trace of annoyance. "What makes you so sure that the KGB thinks we're on a Black Mission?"

"Because there aren't any American or Canadian warships in the area, that's why," Camellion said dispassionately. "Another thing the pig farmers won't do is surface within our area. They won't do anything to force us to use our ASROCS." He put down the rag, raised his head and looked at Bair. "My only worry is that they'll meet the *Night Hawk*, take off Davis and head for the Soviet Union. Should that happen, we lose. We'll lose not only Davis and the secret of his Alpha One unit, but any chance of grabbing the Soviet psionic L-Wave Disrupter."

Duvane pulled back the black flap of his commando watchband and looked at his watch. "We'll know in another thirty-three hours, when we get the report from the U-plane."

The Death Merchant shoved the AMP into a long shoulder holster and got to his feet.

"Let's go to the Bridge."

Chapter Ten

Alone in the hostile Labrador Sea, the *Amphitrite* continued on a northwest course; tension and expectancy were so heavy they were almost as soupy as the fog which enveloped the vessel as it turned at Cape Chidley and entered the Hudson Strait.

What might the Russians in the Eugene Origen *do?*

Now that the Russians had been 100 percent beaten in the first round, what course of action might they take in the second?

Maintained Sam Smokey Bair: *The Russians out there are desperate and unpredictable. Desperate men can be extremely dangerous—in the manner of cowards who are cornered, though the Russians are certainly not cowards. They're not supermen, but they're damned good. The fanatics out there in that submarine might very well trigger World War III.*

Richard Camellion firmly disagreed. *You're wrong*, he said to Bair and to some of the other men who agreed with the Canadian spook. *The Russians are desperate. That's true. But . . . they are not fools. They are not hysterical fanatics of the Hitler type. Because they're not, they won't dare use nuclear weapons. They're too calculating and too pragmatic to make such a fatal mistake.*

Compounding the strain and tenseness was the eerie surroundings. The vessel was now in the northern latitudes, where the nights were almost as light as the days. Add to this the thick fog—so dense that, in the words of Merle

Duvane, "You have to chew your breath ten times before swallowing!"—and the occasional rain, and it all combined to make the passage into Hudson Strait truly ghostly. To a man, including the Death Merchant, the force aboard the *Amphitrite* began to have the subtle feeling that they were in an endless, eerie world that was opening wider and wider to destruction, to a hideousness unknown to most men—to Death. . . .

The vessel was surrounded by rolling fog banks and by a sea whose waves were moderate—four to five feet high, with many crests breaking into "white horses." Beaufort Force 5. Wave speed: 17 to 21 knots.

Suddenly, thirty hours after the short battle with the Soviet commandos, the fog lifted, and the men on board *Amphitrite* could see low stratus and fracto-stratus clouds, along with much lower scud clouds. Even the Death Merchant felt small, insignificant and helpless. Not even he, with all his know-how, could fight the elements.

The weather report from Ottawa came in. Ironically this report was based on the twice daily "send-ins" of the Canadian weather station on Resolution Island. Within a few hours there would be a weird unnatural calm, this anomaly due to *Cyclostrophic* (circle-turning) force. Within hours, this calm would give way to strong winds and a *Katabactic*, that is, cold air flowing rapidly downhill from the mountain ranges of Greenland. There would be mingled snow and sleet. The wind would increase; the water would become angry.

Sam Bair, at the radio, inquired in code (triple scrambled) whether the weather information from the Resolution Island weather station could be considered accurate. There were only fifteen men at the station and it would be a very simple matter for the Soviet force to sneak in and overpower them.

"If the Soviet commandos and the KGB are in control of the station," radioed Bair, "it is possible they are forcing the radio operator there to send false reports. However, we doubt it. The reports from the Resolution station would have to correlate, more or less, with the findings of the station at Arctic Bay on Baffin Island and the weather station at Mayo, in the Yukon."

Ottawa Control replied that they had taken into consideration the possibility of a Soviet takeover of the Resolution Island station; however, the weather reports from Resolution Island were approximately the same as the reports from the Arctic Bay and the Mayo weather stations.

"Which still doesn't prove that the Russians haven't invaded the Resolution station," came Gordon Barret's reply over the short wave. "The KGB would see to it that the personnel wouldn't deviate from routine and would transmit honest findings."

"Any report yet from the rec. U-plane?"

No, there was not. Be patient. . . .

"Be patient," grumbled Basil Taimesser. "I wonder if Barret and Grojean would be so damned patient if they were out here in the middle of a big, wide nothing?"

"A dumb question," Nelson Wiptonfield said, wiping his red face. "They'd be just as anxious as we are."

The men aboard *Amphitrite* waited impatiently. The sub-chaser plowed ahead in water that, after an hour and a half, became very calm—Beaufort Scale Force 1, Douglas Sea Scale 0, speed 1-3 knots. Visbility lengthened and became very good, from eight to sixteen kilometers (five to ten miles). There were no other vessels. *Amphitrite* was alone on the plain of water.

Every crewman was on alert, the sonar men especially so. The ADAWS2 Action Data Automation System was checked and double-checked. Technicians went over the Dardo Firing System, looking for flaws in the timing calculator sensors. Should the Soviet sub toss a missile at *Amphitrite*, the sensors would have only three minutes to detect it, shoot off two ASROCS and destroy the Russian warhead.

Gradually the calm water became less composed. The wind shifted, veered to the north-northeast. Slowly, a heavy gray haze developed, but before it did, one could see bluish-white oases of broken pack ice. The snow came—large, flurry flakes driven by a wind that steadily increased, whipping at *Amphitrite* as it continued west into Hudson Strait.

07.00 hours. The sub-chaser had gone 42.4 miles west. Captain Beach now ordered a change of course—north by northeast.

"We'll proceed 154 kilometers," he said. "I estimate that

will place us parallel with the north coast of the larger Resolution island. At this point," he put his finger on the chart on the table, "we'll be about nineteen kilometers from the northwest coast of the larger island."

Richard Camellion did some thinking—*ninety-six miles north by northeast. Not too bad. Neither is twelve miles from the coast. But the real test will come when we set foot on that forlorn piece of real estate.* . . .

The *Amphitrite* was seventeen kilometers into her new course when Ottawa Control radioed the expected report from the Lockheed U-2A reconnaissance airplane. The *Night Hawk* was only twenty-eight kilometers southeast of Resolution Island.

"I guess that settles it," Major Moan said hollowly, a serious expression in his eyes. "Since she's only seventeen miles from the island, it's not very likely that she'll change course now. So we'll battle it out on the island.

"We'll get there." Beach, who did not like the last part of Moan's comment, turned from the chart table. "The wind is damned strong and the wave speed is 22 knots, but we're moving at full speed. Nevertheless, we are losing half a knot due to the severity of the wind and water."

The Death Merchant, looking out of one of the snow-beaten bridge windows, stared into the white haze. "Captain, how much time do you estimate we'll use from the total schedule?"

Captain Beach tured to his first officer, W.D. Artbreak, who was making computations with a slide rule and writing them down on a pad.

"What do you have, Will?"

Artbreak pushed back his peaked officer's cap and put down the slide rule. "I calculate about six hours and thirty minutes," he said, looking from Beach to Camellion, "give or take an hour. It all depends on what the weather does. The wind could decrease."

"Ottawa said it won't," Sam Bair reminded him. "We can't expect fate to give us all the goodies."

"But the wind might," insisted Artbreak, a short, plump man. "No weather report is ever gospel."

"We'll assume that the weather will continue to be against us." The Death Merchant turned from the window. He blinked at Beach and Artbreak and dropped to a chair.

"Okay, so we'll lose—let's assume—seven to eight hours. Even with a nine-hour loss, we would still have enough time to get around to the southwest side of the island."

Smokey Bair and Major Moan started to speak together. "Go ahead," Moan said, letting Bair have the floor.

"Look, Chester! Have you considered the weight we'll be lugging in those tubes behind the Dragon Chariots," Bair said to Camellion. "We'll be lucky if we make four knots."

"I figure three knots tops at a hundred feet," Camellion replied. "Even so, we'll still have time or have you forgotten that the Ruskies will be on the island for three days. Even with our having to set up tents to change, we'll still have time. Not lots of it but enough."

Major Moan, one booted foot on the floor, the other dangling from the chart table, made a disagreeable face. "That's what worries me—changing from diving suits to surface clothes. Another thing, how do we know the Soviets won't send out scouts on snowmobiles. They know we're somewhere out here. They're not going to ignore us."

"We're counting on the Soviets looking for us on land," Bair said heartily, stroking his narrow chin. "But figure it out for yourself. If they look anywhere, it won't be four or five miles west of the weather station. It will be on the other side of the island, to the north, or to the northwest. Or to the northeast. You know how it is. Hide something right under someone's nose and they'll never see it. The Russians aren't any different than we are. They're human, too."

"Duvane might give you an argument on that," chuckled Captain Beach. He removed his pipe and tobacco pouch from the left pocket of his uniform coat. "He's the most 'anti' man I've ever met—anti-black, anti-Semitic, anti-Spanish, anti-abortion, anti-bussing, and only the good Lord knows what else he's against."

Camellion smiled slightly. "When it comes to race, the only thing Merle is right about is the Russians. He puts the Ruskies where I place them and a creepy crud named Galloway—lower than a beltbuckle of a crippled cockroach, nor do I mean to insult honest cockroaches."

"And who is this Galloway?" asked Bair with an amused grin.

"A backstabbing son of a sow who lives in southern California! His hot air makes the Santa Ana seem icy cold."

(He doesn't know it but the cold breath of Death is not too far away from blowing on him!)

Major Moan, always somber and seemingly annoyed and impatient, demanded Camellion's attention with his hard gaze. "I think it's time we activate the Corvus dispenser[1]. That Soviet submarine could have its radar trained on us right now."

"They could have—yes," Camellion agreed in a calm voice, toying with the zipper of his Overland jacket. "But it's also possible that the Soviets aren't doing anything of the kind. This is a large area, and the Soviets can't be sure where we are."

"Exactly what I am saying," went on Moan heavily, motioning furiously with one hand. "It's because they don't know our location that they'll begin probing with radar. And here we are as naked as a honeymoon couple at midnight!"

An interested expression fixed itself on Captain Beach's face.

Smokey Bair said, "He might have a point, Giffwangle. I think he has."

"I think he hasn't," Camellion said matter-of-factly. "First of all, the pig farmers in the sub can't search this entire area. They don't have the time. Second, if we toss up decoy clouds of 'window' chaff, we will make it easier for the *Eugene Origen* to find us, due to the height of the clouds, something like two thousand feet."

Major Moan appeared dumbfounded. "But damn it! It's the decoy clouds that will protect us!" he said in a loud voice. "Can't you understand that?"

"And can't you understand that once the Soviets ping in on the 'windows,' they'll know the general area we're in. Modern radar knows the difference between a solid target

---

1. Knebworth Corvus chaff-dispensing system. A series of multi-barrelled rocket launcher, control and firing panel and chaff-dispensing rockets, designed to deploy a number of chaff— antiradar—clouds around a vessel threatened by missile attack. These clouds form a series of decoys to the radar homing device in the missile, and thus provide a variety of alternative targets for the missile to home in on. Different types of cloud pattern can be selected, depending on the form of threat posed.

The chaff, or "window," is usually silver metallized nylon filament, aluminum coated with lead-loaded paint and lacquer, or glass fibre coated with aluminum.

and a decoy 'window.' We throw up decoy clouds and all we'll do is give the submarine our general position, and that will let them plot our general destination. No dice! I say we don't do anything that will give the pig farmers even a hint of where we are."

"It seems sensible when you put it that way," Bair said.

Captain Beach said quickly, "It's a risk, Mr. Giffwangle, but not a risk that could prove fatal. The Dardo would warn us about any incoming missiles from that Soviet U-boat."

"It seems I'm out-voted," Moan said stiffly. His tall, muscular frame stiffened and he jutted out his jaw. "Very well. We'll cruise along without activating the Corvus system."

The weather did not become more treacherous but neither did the wind and snow decrease in severity. In the center of a silent white fluffy nothingness, *Amphitrite* cut her way through waves that remained harsh—and large, between five and nine feet high, their speed twenty-two knots, their length between 100 and 200 feet. Captain Beach and his officers had to exercise the utmost caution, for under such adverse weather conditions, a vessel of *Amphitrite's* cut and tonnage could drift leeward at about one knot. Reaching across the wind, the leeway would be well over ten degrees.

Fighting the wind and the water, the sky and the sea, the sub-chaser finally reached the end of her passage north by northeast. She had come 154.7 kilometers.

In the bridge, Captain Beach told Camellion, Bair, Moan and Duvane that "We're just about twenty miles from the northweat coast of Resolution. Now we'll proceed northeast for ten miles, then twenty miles due east. After that, you men can go to work.

"Lowering the Dragon Chariots into this sea won't be easy," Duvane said, scratching the back of his head. "I'm going to be interested in seeing how you navy boys do it."

"It's all a matter of knowing how, Mr. Duvane," Captain Beach said.

The Death Merchant finished chewing a lemon flavored protein tablet. "Captain, how much time have we lost from the original schedule?" He addressed himself to Beach but looked at William Dearl Artbreak, the first officer.

"Four hours and thirty-seven minutes," Artbreak responded promptly. "But we still have thirty miles to go and have to place the six Dragon Chariots in the water. We'll lose time there. How much"—he shrugged his shoulders—"we'll have to wait and see."

On this, the last lap of the voyage, Camellion, Major Moan, and Sam Bair went over last minute strategy with the thirty Hell Eater commandos, and Canadian Navy experts made last minute checks of the six Dragon Chariots. The commandos themselves would pack the aluminum and plastic tubes that each swimmer delivery vehicle would tow.

By the time *Amphitrite* had completed the last leg of her voyage, the six SDVs were ready and waiting to be lowered into the choppy water and the commandos had packed the six UTCs (Underwater Transport Carrier). At 22.00 hours Amphitrite dropped 300-foot-long sea anchors—two at the bow—both port and starboard—two at the stern, one center port, and one center starboard. The *Amphitrite* had arrived at her destination. She was 30.7 miles from the northern coast of the larger island of Revolution. The smaller island was only forty-one miles north of the ship.

Preparations were made to lower the six DCs into the water, work that was tedious and time-consuming. Men had wheeled the eighteen-foot long vehicles—each one on its special six-wheeled dolly—into positions close to the jib crane whose boom could swing through the cargo doors.

Camellion, Major Moan, Sam Bair, and some of the other Canadian and American intelligence people watched technicians making a last minute checkup of the SDVs and the UTCs. Each vehicle had to be in perfect condition, the batteries at full strength in order to take the vehicles the sixty-two miles from the *Amphitrite* to that point on the southwest coast of the island where the force would go inland. Then sixty-two miles back to Amphitrite. Just to be on the safe side, each UTC contained a spare set of batteries and spare air tanks. In the UTC that would be towed by Camellion's swimmer delivery vehicle, there were also two deep-dive dry suits and air tanks. They would be used by Dr. Wayne Davis and Ursula Czerweny.

"I'm still in doubt about those diving suits," Charles Fond said worriedly. "I can't believe it. Sixty-two miles in that icy water." He turned and raked Major Moan with distressed eyes. "You're sure those dry suits will protect us from the cold?"

"Positive," Moan said flatly. "They've been tested in water as cold as twenty degrees below zero. The suits have a dual electrical heating system, and it's the same with the underwear we'll be wearing. The worst that can happen is that we'll get a bit chilly."

Fond moved a hand nervously across the gray hair of his left temple. "And what happens if both electrical systems go on the fritz? What do we do then?"

The Death Merchant smiled. "What do you do if the sun turns into a nova?"

Remarked Fred Thumm lazily, "I'd like to know how we're going to get those damned SDVs into the water, plus those aluminum carriers."

Cyrun Moan's expression became hard. "It isn't likely that both electrical systems would fail together. But if they should malfunction at the same time, well . . . you'll be unconscious in ten minutes, dead in fifteen. But it's not likely that both could quit working simultaneously."

The Death Merchant answered Thumm. "It's a simple but tricky process," he said. "The vehicles will be lowered, one by one, into the water, each one attached to a line to keep it from floating away." He punched a finger at the nearest Dragon Chariot. "As you can see, the Underwater Transport Carrier is attached to the side of the Swimmer Delivery Vehicle. Once we're in the water, we'll release the lines that secure the SDVs to the vessel and unclamp the cables holding the UTCs to the SDVs. Lines are already attached to the UTCs. Once the UTCs are free of the SDVs, they'll stretch out behind us for thirty feet."

Thumm nodded understandingly. "Uh-huh. Now suppose you tell me how we get from here into those weird looking underwater deals? Do we get into the SDVs before they're lowered into the water?"

The Death Merchant and Sam Bair exchanged amused glances. Even Major Moan, a stranger to humor, smiled slightly.

"We go into the water by means of rope ladder," the Canadian commando officer explained. "After all, we're on the third deck. From the open door it's only twenty feet to the water. It's not as though we had to jump."

Thumm merely shook his head.

Roger Barnkoff opened his mouth to speak, but closed it when one of the Canadian Navy technicians walked up to the group and said to Major Moan, "Sir, we're set to launch. You had better get your men suited up. . . ."

The six Dragon Chariots, spread out in a line, each one twenty feet apart from the other, moved through the water at 110 feet below the choppy surface of the Hudson Strait. A wried procession! Each Dragon was constructed in the general shape of an oversized torpedo, a giant tube that had five metal seats bolted to the top. There were other protrusions on the top of the strange looking vehicle—a two-foot high rounded "bump" just in back of the nose, and a conning tower-shaped structure on the top stern. The "bump" in front contained the instrument panel, the electric motor control, the steering diving control and the sea cock. The rear "conning tower" was a locker in which spare breathing sets were stored. The propeller, rudder, and a hydroplane protruded from the nose of the stern. There were two more hydroplanes on the side of the craft, one to port, one to starboard. The "guts" were inside the rounded tube part of the craft—an electric motor, eight batteries, pump, the aft trim tank, and the forward trim tank; air tanks and hydroplane mechanism in the center.

The launching of the six swimmer delivery vehicles had gone smoothly, and the Canadian and the American intelligence officers, in spite of their nervousness over the long underwater swim, had behaved liked seasoned pros. The Death Merchant was also pleased that he had been right about Merle Duvane.

Several hours before the SDVs had been launched, Sam Bair had gotten Camellion off to one side and had tactfully asked him about Duvane's drinking. "He seems to have two hollow legs," Bair said. "I personally couldn't care less, but a man like that could endanger all of us once we're on the island."

"Some men can handle their firewater; others can't. Duvane can," Camellion told Bair. "He'll be cold sober when the situation demands a clear head. You'll see."

They saw. Duvane had suited up cold sober. Now he sat behind the Death Merchant, grumbling as usual, muttering that the entire force should have been composed of blacks.

"They'd all be expendable. Who'd miss thirty or forty jungle bunnies?"

The Archie Bunker of the CIA! "Merle," Camellion spoke into the throat mike, "Why don't you shut off your mouth. When it comes to racism, you have a very clear mind. It isn't at all cluttered up with facts or knowledge."

"Screw you, Wigglewaggle."

Thinking of the two vehicles behind the Dragon Chariots, Camellion switched off communication with Duvane and switched UTEL to full cover, so that all the commandos could hear, including the commandos in the two Sea Stallions.

There were some differences between the American-made Sea Stallions, used by U.S. Navy SEALS, and the Canadian Dragon Chariots. The main difference was that the men sat *inside* the Stallions. The Stallions had slightly more power; nor did they have any storage space, such as a conning tower compartment outside the hull. The control panel of the Stallion was also inside the vehicle.

"How are you fellows in the Stallions doing?" asked the Death Merchant. "Any problems?"

"No sweat," Clint Farr, one of the Hell Eaters commented. "These American babies are all right, very easy to handle. Anything else?"

"No. Just keep a sharp lookout, as much as you can in these tar waters."

The minutes moved into hours. The hours dragged by. The eight-swimmer delivery vehicles moved silently south through the dark water, the pilots steering strictly by compass, contacting each other every five minutes to make sure each vehicle was in position and on the correct heading. For purposes that were pragmatic, the force, in this watery environment, was defenseless. The commandoes did carry shock rods and underwater shot tubes, but should the Russians discover them and attack with naval infantry, the mission would come to a halt and dissolve in total failure.

They did have one weapon in their favor. A day and a half earlier, at 0.700 hours, a special transponder had been dropped from the *Amphitrite*. A transponder, or pulse repeater, was a device that received pulses from one circuit and transmitted corresponding pulses at another frequency and waveshape into another circuit.

The transponder dropped by *Amphitrite* was slightly different from the usual transponder. It had not sunk to the floor of the ocean. Special floats had sprung out at a depth of only sixty feet below the surface, and there the transponder remained. Instead of receiving a continuous stream of pulses that it would rebroadcast, the transponder would receive only one short "narrow-band" signal from *Amphitrite,* this one signal activating its own pulse transformer, which would broadcast pulses in a widespread trapezoidal pattern.

It was hoped that the detection equipment aboard the *Eugene Origen* would detect the decoy pulses coming from the transponder. By the time the Russians realized how they had been tricked, the Canadians and the Americans would have invaded the weather station and have rescued Dr. Davis and his secretary . . . if everything went as planned. . . .

The time had to come and it did. Erwin Climers, the pilot of the Dragon Chariot on which the Death Merchant rode, announced in a calm voice, "In another ten minutes we'll be twenty miles west of the southwest coast, or twenty miles due west of Tower Rock."

"The rest of you heard?" Camellion said.

A chorus of "yeses" came back over the UTEL.

Nine point six minutes later the eight vehicles turned and headed due east. To a man, the force was relieved, not only because they wanted to get on with the most dangerous part of the mission but also because the deep-dive Endus suits were becoming uncomfortably chilly. While the electric heating units in the suits and in the underwear were functioning without a single flaw, they could not keep out the bitter coldness of the water indefinitely. Six hours was the maximum safety limit. Already the force had been in the water seven hours and sixteen minutes.

Merle Duvane suddenly spoke up. "Say, Wigglewaggle, did I ever tell you how you can recognize a hospital zone in Moscow?"

"Negative."

"All the guards have silencers on their machine guns."

* * *

The pilots of the SDVs shut off the electric motors when the vehicles were 160 feet from the shore, from where the waves were breaking furiously across craggy sea stacks. A hundred feet from the shore, the pilots opened the sea cocks and let the water flow into the tanks of the vehicles. Slowly the SDVs sank to the bottom, which at this point from the shore was only 107 feet deep. The men on the Dragon Chariots and in the two Sea Stallions unstrapped their seat belts, left the swimmer delivery vehicles and, after attaching ten-foot tordo-lines to each other, grasped the cables attached from the SDVs to the Underwater transport Carriers that had floated upward and were tugging at the SDVs, lifting their sterns slightly off the bed.

The men took the lines in tow and swam upward to the surface where they began swimming in the choppy wind-whipped water, filled with crystals of water ice, toward the shore. Now they could hear the roar of the waves ahead and see where the water plunged against the rocky coast and foam tumbled forcefully from the crest of fifteen-foot high waves.

Soon they no longer had to swim. Standing on the bottom that sloped upward, the men began to fight the water slamming against their backs as they fought to get on the shore and tugged at the lines of the UTCs.

It took the better part of half an hour for the force to fight its way through the raging, roaring surf, stagger to the beach and pull in the eight UTCs through the rocks and across the sand and snow and ice-covered pebbles.

It was snowing only lightly and it was night; yet there wasn't any darkness. There was only a twilight that revealed stark desolation, all of it more dreamlike and supernatural than a combination of earthly features . . . a landscape such as Milton or Dante might have imagined . . . inorganic, desolate, mysterious—and deadly.

Snow covered the rocks and uneven terrain. There was a "water sky"—a dull greyish cloud hovering near the horizon, the reflection upon the sky of the sea's dark color. The water itself, filled with crystals of slush ice, appeared oily. The men were very cold, their fingers and toes beginning to hurt. The electrical heating units in their suits had reached the limits of their maximum efficiency; either the men must soon change into warm land clothes—or freeze to death.

It was the wind that had increased the cold. Oddly, wind

turbulence in the Arctic regions is less than in southern climes, but when the wind does awaken, an already cold climate becomes, due to wind chill, harshly colder, and ground drift cuts visibility. A moderate wind of 10 mph is sufficient to move granules of dry snow across the land. At 20 mph the drift is high and dense. At 30 mph the hard snow spicules sting your face like a thousand needles.

The 30 mph wind had compacted and shaped the snow on Resolution Island, sweeping it off small ridges and packing it into hollows. Using hard, abrasive snow particles, the wind sculptures the snow into long fluted ridges called sastrugi.

Major Moan's voice, shivering with cold, came through the Death Merchant's headphones. "That long ridge over there, Giffwangle. That's a good place to unpack the tubes, set up the tents, turn up the heaters to full blast and get out of these damned diving suits. . . ."

So cold he would have welcomed dropping into hell, the Death Merchant agreed. . . .

Chapter Eleven

The large workroom of the Canadian weather station was very warm, the four blowers tossing out heated air from the central oil burning furnace. But Colonel Aleksei Vladimir Dolgov, a special assignment agent of the KGB, was concerned with neither heat nor cold. Nor was Major Khairlon Mukhanovich, the commander of the Soviet *Morskaia Pekhota* contingent aboard the *Eugene Origen*.

There were forty-six other Russians spread out in and around the weather station. Six were KGB special *Boykevso-kvivliie* agents who had been on board the *Night Hawk*. The remainder were Soviet commandos from the *Eugene Origen*.

The fifteen Canadians, who had operated the weather

station, sat on the floor against the south wall, their hands tied securely behind their backs, four commandos, dressed in black fatigues (hence "Black Berets," the nickname of the Soviet naval infantryman), guarding them with Vitmorkin machine pistols.

Doctor Wayne Davis and Ursula Czerweny sat dismally at a small table. In his middle forties, Davis was a solid man with pleasant features. Ursula Czerweny was a rather pretty blonde whose face revealed the terror she felt. Both she and Dr. Davis were wearing sheepskin insulated boots, nylon taffeta insulated "Sno" pants and chamois cloth shirts. Never had they felt so lonely and so helpless.

"Something is wrong, *Tovarishch*[1]." Mukhanovich spoke in Russian to Colonel Dolgov who was staring out of one of the small windows into the bleak swirling whiteness. "The Canadians and the Americans didn't follow us all this way to sit by and do nothing. Why, we don't even know where they are. We should have taken time to find the enemy ship before coming ashore. We're sitting on a timebomb."

Turning from the window, Dolgov scrutinized the Black Beret commander with serene but calculating eyes. As tall as Major Mukhanovich but ten pounds lighter, Dolgov was a broad shouldered, craggy faced man who was used to stress and danger.

"The Americans and the Canadians don't want to start a war," Dolgov said in a low voice, walking toward Mukhanovich who was standing by the shortwave sets, holding a mug of hot tea in his hand. "They don't dare make direct contact with us—with either the *Night Hawk* or the submarine. They're afraid we'll use a missile against them, and then they would have to retaliate. We would destroy each other. No one would win. We'd all lose."

Interjected Viktor Tcherniak, one of the special KGB agents who had been aboard the *Night Hawk,* "Comrade Khairlin Mukhanovich, you're a combat officer; your training forcing you to view every situation in terms of violence. We're not here to search out and destroy the enemy vessel, and we're on a very tight schedule. If the submarine had gone chasing all over the place looking for the ship, we'd be here another three or four days. Who knows what the Americans might decide to do during those

---

1. "Comrade."

three or four days? The sooner we leave this barren little island and head for home, the safer we'll be."

As Tcherniak talked, Colonel Dolgov pulled a chair from the long radio table and sat down next to Ilyador Pankin, the Black Beret who was tending one of the two radio transmitters that had been brought ashore from the submarine. For two days the Soviet force had been master of Resolution Island, the *Morskaia Pekhota* taking over the weather station without firing a shot. Major Mukhanovich and a group of Black Berets had come ashore in ELMO-7s and had sneaked up on the weather station personnel. That's all there had been to it. Major Mukhanovich had been second in command of the Soviet commandos. After Colonel Lavrenty Kossior, the commander, and the forty-eight commandos had not returned from the attack against the *Amphitrite*, he and the forty-eight had been presumed dead, and Moscow Central had placed Major Mukhanovich in command.

Moscow had blamed Colonel Kossior for the failure of the attack and had warned Mukhanovich, Dolgov, and Commander Mikhail Servich, the skipper of the *Eugene Origen*, that more failures would not be tolerated.

Protect yourselves but do not look for trouble! Moscova had ordered. The next phase of the operation had gone smoothly and without any complications. Word was radioed to the *Night Hawk* that the island was secured. Captain Lawson Jebson had anchored the *Night Hawk* two miles south of Resolution Island. Three hours later, the *Eugene Origen*, a large Delta type submarine, had come to a full stop a mile and a quarter southeast of the *Night Hawk*.

The Soviet force had waited, the radar and sonar of the submarine searching, probing, but finding nothing. There wasn't a trace of *Amphitrite*. There was a possibility that the Canadian vessel had anchored north of the island. *Nyet*. The Canadians and the Americans might be desperate but they weren't fools. To land on the north coast and come south would be literally suicide. The radar at the weather station would pick them up. Where then was the enemy ship?

Colonel Dolgov had his own private thoughts about the Americans and the Canadians. It did seem unlikely that they would come all the way from Newfoundland merely to observe. He was still trying to dredge up from his mind another possibility when he heard Major Mukhanovich say in a voice that was heavy with frustration, "Moscow wants us home, yet we have to stay here for the next day and a half and protect those scientists while they conduct some kind of weird experiment. It doesn't make sense."

"We have our duty," said Yuri Novosti, another KGB officer, who was pouring a cup of coffee. "I would advise you to do yours, Comrade Khairlin Mukhanovich."

"It's not supposed to make sense to us," Colonel Dolgov said acidly, and although he knew all the details about the experiments to be conducted with Professor Josef Demokinin's psionic L-Wave Disrupter, he saw no reason to make the volatile Mukhanovich privy to such sensitive information, even if he had been permitted to. "Our job is to follow orders. That means that all we have to do is protect the three scientists from the Americans and the Canadians. The three will conduct their experiment; then we shall go home—home with our prize." He turned his head slightly and smiled at Dr. Wayne Davis. "I'm sure, Doctor Davis, that after you confer with our specialists in Moscow, you will be more than anxious to reveal the secret of your Alpha One unit."

"We're a long way from the Soviet Union." Dr. Davis's personal pride, plus his pride as an American, made him feel that he had to defend himself with a reply. "A lot can happen between here and that big pigpen you call the Soviet Union."

"Dyn sookynsyn zho-punchnik!" snarled Boris Zabikkitski, one of the KGB agents. Quickly he stepped toward Dr. Davis, his right hand upraised. Dr. Davis glared defiantly at him.

"Boris! That's enough!" lashed out Colonel Dolgov. "We don't mistreat our prisoners."

Zabikkitski, a thickset, ugly-faced man with watery eyes, pulled up short, his savage stare protesting, but he knew better than disobey.

Pavlik Zdebskis, a tall, cadaver-thin KGB officer, uttered a long, low laugh. "We might not even need Dr. Davis's psychotronic device if our own secret weapon works as well as the scientists anticipate."

"That's quite enough, Pavlik," warned Colonel Golgov, angered that Zdebskis should even hint at the nature of the experiments in front of Major Mukhanovich and the other commandos in the room.

There was a loud BEEP from the transceiver to which was attached a scrambler and a frequency hopper[2]. The submarine was on the radio. The dots and dashes came rapidly. Ilyador Pankin's hand and pencil flew with equal speed over the pad.

The message from the *Eugene Origen* was the best kind of news. Ilich Efindiyev, the chief KGB officer aboard the submarine, was going to bring the three scientists to the island, and he wanted Major Mukhanovich and ten commandos to return to the Delta sub in one of the power boats and return to the sub. Mukhanovich and the ten commandos would then escort Efindiyev and the three scientists to the island.

The best news of all was that the sonar of the *Eugene Origen* had picked up high frequency pulses fifty-one miles southwest of her present position. The enemy vessel had been found. Apparently, since the pulses were stationary, *Amphitrite* had dropped her sea anchors and was waiting. Analysis of the situation indicated that the enemy subchaser did not pose a threat to the Soviet Force. If the Americans and the Canadians were going to attack, they would have done so before now.

More important, Moscow Central agreed.

The communication ended with a request to Confirm and—Were there any questions?

"Acknowledge the message and ask Comrade Ilich Efindiyev if he wants Major Mukhanovich to bring Dr. Davis and his secretary aboard the submarine," Colonel Dolgov instructed the pinched-faced Pankin whose finger began tapping out the message on the brass handkey.

At once, back came the reply, which Colonel Dolgov read over Pankin's shoulder as the commando wrote it down on the pad.

2. Operates in such a manner that the transceivers—transmitter/receiver—at each end of the communication very rapidly skip from one frequency to another. There are sixteen different frequences in use at any given time and each frequency is used for only one/twelfth of a second before the units hop to another frequency. Since twenty-four different frequencies can be programmed into the unit and the sixteen operational channels selected from these twenty-four can be used, about 50-billion choices of frequency and programming sequences can be selected. Unless one knows the frequencies, it is impossible to monitor the units.

Nyet. The two *Amerikanskis* would remain on the island until the experiment was completed. It was possible that when Dr. Davis saw how the L-Wave Disrupter worked, the scientist in him would overcome his patriotism. It was possible that he might confide in Professor Demokinon and the other two parapsychologists. Please confirm.

"Confirm and sign off," Dolgov ordered Pankin. His voice, all business, did not betray the disgust and the anxiety he felt. The *Amphitrite* was out there waiting, only eighty-two kilometers from the sub and yet they were still going to bring the scientists and the device ashore.

The fools!

Colonel Dolgov turned to the circle of anxious faces. "Major Mukhanovich, you are to take ten of your men and return to the submarine. You are to escort Comrade General Efindiyev and the three scientists to the island. You are instructed to leave at once."

"Good. Now we're getting some action. Was there anything else?" Major Mukhanovich heaved his big frame out of the chair and stood erect. "Was there anything else?"

"They think they've located the Canadian ship," Dolgov said. "In theory, it's eighty-two kilometers southwest of the *Origen.*"

Mukhanovich's face broke out in a smile. "Well now. Now that we know where the enemy ship is, she shouldn't be much of a threat. I think we can ignore her."

He motioned to one of the commandos guarding the Canadian weather personnel. "Vitali, get nine of the other boys and we'll get going."

Vitali Bakholdin, a mean-looking brute, stood up. "What about the guards outside? You want any of them to go with us, Comrade Major?"

"*Nyet.* I'll have them rotate with the men inside every half-hour," Mukhanovich said, then looked at Colonel Dolgov. "There will be more than enough men, Comrade Colonel, to protect the station until we return. You need not worry."

"I think we'll be able to manage," Dolgov said sarcastically. "I don't think you and ten men would make that much difference should the Americans miraculously appear." He would have liked to smash Mukhanovich in the mouth—and General Efindiyev, too, for that matter. Efindiyev was another idiot. They were both fools who were leaving too much to chance. Worse, it was with the approval of Moscow!

In Dolgov's opinion all of it—bringing the scientists to the island—was as silly as Efindiyev's ordering Captain Jebson to remain on board the *Night Hawk*. However, Dolgov did have to admit that Jebson was not about to sail off, not under the guns of the *Eugene Origen*. That *cvevkoskeien*! Jebson actually thought that he and his crew would eventually be brought aboard the sub and taken to the Soviet Union. Another fate was in store for Lawson Jebson whom Dolgov despised as a traitor. The Canadians and the Americans were only doing their duty, doing what they had to do to protect their nations. Not so with Jebson. He was a Canadian working against his country. To Dolgov, there wasn't anything lower than a traitor.

Colonel Dolgov was suddenly conscious of the wind whistling outside the weather station . . . a moaning that made him vaguely uncomfortable. Again he tried to convince himself that there wasn't anything the Americans could do.

Or was there?

Chapter Twelve

The Death Merchant and his men had done a lot of sowing. Shivering with cold, they had unpacked the underwater transport tubes, erected the white tents, turned on butane heaters, and had changed to Arctic clothing, their outer garments hooded white sub-zero combat suits heavily insulated with goose down. Their feet were protected by cold weather pac boots with an inner lining of soft, warm felt that insulated against the cold and absorbed perspiration. Like the submachine guns and other long weapons, boots and equipment bags were covered with white canvas to blend in with the snow.

They had taken down the tents and were hiding them and their swim suits and air tanks in the snow when Fate smiled slightly on them. The snow stopped, the result: an increase in visibility, but only for a few hundred feet. The harsh wind still swirled the wind off drifts and rocks.

"Make a final check of equipment," Camellion ordered the men. "Make sure that all your weapons are on safe. A shot could give the whole show away."

He adjusted the wind ruff of the hood encircling his face and pulled down the fog-X goggles. Composed of thermal pane-type lens, the goggles would not fog and would eliminate snow-glare. . . .

The Death Merchant and his force had sown. Now it was time to reap.

They moved east, single file, two scouts several hundred feet ahead of the main party. Every few minutes they would report to Camellion and Major Moan by walkie-talkie.

Everywhere was desolation and vast emptiness—contrast. Where the wind had blown the snow totally from the surface, there was stark brown or black rock. During the summer months, Resolution Island would be free of snow and the temperature would rise as high as 50 degrees at high noon. The firs, tamarack and jack pine in the northern part of the island would feel gentle breezes and pink lousewort, purple saxifrage, and Arctic chamomile, the daisy of the north, would bloom. But now there was only a white barrenness, a plain of snow drifts constantly being shaped and reshaped by the wind.

Completely covered from head to foot and resembling creatures from another planet, the force moved east by southeast. By 09.00 hours, they had covered a mile. Four and sixth tenths miles to go. Four and six tenths to the Canadian weather station. . . .

The Death Merchant touched Major Moan on the shoulder. "Call a halt on the walkie-talkie. It's time to send the signal."

On Moan's orders, the men got down behind and beside drifts, careful to keep their Steyr-Mannlicher AUG[1] automatic rifles free from snow. The AUGs looked like something straight out of Star Wars, with the magazine behind the frame handle, which, at the bottom center, housed the

---

1. "Army Universal Gun."

trigger. A fold upward handle was just to the rear of the handle. The stock looked oversized; yet the weapon was well-balanced and was quick to line up on a target because of the fixed optical sight that magnified one and a half times and featured a black ring as a reticle. There was no selector switch. One merely pulled the trigger four times in quick succession to switch the weapon from semi-automatic to full automatic.

The Death Merchant reached into one of his white-covered shoulder bags and took out a metal box no larger than a small card file. Containing a time-code generator with a carrier tap transmission choke coil, the device had only one function: to broadcast a long high-frequency signal. The Death Merchant opened the box, extended the four-foot antenna, threw the toggle switch, waited until the blue eye glowed, then pressed the button. The men on *Amphitrite,* picking up the signal, would not activate the transponder that had been dropped over the side of the sub-chaser.

"How long will it take for them to get to get the transponder in operation?" Sam Bair, down on his haunches beside Camellion, stared at the Death Merchant through his amber-lens goggles.

"All they have to do is push a button," Camellion said. He shifted the M-11 Ingram submachine gun, in its case on his belt, to a more comfortable position. "The transponder is sending out pulses right now. Let's hope it fools the Russians."

Major Moan offered, "It could backfire. Should the Russians investigate and find out that it's only a transponder, they might guess what is going on. No telling what they might do."

The Death Merchant nodded. "Another reason why we had better put ballbearings in our feet and get going. Let's move out. Major, warn the men to be very careful. Not all of the surface is what it appears to be."

He was referring to the snow-filled crevasses . . . deep, wedge-shaped clefts that varied in width from a foot to ten feet and were often fifty feet deep. Wide crevasses appeared as large depressions in the earth, unless the snow was very thick, with rims of recently compacted snow a dull eggshell white. Further down snow turns to ice, light green at first, then deep bottle green, falling away into the cold blue and the inky black of the abyss.

The force moved over the dead, cold land that, frozen and rockhard, could not absorb any moisture. Pushing themselves to make speed, they bypassed crevasses, moved between large drifts and crept across flat spaces of rock swept clean by the wind. Fortunately, their bodies were well protected against the whip of the wind, the outer nylonpolythene shell of the combat suits impervious to the cold. Finally, when they were within sight of the weather station, the force was weighed down, not only with killequipment but with exhaustion.

Lying flat between drifts, Camellion, Bair, Major Moan, and some of the intelligence people studied the station through binoculars. Shaped like one of the sections of a swastika, with the left leg pointing north and the right leg pointing south, the prefabricated one-story structure would never appear on any picture postcard. Against the north side of the horizontal structure were two oil tanks that furnished the fuel for heating. A short distance to the southwest was the shed where the snowmobiles were kept. To the south, only a hundred feet from the building was an English-type thermometer shelter, the four cups of an anemometer, on top of a twenty-foot pole, spinning furiously in the wind. Just north of the snowmobile shed was a forty-foot steel tower anchored with guy wires. To the southwest of the southwest corner of the main building was another cable-anchored tower. Stretched between the two towers was the short-wave antenna.

"You two have the know-how," said Sam Bair, who was lying prone between Camellion and Major Moan. "How are we going to do it. Do we just storm the place?"

A low noise rumbled from Major Moan's throat. "I've always had an ambition to throw an egg into an electric fan, but never to commit suicide. First we do a complete recon."

"Including a recon of the harbor," added the Death Merchant, adjusting the focus knob of the Bausch & Lomb binoculars. "The harbor is only a mile south of here. We must know what's in that harbor."

Major Moan pulled out his Dessex walkie-talkie. "We're about sixty meters northwest of the weather station. I'll have four of the boys swing around in a large circle to the east, then move south to the vicinity of the harbor."

"Negative." The Death Merchant's almost cruel tone was an order. He continued to look through the binoculars.

"I want to eyeball that harbor myself. If—hold on! Take a look at that! Two of our pig farmer friends are by the fuel tanks."

"Yeah, I see the sons of bitches. They're all in white, just like us," Bair said. "I doubt if they are part of a genuine welcome wagon."

"There's no doubt more of them in front," Major Moan said, staring at the two Russian commandos through his binoculars. "Maybe by the snowmobile shed. They won't be a problem. We can kill them with silencers. But we'll have to get them all at once."

He took the binoculars from his eyes and glanced at the Death Merchant, who was shoving his own pair into its case and was getting ready to belly-slide back from the drifts.

"I'll go with you to the harbor," offered Moan.

"The men need a trained officer with them," Camellion droned. "You stay here. I'll take two of your boys and Duvane."

"Duvane!" Moan seemed astonished. "That damned boozer!"

"That damned boozer is worth five of your best men," Camellion said with a twisted smile. "He's an expert killer."

"He's a damned comedian!" snorted Moan.

Moan was surprised when the Death Merchant agreed with him. "Sure he is. In fact, all expert terminators have one thing in common with comedians—timing."

Camellion, Merle Duvane, and two of the Hell Eaters had worked themselves to within 150 feet of the harbor, crawling the last sixty feet on their stomachs, wriggling like white clad worms to a twisted line of snow-covered boulders to the northeast of the harbor, which was actually a large cove filled with numerous chimney stacks developed by wind and wave erosion, some of the rocks as tall as thirty feet. It would have been impossible for a craft of any size to have navigated the waters of the cove. But the harbor was ideal for small boats, launches, and the like; even in stormy weather they could pull up to the pier made of wood supported by steel girders. While the rocks were numerous, small boats could easily maneuver between them.

More important, the rocks acted as a water-break, preventing the waves from striking the pier with full force.

"It's not much to look at, is it?" whispered Sergeant August Voges.

"The water ain't so inviting either," commented Fred Webber, the other commando with Duvane and the Death Merchant, the latter two of whom were scanning the stormy waves through binoculars. The waves had a leaden color, and there were small ice floes. Crystals had coalesced and squeezed part of their enclosed salt content toward the surface of this "young ice," so that it was covered with brine, gray and tacky. The ice was elastic and, when broken, razor sharp.

A slight mist hung over the water; yet one could see for miles. There, two miles to the south, was the *Night Hawk*, riding easily in the waves.

"Do you suppose they've brought Dr. Davis and his secretary ashore?" Duvane said. "If they're still on board, we'll never get to them."

The Death Merchant, not replying, was busy adjusting the focus knob of the binoculars, his eyes fixed on the low, curved silhouette of the *Eugene Origen*.

"Merle, take a look to your left," he said. "About a mile and a fourth southeast of the fishing boat. It has to be the Soviet sub."

"It sure as hell isn't a whale!" Duvane said, focusing in on the large Soviet Delta sub whose top hull and sail showed darkly against the background of sky and water. "By God! Either we got here too late or just in time. Take a look at those motor launches!"

The Death Merchant looked. He stared at the three motor launches that were close to the submarine, their bow and stern lines held by sailors while men moved from the hull of the sub into the large motor boats.

"We arrived just in time," Camellion said, a hint of force in his voice. "I'd say they're getting ready to come to shore, and that means to the weather station."

"I estimate from fifteen to twenty men in each launch," Duvane said, sounding unhappy. "It's difficult to tell from this distance."

Camellion returned the binoculars to their case. "We have forty-one men counting ourselves. With the number of pig farmers who must be back at the weather station, there must be sixty to seventy of the commie trash."

Rip Elmier said with conviction, "Let's not kid ourselves. The only way we're going to whip those commie bastards is to ambush them."

"It's either that or run like hell," Fred Webber growled. "They're not supermen but neither are we."

All this time, the Death Merchant's clever mind had been working in high gear, analyzing all the possibilities. From the pier to the weather station the distance was not quite a mile, a mile swept almost clean of snow by the wind. On either side of the hundred-foot wide area were long, weirdly shaped *sastrugi*, wave like ridges of hard snow.

It can be done. Camellion was positive. It must be done because there isn't any other way.

"Well, by God! Let's do something!" urged the impatient Duvane.

"We will. Motivation got us started. Habit will keep us going." The Death Merchant pulled out his walkie-talkie, extended the antenna, switched on the set and began giving orders to Major Moan and Smokey Bair. Twenty men would take positions around the weather station; the rest of the force would ". . . get the lead out of their tails . . . and spread out behind the ridges of *sastrugi* east of the area from the wharf to the weather station."

"Why not on both sides?" Major Moan's voice, coming through the walkie-talkie, was almost a demand. "Hell, we can trap them in a crossfire."

"No deal," barked the Death Merchant. "There's too much chance that the Ruskies at the weather station will spot the boys if they try to cross from the east to the west; and we don't have time for the men to move from their present positions to the west of the trail."

"Listen. I think—"

"I am not interested in what you think. We haven't the time to indulge in perspicacity. One mistake and we'll have grass growing over our heads come summer," Camellion said. "Do what I tell you. Place twenty of the men in positions that will enable them to storm the weather station at the same time we open fire on the pig farmers coming in on the launches. Take the rest of the force and place them behind the snow ridges to the east, so that you can toss lead at the Ruskies when they are, say, a hundred and fifty feet south of the station. Over and confirm."

"I understand," Moan said, sounding as cranky as an old

maid who had discovered a man wasn't under her bed. "Where will you and Duvane and the other two boys be?"

"We'll move back north and meet you behind the ridge east of the station," Camellion replied. "Hop to it, and tell the men to be very, very careful. If we're spotted and a Ruskie fires one shot, the entire ball of wax will melt in failure. You got it?"

"Affirmative—but I don't have to like it. Anything else."

"Negative. Out."

Camellion switched off the walkie-talkie, pushed down the antenna and shoved the set into its case. "All right, guys. Let's move back and line up with the others."

"First we move up, then we go back. The next thing you know we'll be moving sideways," muttered Duvane, wondering what *perspicacity* meant.

The force had deployed itself with no time to spare. Five commandos had burrowed into the snow only a hundred and six feet north of the weather station; another five were behind snowdrifts to the west. To the east, twenty-three feet from the snowmobile shed, were three more impatient "Hell Eaters." Seven more commandos had belly-crawled in the fluffy snow and ice to within ten feet of the radio tower southwest of the station.

The instant these commandos, under the leadership of Lieutenant Buster Altengid, heard firing from the ridge to the east, they would storm the weather station.

The rest of the commandos and the Canadian and American intelligent agents waited with equal impatience, scattered in various positions around the closest snow ridge east of the station—some on the summit, on the low part, of the long *sastrugi*, which, at its highest point, was fifteen feet high; others lay behind gaps in the ridge and at either end.

Duvane, lying next to Camellion, a 9mm M-11 Ingram in his right hand, chuckled mirthfully, "Some nut once said that strangers are friends we haven't met. He sure as hell wouldn't apply that crap to the Ruskies in either the weather station or the launches coming in."

Jacob Hall, on the other side of Duvane, said worriedly, "What bothers me is that damned submarine. It has not only twin 35mm guns but a 75mm deal on deck. That's a lot of fire power."

"So what?" said Roger Barnkoff, lying next to Hall in the gap. "The submarine is three and a half miles out—four miles from here." He considered for a moment. "Of course, it could move in closer."

The Death Merchant removed his Duvex gloves, their removal still leaving his hands warm in frogman's textured rubber duprene gloves—thin but giving sure grip protection against the cold, due to the millions of tiny air cells trapped in the foam rubber, these retaining moist body heat. The other men had similar dual gloves.

Camellion pushed the earplug, connected to the walkie-talkie, more firmly into his right ear, anxious to get the report from Fred Webber whom he had posted two thousand feet to the south, in a position in which the commando could observe the pier.

Webber's voice finally came in through the earplug. "The launches have pulled in. There's twenty men to a launch, not counting the pilots. All carrying weapons—most of them anyhow. AKMs and Dragunov machine guns. Four of the Ruskies are carrying a small crate. Hell, they're treating it as though it were filled with nitro. Any special orders? Over."

"Good job, Webber," said Camellion. "Remain where you are. When you hear firing, head back this way. Over and acknowledge."

"Understood—out."

Camellion pulled the plug from his ear and turned to Major Moan. "The pig farmers are on their way. Pass the word, and tell the men not to fire until I give the signal with a shot; then they can open up with everything they've got—and listen. The Russians are carrying a small crate. It could be their L-Wave Disrupter. I don't want one bullet to hit that crate."

Moan switched on his walkie-talkie, and as he spoke to the men, giving orders in a low, firm tone, the Death Merchant checked his two .44 "Backpacker" Auto Mags. Matter-of-factly, Merle Duvane, pulled back the slides of his two Safari Arms MatchMaster auto-pistols, then pushed the catches to SAFETY.

"It's a good day for a fire-fight," he said laconically to Camellion.

"We have two minutes to pray and one second to die," Camellion mused, knowing that the Cosmic Lord of Death would soon claim his own. . . .

Chapter Thirteen

"Jack and Jill went up the hill to fetch a pail of water," muttered Duvane, watching the Russians approach in the distance. "Jill forgot to take her pill and now they have a daughter."

"And if you're not careful, you're going to have an AKM in your gut," said Camellion, his amused tone mystifying Major Moan, who considered both Duvane and Camellion freaks with a death-wish. Here they were, on the verge of death and yet were making jokes. Automatically, Moan began to think in German. *Ya, der Todesengel!* That was Giffwangle. And that damned Duvane! A *besserwisser*—a know-it-all. A man whose mind was cluttered with minor information and misinformation about everything. Moan sighed. *Es geht alles vorueber, esgeht alles vorbei*[1].

The Russians, all decked out in white parkas and moving in small groups of twos and threes, came forward at a leisurely pace, neither hurrying nor dragging their feet. While some of the commandos carried their weapons loosely in their hands, others had their AKM assault rifles or submachine guns slung on leather straps over one shoulder, an indication that they felt safe and secure.

In back of the first thirty commandos were four men carrying a crate on a square wooden pallet with handles, a crate about three feet square. Beside the men carrying the crate walked three men in heavy coats—civilian coats and the familiar round fur hats on their heads. Civilians!

The Death Merchant stared coldly at the three men. *Sci-*

---

1. "Everything passes, everything has its day."

entists! Scientists who are with the L-Wave Disrupter! You'll never get to use it, Comrades.

Second by second, step by step, the Soviet column drew closer to the weather station . . . drew closer to certain death. Within seventeen minutes, the first of the Russian commandos were parallel to the first of the Canadian commandos waiting behind the snow ridge, these first "Hell Eaters" some seventy-five feet to the left of the Death Merchant and the intelligence officers around him. Knowing human nature the way he did, Camellion glanced from the left to the right. The men were impatient, impatient to kill.

He waited—*And everyone else had damned well better wait, too!*

Camellion switched off the safety of the Ingram and pushed the selector switch to automatic. The seconds slipped into minutes. The minutes crawled by. Just as a watched pot never seems to boil, victims always seem to move with extraordinary slowness. Three minutes! Now, almost all of the enemy column was strung out in front of Camellion and his killer force.

"In three months it'll be Christmas," growled Duvane. "We going to wait until then?"

"Nor Easter." The Death Merchant sighed in with the Ingram on a tall, hulking Russion who walked as if he were trying to tiptoe, and barely touched the trigger of the dandy machine pistol. The Ingram snarled, shattering the stillness of the early morning. Three 9mm Parabellum projectiles, having bored into the Russian's right side, were still pitching the mortally wounded man to the ground when the snow ridge erupted in a tremendous roar of gunfire, a thunderous chorus of Ingrams, Sterlings, and Steyr-Mannlicher AUG A-Rs. High-velocity jacketed hollow-points and jacketed flat-point slugs sliced into the Soviet commandos the way hail strikes the roof of a greenhouse. In less than ten seconds 23 of the Soviet commandos were riddled, were stone dead before their bodies had time to even crash to the ground. But after that first deadly blast there was that slight lag time on the part of Camellion's force, that five to six seconds pause in which the gunners had to realign their sights on new targets, all of which gave the *Morskaia Pekhota* commandos—those who had weapons in their hands—time to spin to the east and rake the snow ridge with a vicious hail of AKM and submachine gunfire, the projectiles creating tiny geysers of snow, scores of the steel-cored 7.62mm projectiles ricocheting as they struck granite rocks. Many of the enemy slugs came very close to Camellion and his men. Five came as close as possible. Two of the Canadian commandos cried out and died. One man had a projectile squarely through the mouth. He slid into eternity with the back of his head blown out. The second man ended life on planet Earth with a bullet through the upper chest. A short cry. Then the forever blackness. . . .

Very well trained, the Soviet commandos adjusted to the emergency with a speed that surprised even the Death Merchant. Knowing better than to remain stationary and/or to flop to the ground in the open, the Russians took the only course of action possible: firing short bursts from their AKM assault rifles and Dragunov sub-guns, they charged the snow ridge, Major Mukhanovich screaming, "Kill them! Kill them!"

There wasn't anything that the Death Merchant and his people could do—except to keep down and do a lot of hoping. . . .

The split second that Lieutenant Altengid heard the duddle-duddle-duddle of Camellion's Ingram, he said *GO* into the walkie-talkie, and the twenty Hell Eaters hidden on all four sides of the station went! However, they didn't begin the attack with automatic weapons. Instead, four of the Canadians—one on each side of the building—sighted in on the patrolling guards—now rigid with alarm!—with .22 Ruger auto pistols to which silencers had been attached. *Pyfftt. Pyfftt! Pyfftt!* The two Soviet commandos to the north fell apart with .22 slugs in their bodies. Concurrently, the pig farmer to the east, the two to the west, and the two walking in front of the main doorway to the south began going down. Except for one of the Russians to the west. A .22 bullet had deflected against a rib and, while the man was in pain, he was not seriously wounded nor unconscious. With determination, he tried to swing his AKM assult rifle to the west and rake the snow bank. He didn't succeed. The Canadian Hell Eaters were now charging and one of them ripped him open from Adam's apple to groin with a short burst of AUG fire, the .223 slugs ripping him open and knocking him six feet back into the snow.

Lieutenant Buster Altengid and the other nineteen Canadian commandos now had one goal only: to get inside and secure the weather station building.

There were twenty-eight of the *Morskaia Pekhota* inside the building. A half-dozen were in the north/south wing in which the bedroom cubicles were located—going through the personal belongings of the meteorologists, seeing what they could steal. Some of the Ruskies were in the Mess, in the horizontal section, stuffing their faces on good "Capitalist" food, while others were in the recreation room, wondering about the strange Western game known as pool. A ridiculous game! Hitting colored balls with long sticks. *Veprosy skogo nyana noi*! Other Russians were in the general operations room with its weather charts and instruments.

Colonel Aleksei Dolgov, sitting on a chair by the radio table in the operations room, knew in that half-wink of a second that somehow the enemy had executed a super-slick maneuver and that—considering the tremendous firing to the south—Major Mukhanovich (*That fool!*) had walked into a clever ambush.

Throwing himself sideways from the chair to the floor and pulling a 16-shot Vitmorkin machine pistol from a hip holster, Dolgov shouted to the commandos and the KGB agents in the room, "Get to the windows! Stop them from coming in!"

Also in that moment he thought of his Prime Directive from Moscow Central: *Should the Amerikanskis even get close to Doctor Wayne Davis, kill the scientist and the woman. At all costs, do not let the Amerikanskis take the scientist from your custody.*

While the cursing men rushed to the windows, Dolgov glared at Dr. Davis and Ursula Czerweny, both of whom had thrown themselves to the floor and were lying flat on their stomachs, their faces masks of stark fear. They looked across the ten-foot space at him, at the black muzzle of the long-barrelled machine pistol in his hand. Fully expecting him to shoot, there was fear, yet acceptance, on their faces.

Dolgov did not pull the trigger, his decision based not on any compassion but on indecisiveness and on pragmatism involving his career. Suppose he killed Dr. Davis and the woman and the *Morskaia Pekhota* succeeded in fighting off the Americans and won? How then would he be able to explain his action to Moscow. His superiors would say he acted in haste! On the other hand, if he didn't kill them and the Americans won—what difference would it make? He would be dead and beyond the long arm of the KGB. *Nyet*, he wouldn't kill the two Americans. *Da* . . . he would wait.

"OHhhhhhhh!" Safar Abdulov fell back from a window, blood streaming down his face from his forehead that had been hacked open by several 9mm submachine gun slugs. Pavel Kiktev was the next to die. His mouth open, looking as silly as a penny waiting for change, he fell back from one of the windows in the north wall, several slugs in his chest.

The usually peaceful station, where monotony was an occupational hazard, became a battlefield of quick and violent death. Within seconds, every double-paned window in the building was shot out, the floors littered with glass.

Canadian commandos tossed half a dozen fragmentation grenades through the east and west side windows of the north/south section, the thundering explosions ripped apart the fiberboard partitions and turned four of the Russians into bundles of ripped bloody rags. The last two pig farmers fled, running down the hall to the south, one staggering and in pain from a dozen pieces of shrapnel that had peppered his back.

There was a definite method and procedure to the attack of the Hell Eaters. While four Hell Eaters tossed 9mm Sterling machine gun slugs and .223 caliber AUG projectiles through the shattered windows of the N/S section and through the windows of the east-west portion of the building, another commando tossed two grenades against the door on the north side of the east-west section. This door opened to a narrow hallway that lead to the stores, the kitchen, the mess, and the first-aid room.

The grenades exploded, the savage blast tearing the door off its hinges and throwing it inward, creating more panic and confusion among the *Morskaia Pekhota* in the mess who, during those short moments, were lying prone on the floor and trying to decide which course of action to take. Should they rush to the north or the south windows? Go to the operations room—or what? Unlike commandoes of the Western nations, Soviet soldiers are not urged to take the initiative but to listen to and obey their officers. This brainwashing now worked against them. They hesitated. The Canadian Hell Eaters did not.

The exploded door had slammed into Aleksandr Aistov, one of the Russians who had escaped from the bedroom, the big smash breaking four of his ribs whose jagged ends punctured his lungs. Blood bubbling from his slack mouth, Aistov lost consciousness and melted to the floor as two more Hell Eaters fired through the north side windows, raking the already shattered room with slugs. At the same time, three other Canadian commandos stormed through the wrecked doorway—right into the AKM fire of Dmitri Darensky, the pig farmer who had been in one of the bedroom cubicles and whose back had been stabbed with shrapnel.

No coward was Aistov. Although in intense pain, he swung the Kalashnikov assault rifle around in the direction of the Canadians and squeezed the trigger, muttering, *"Idyi zho ssat ya natyb yahachoo!"*[2] The burst of 7.62mm projectiles ripped open the stomach of James Gukmiller, the first Canadian through the door, the slugs stabbing all the way through his body and hitting Wilbur Lively, who said "Aw hell!" and fell back with Gukmiller.

Clint Farr, the third commando, was luckier—and very fast. In a crouching position, he snarled, "You Russian son of a bitch!" and knocked Aistov back across the room by putting three .223 AUG projectiles into his chest. Simultaneously Farr swung the AUG in a raking arc and chopped apart four Russians who had scrambled up from the floor of the mess hall and had rushed into the area way. Tiny bits and fluffs of black cloth jumped outward from their uniforms as the slugs stabbed into their bodies and killed them.

Farr himself would have been turned into bloody cold cuts moments later if it hadn't been for Wayne Bohmer and Norman Schneider, two of the Hell Eaters from the south. Bohmer and Schneider thrust their AUG A-R through several shattered windows on the south side and butchered the remainder of the *Morskaia Pekhota*. The other five commandos from the south linked up with Lieutenant Altengid and prepared to polish off the operations room where Yuri Novosti and Pavlik Zdebskis, two of the KGB agents, were already dead.

2. Too vulgar to be stated in English.

Lieutenant Altengid, forty feet from the south door, tossed a grenade and, with the other men, dropped to the snow. The grenade exploded, the blast further increasing the fear of Colonel Dolgov, the four commandos and the four KGB agents in the large operations room through which the wind now howled, every single double pane of glass having been shot out.

Altengid and his people were too sensible to charge like wild bulls through the blasted door. Instead, rushing to the south and the east walls, under coming of AUG and submachine gunfire, Mel Gills and Doyle Cuppi—to the east—and Orvel Hidge and Tony Bensin—to the south—tossed frag grenades through the windows, grenades in which the fuses had been removed—duds! *Plunk-plunk-plunk-plunk.* The grenades rolled across the floor, two coming close to Boris Zabikkitski and Sergei Volnov.

"Svi s Bogóm!" yelled Viktor Tcherniak and, forgetting himself, stood up at the same time that Lieutenant Altengid and two Hell Eaters rushed through the door, their AUGs spitting slugs. Concurrently, Mel Gills and Doyle Cuppi fired through several of the east wall windows, the lines of slugs taking out Viktor Tcherniak and Sergei Volnov, both of whom jerked violently when the projectiles cut into their bodies.

The roaring of weapons filled the air, the wind, whipping through the broken windows, mixing the burnt, acrid odor of gunpowder with that cold, crisp smell of the Far North.

The big head and the neck of Boris Zabikkitski dissolved in a burst of flesh and bone and blood-spray as two of the commandos with Lieutenant Altengid hosed down the area with a tornado of slugs. Stanislav Utemov went down with half a dozen 9mm slugs in his chest and stomach, followed by Josef Kinskoboski, who, when two .223 projectiles struck him, one in the gut and one in the stomach, looked like a man who knew there was a party going on and he hadn't been invited. Slugs, as thick as popcorn, zipped across the room. The two Drake short wave sets exploded. More commando bullets turned the transceiver—brought to the station by the KGB—into junk.

Tony Bensin sighed, fell sideways and died when Ilyador Pankin, trying to crawl to one side of a filing cabinet, fired off three rounds with his Vitmorkin machine pistol. One of the HV 9mm slugs barely grazed the right side of Lieutenant Altengid; another cut into a Draper thermograph and wrecked it. The third projectile caught Bensin in the left side of the chest. He dropped without a sound, without a murmur or a sign. . . .

Then Pankin and Dmitri Zevkesski caught Hell Eater slugs and went down, their bodies riddled. Porfiry Galkin, a machine pistol in his right hand, got off his last four rounds, three of which went wild, the fourth hitting Austin Poe in the left front thigh, six inches above the knee.

All this time, Colonel Aleksei Dolgov had kept down between two filing cabinets. Now, seeing all his comrades falling around him, he knew that he, too, would soon be dead. But, by God, the *Amerikanskis* would never get their hands on Dr. Wayne Davis, who was lying flat on the floor, his hands over his head. Next to him lay Ursula Czerweny, paralyzed with naked fear.

Extending his right arm, Dolgov aimed down on Dr. Davis, his line of vision following the front and rear sights that were aligned on the top of the scientist's head. But Dolgov never got to squeeze the trigger.

Seeing Dolgov's extended arm, Orvel Hidge snap-aimed and sent a dozen 9mm Sterling SMG slugs at the limb. Dolgov shrieked when his forearm disappeared in a bloody cloud of shredded flesh and chips of bone, his eyes almost jumping out of their sockets when he saw his hand, cut off at the wrist by two hollow pointed projectiles, fly to the left, only a hair-of-a-second after muscle reflex caused the forefinger to squeeze the trigger. The Russian machine pistol roared, but the bullet did not hit Dr. Davis in top of the head. The force of the nine-millimeter projectiles that had severed the hand at the wrist had moved the hand upward, and the projectile, moving at a slant, struck Davis in the rear of his left leg, just above the ankle, the bullet breaking the fibula.

With blood pumping from his wrist stump, Dolgov felt the world spinning around him. Almost unconscious from loss of blood and shock, he never saw the slugs that slammed him into eternity. Nor did Georgi Pekin, the last KGB agent. Mel Gills cut them both apart with a long burst of AUG automatic rifle fire.

The Canadians now controlled the weather station; it had been taken. . . .

* * *

Outnumbered two to one, the Death Merchant and the men with him met the charging Morskais Pekhota head on. Dodging, ducking and weaving from side to side, Camellion had discarded his Ingram, not having had time to reload the weapon. With a .44 Backpacker Auto Mag in each hand, he fired with a deadly, methodical accuracy, the tremendous roaring of the stainless steel auto pistols echoing up and down the coastline. One powerful .44 magnum cartridge went all the way through the bodies of two Soviet "Black Berets" and hit still a third Ruskie in the shoulder, shattering the scapula.

Major Moan, Sam "Smokey" Bair and the rest of the men with Camellion fought with equal force and determination. There were, however, too many Russians. Within a matter of minutes, the Soviet force was closing in hand-to-hand combat with the Americans and the Canadians. Now it was man-to-man, eyeball-to-eyeball.

"I don't love you, but Jesus does!" muttered Camellion and shot one Russian squarely in the face with the left AMP. As the man's face and head exploded in a burst of blood and gore, the Auto Mag in Camellion's right hand thundered and a .44 projectile blew open the chest of an ugly-faced Ivan aiming down on Fred Thumm, who, at the moment, was pulling a 9mmP Beretta auto-loader from underneath his parka.

To save ammo, the Death Merchant slammed the short barrel of one AMP against the temple of a Russian trying to crown him with the butt of an AKM . . . used a short, but vicious snap-kick to the groin to slam a second pig farmer, and crushed the forehead of a third dummy with the barrel of the other AMP. An AKM bullet tore within half an inch of his left temple, ripping through the hood lined with rabbit fur and barely missing the elastic strap holding the fog-X goggles in place. Another slug went through the leather case on the belt and wrecked the walkie-talkie, but Camellion didn't notice. He was too busy using a right-legged *Yoko Geri Keage* side snap-kick, his foot landing in the gut of Leonid Rok. The Russian commando cried out in agony, doubled over and went skidding back in the snow to Major Moan, who instantly shoved an ST-23 fighting dagger into the region of the slob's left kidney. Out came the knife, the eight-inch blade covered with thick blood. Down went the dying Soviet commando.

Moan would never know that he was only seconds from death and that it was Merle Duvane who saved his life. A Safari Arms MatchMaster auto-pistol in each big ham of a hand, the tall and muscular Duvane was fighting with a coldness of purpose more frigid than the snow and ice around him. He snap-aimed on an Ivan swinging a Tokarev pistol toward Major Moan, grinned and pulled the trigger, the Federal 230-grain .45 ACP bullet banging the pig farmer in the right jaw, the big flat-nosed bullet flattening out and tearing off most of the man's lower jaw. With a strangled cry of pain and shock, the Ruskie nosedived to the ground in a wide spray of blood, falling in back of Roger Barnkoff who knew he was as close to death as he would ever get without actually dying. Barnkoff was struggling with Kaarlo Galkin and Aleksei Diakonov, Galkin's right hand around Barnkoff's right wrist, preventing the CIA man from turning the Colt Python revolver against either Galkin or Diakonov, the latter of whom had both his hands around Barnkoff's left wrist and was trying to kick him in the groin with his left foot, Barnkoff constantly blocking the Ivan's foot with his own left leg.

It was Basil Taimesser who, coming to Barnkoff's rescue, came in from behind the two Russians and shoved the muzzle of a S&W Highway Patrolman revolver against Aleksei Diakonov's right hip and squeezed the trigger. A big roar! And the .357 magnum projectile tore through Diakonov's hip, tickled itself all the way through the pig farmer's intestines and took its exit out the other side, breaking the left ilium, or hip bone, in the process. Diakonov, crying out in hideous pain, sagged faster than tissue paper that had lain in the rain all night, his termination increasing the fear in Kaarlo Galkin whose fingers tightened on Roger Barnkoff's right wrist. But with Barnkoff's left arm now free, Galkin's doom was a certainty. His breath coming in gasps, Barnkoff slammed Galkin in the right temple with a left *Ken Tsui* bottom fist. Quickly, he then used a left-handed *Yon Hon Nukite* four-finger spear stab to turn the Russian's Adam's apple into applesauce. Gurgling and strangling to death, the upper portion of his windpipe smashed, Galkin's knees buckled. His eyes wild, he wilted, tried to wail in agony and began the quick process of dying.

Everywhere, men were grunting, groaning and gasping,

each man knowing—friend and foe alike—that this struggle was to the death, that there were no rules. Each side had only two objectives—to kill and to survive. . . .

The Death Merchant, not wanting to have his Auto Mags twisted from his hands and perhaps lost forever in the snow drifts, dropped the big weapons in their springhold hip holsters and jerked out an 18" long steel Ko-Budo Sai, a vicious *trisula*, or trident, shaped weapon whose center blade was separated from the handle by a large handguard of forked design. The main blade, or shaft, was made of chrome steel and was wedge-shaped, each side as sharp as a razor, the end as pointed as an icepick. In the hands of a kill-master like Richard Camellion, the Sai was as deadly as an H-bomb, a weapon of pure death, which Camellion used with an almost preternatural accuracy.

Oleg Szamuely, Gleb Struve, and Zhores Medvedev thought they would make short work of the Death Merchant, Struve coming in from directly in front, Szamuely from the left—he was swinging an empty AKM A-R like a baseball bat——and Medvedev—a commando knife in one hand, an empty Stechkin machine pistol in the other— from the right. All three Russian commandos paused for the barest fraction of a second when they heard the Death Merchant laugh and say *"Mine eyes have seen the glory of the coming of the Lord. He was roaring down the alley in a '57 Ford!"*

"Yop tva-yoomat!" snarled Szamuely and tried his best to shatter Camellion's skull. The Death Merchant ducked the AKM and, as he buried his heel in Szamuely's gut with a left-legged *Sokuto Geri* sword-foot kick, he first sliced Zhores Medvedev across the right wrist, then let him have a quick one-two stab in the stomach with the blade of the Sai. Medvedev gasped loudly and started to fold while Szamuely, who had dropped the AKM, staggered in agony against Pytor Burzinski who was doing his best to get his hands around Charles Fond's throat.

At the same time that he stabbed Medvedev, Camellion ducked a vicious right-handed *Nukite* chop by Gleb Struve that would have caved in the left side of his neck had it landed. He also barely managed to deflect Struve's left-handed *Tettsui* fist hammer that could have easily fractured his collarbone; however, Camellion managed to jerk to the left so that the Russian's fist landed on the knob of the Death Merchant's right shoulder. Before Struve could regroup his reflexes, step back and try another series of blows, Camellion stabbed him just below the breastbone with the Sai.

All this time—not more than five minutes had passed—the Death Merchant had been concerned about the crate and the three civilians who had not charged the Americans and the Canadians with the *Morskaia Pekhota*. Camellion was positive that the crate contained the Soviet psychotronic L-Wave device.

Now, Camellion's worst fear was confirmed. The three Russian scientists had picked up the crate and were struggling south with their burden, their intention to get back to one of the motor launches, then to the submarine.

The three scientists didn't get far. There was a crack of an AUG from one of the south windows of the weather station and Professor Josef Demokinin howled and went down, a .223 caliber bullet in his left leg. Two more cracks and Professor Leon Kirensky and Professor Egin Stalokov hit the snow, slugs in the lower parts of their legs.

Merle Duvane was busier than a one-toothed mouse in a roomful of cheddar. He had holstered his empty MatchMaster auto-pistols, had removed his outer gloves and had slipped the first two fingers of each hand into extra-large *Karate Keys*. Not a key, each Karate Key (while it did have a link chain to which keys could be attached) was actually a small set of ultramodern "brass knuckles." Machined from solid aluminum bar stock, weighing less than an ounce, and 2½-inches on all four sides, the Karate Key was square with an open, horizontal slot in one end and two holes in the other end. To use the device, one merely slipped the first two fingers (or the two middle fingers) through the holes and closed the hand into a fist, an arrangement that permitted half of the "key" to protrude, a protrusion that could crack and break bones.

Merle Duvane was doing just that, using the Karate Keys with a natural-born talent. At times, he used both fists the way a boxer would—a right cross, or a left uppercut or a straight-in jab, each time the Karate Keys on his hands either cracking or breaking bones; and he also used his feet to kick Russians trying to get at him from either side or the rear.

Captain Yuri Dzhirkvelov died within seconds when Duvane first made the Russian pitch forward by slamming him in the stomach with a short *Mae Geri Keage* front snap-kick, then, as the agonized Soviet commando fell toward him, Duvane smashed him in the left temple with a tremendous right-handed blow, the Karate Key shattering the temporal bones as though they were tissue paper. Almost all in the same lightning quick motion, Duvane half-turned and let Gennadi Sychin have a terrific right uppercut and, at the same time, flattened Suren Aksenpiv's intestines with a TNT *Mawashi Geri* roundhouse kick.

Sychin, his lower jaw broken by the Karate Key, wilted with all the speed of a dead flower, and so did Suren Akempiv who, because the common iliac vein had been ground to pulp, was bleeding to death internally.

Geli Okulov, a 220-pound Russian commando, had been a drinking comrade of Sychin. Filled with hate for Duvane and determined to revenge Sychin, Okulov charged the CIA street man, a commando knife in each hand.

"Here's your crackerjacks—but no prize!" muttered Duvane. His left leg shot out like a piston, in a *Sokuto Geri* sword-foot kick, the sole of his foot landing solidly in the middle of Okulov's broad chest.

"UHHHuhuhhhhhhh!" Half unconscious, Okulov let the daggers slip from his fingers, looked as if he wanted to tap dance but didn't know how, and staggered back—right into the waiting arms of James Burke-Whit, the Canadian intelligence officer. Burke-Whit struck faster than a mama Black Mamba. His left arm shot out, went around Geli Okulov's thick neck, and tightened at the same time that he crashed the heel of his right palm against the back of the Russian's head. Snap/crackle/pop! The Russian's neck snapped. Burke-Whit released the limp body, stepped back and—died instantly!

Vasili Sitnokov caved in the back of the Canadian's head with the barrel of a Dragunov submachine gun. But Sitnokov was far from safe. Just as a bullet cut through the front of Fred Thumm's hood—so close to his face that it skimmed through his shaggy black mustache—Thumm shoved the blade of a Gerber Mark-I. knife into Sitnokov's right side and slammed the barrel of an empty S&W Military & Police .38 revolver against the back of the Russian's neck.

* * *

The Cosmic Lord of Death was having a feast. The end of life came for Jacob Hall. Major Khairlin Mukhanovich first staggered him with a Nukite chop to the neck, slammed him in the stomach with a *Ken Tsui* bottom fist, then speared him in the throat with a *Yubi Basami* knuckle/fingertip strike. Helpless, choking to death, the ONI agent began going down, a great roaring in his ears, the world turning black around him. As Hall fell, the elated Mikhanovich jerked the S&W .41 magnum from Hall's Jerry-Rig holster.

Snarling in rage and frustration—he knew that his world and his career were crashing around him—the *Morskaia Pekhota* commander spun, caught sight of Basil Taimesser who had just killed a Russian commander by beating his head in, raised the revolver and fired. The big revolver roared, the JFP Hi-Shok bullet smashing Taimesser in the lower right side, the impact almost picking him up off his feet as the projectile cut through his liver and tore out the left side of his back.

Major Mukhanovich aimed and again pulled the trigger. This time a large .41 magnum bullet sent Nels Whiptonfield's head flying apart in all directions.

The self-satisfied commando chief didn't get a chance to fire a third time. Before his mind could put together what was happening, there was a terrible pain in his right hand, his arm flew upward and so did the big Smith & Wesson revolver, flying out of his hand.

The Death Merchant had kicked the weapon out of the Russian's hand, breaking several of the bones in his hand; yet Major Mukhanovich was far from helpless. He still had his good left hand, both legs, and was one of the most renowned experts in *Koshoryu Kenpo* in the Soviet Union. Kenpo, a deadly martial art[3] had originated in Japan.

Mukhanovich, recovering very fast, threw up his left arm, blocked the Death Merchant's right arm and the Sai, and attempted to ice the Death Merchant with a left *Hiza ate* knee-lift. And missed when Camellion, seeing the blow coming, twisted to one side and tried a left-legged side sword kick. Camellion missed. The commando chief back-

---

3. Kenpo—sometimes spelled Kempo—is the Japanese pronunciation of the Chinese ideograph representing *ch'uan fa*, or fist law. The origins of the system date back to about A.D. 525 when the Indian monk Bodidharma—Daruma in Japanese—traveled from India to China to spread Buddhism.

stepped and rapidly countered with a *Nokki Tok* spin kick which the Death Merchant did more than avoid. Camellion let the Sai fall point first into the snow, grabbed Major Mukhanovich's flashing foot with both hands and twisted to the right with all his might.

The Russian howled, but was helpless to prevent his body from twisting around so that, as he fell heavily, he crashed downward on his face. Though in pain, he tried to roll over and scramble forward at the same time. He was too slow. Camellion leaped high, came down and kicked Mukhanovich in the coccyx or tailbone. Paralyzed with pain, the Russian screamed in agony and in fear. The end of his life was approaching and he knew it. The end came when the Death Merchant kicked him first in the neck, then again in the left temple. He then stamped on the back of the Ruskie's neck with his right heel.

Major Khairlin Mukhanovich would never move again. . . .

Men continued to die. Sergeant August Voges sank to his knees after he was knifed by Georgi Kelviskiv, but with one final effort Voges managed to bury his own double-edged blade into Kelviskiv's belly as he fell. Rip Elmeir and Erwin Climers died from 9mm DM Makarov pistol slugs, followed by the two Soviet commandos who had killed them.

Picking up the Sai from the snow, the Death Merchant saw that white clad bodies littered the snow ridge. Since both the Russian and the Canadian commandos were wearing white, the only way to tell East from West was by their snow goggles. The Canadians wore goggles with amber lens, the Russians, green.

Camellion tore across the snow to where Will Donovan and Sam Bair were fighting a group of Soviet commandos. As the Death Merchant tore across the snow, he saw that Duvane was also headed for the group of struggling men. Off to one side, Fred Thumm, Charles Fond, and Roger Barnkoff were giving good account of themselves. Major Moan was still in action, at the moment cutting the throat of Gilgan Mimsky with his ST-23 fighting knife while Stephen Karanko was wiped out by Charles Fond, who first took Karanko down in a wraparound sweep, then mashed his windpipe to pulp with a series of short left kicks.

Crouched only twenty feet from where Wilbert Donovan and Smokey Bair were struggling with the last group of

Russian commandos, General Ilich Efindiyev was taking out the empty magazine of a Vitmorkin machine pistol, preparatory to shoving in a full 16-round clip.

Damn! Camellion realized that if the Russian succeeded in reloading the machine pistol, he could easily turn the tide of battle—*And I'm not that much of an expert with a Ko-Budo Sai to try to throw it. I might miss*.

The Death Merchant took a long shot. He tensed, ran forward and jumped, half-turning his body as he executed a spinning backkick, the effectiveness of the technique lying in the duality of eluding and countering in one smooth, fluid motion. His torso spun 180 degrees, the power traveling along a waist-high plane, the force delivered with the heel of the extended leg. In this case it was the heel of the Death Merchant's right leg, his heel crashing like a battering ram against the right side of General Efindiyev's hood and face. Knocked to the left, his upper and lower jaws broken, Efindiyev lay unconscious, drowning in his own blood.

Donovan, an expert in Chuka Shaolin, was hard pressed, holding off five Morskaia Pekhota with the help of Sam Bair. But all the expertise in existence couldn't compensate for sheer numbers. Bair and Donovan were within seconds of losing when Camellion and Duvane arrived.

A one-two-three punch by Duvane with his Karate Keys and Vadim Stepakobsky folded unconscious, his lower jaw broken and several of his upper vertebra fractured.

Vitali Bakholdin, trying to get to Donovan by using a series of chops, screamed like a wounded mountain lion when the Death Merchant buried the blade of the Sai between his shoulder blades.

Sam Bair ducked a *Sangdan Yikwon Taerigi* high back fist, grabbed Fredrenko Kuznestov's arm, pulled and presented the Soviet commando with a *Mawashi Geri* roundhouse kick that landed in the left armpit. Almost paralyzed with pain, Kuznestov did not see Bair's left hand flash out in a four-finger *Nukite* spear stab, but the Russian did not feel the "spear" bury itself in his solar plexus. A minimoment before Bair used the *Nukite* stab, the Death Merchant chopped Kuznestov across the left side of the neck with the Sai.

Vasilevich Stupar and Mikhail Belurus, both fighting Donovan, suddenly realized that their situation was hopeless. Not only were they fighting Donovan, but Bair, Duvane, and Camellion. Better to surrender to the Amerikanskis than to die.

A wild look on his face, Belurus stepped back. As he was raising his arms, Camellion's Sai blade stabbed in and out of his left side. Stupar died seconds later. Seeing Belurus die, he had hesitated only a moment. During that blink of an eye, Smokey Bair killed him with a left *Nukite* chop to the neck and a *Ni Hon Nukite* two-finger spear stab to the throat. Stupar crumpled, making choking sounds. . . .

The Death Merchant looked at Will Donovan, then turned his goggled eyes to Merle Duvane who, while shoving fresh clips into his Safari Arms MatchMasters was looking grimly up and down the length of the long sastrugi. Except for the moaning of the wind, there was a strange quietness gripping the area.

"It would seem we've won." Major Moan pushed up his fog-X goggles and began counting the Hell Eaters who were still on their feet. Nine were standing. If other Canadian commandos were alive, they were either in the weather station or were on the ground, wounded and unconscious, perhaps dying.

The Death Merchant shoved the Sai in its special holster and, noticing that Major Moan had pulled out his walkie-talkie and was contacting the weather station, stared at the three Russians in civilian clothes who had been shot in the legs and were lying close to the crate.

Camellion motioned to some of the approaching commandos. "Go down there and see if those pig farmers are alive. Don't waste them. I suspect they're scientists and that the crate contains a device we're after. Be damned careful and search them for weapons. . . ."

"Suppose they're alive, sir?" one of the commandos asked. "What the hell do you want us to do with them?"

"Drag them to the weather station; we'll take them back with us to the Amphitrite."

The five commandos moved off toward the west, their AUGs held at the ready. Fred Thumm—his snow goggles had been torn off—and Charles Fond, unhooking the Ingrams attached to their belts, stepped closer to Camellion and Moan, the latter of whom, smiling, was shutting off his walkie-talkie.

"What about the Soviet submarine?" Thumm said in a level voice.

"What about it?" Donovan's tone was smug. "This is the

second round they've lost with us. All the *Eugene Origen* can do now is go back to mama Russia."

"Lieutenant Altengid said the station is secure," Moan said heartily. "They killed every Ivan in the place . . . but, they did lose some men. Dr. Davis and the woman are there and safe. Davis was wounded in the leg, but it's not serious." Moan rubbed his gloved hands together. "Gentlemen, I'd say we have accomplished our mission. All we—"

Moan's walkie-talkie buzzed. Moan again pulled out the small transceiver and switched it on. The frantic voice of Fred Webber jumped out of the set. "The Soviet U-boat is moving straight in and she has men on her deck around her seventy-five millimeter cannon."

Duvane finished lighting a cigarette. "Damn it to hell! How do we fight a damned cannon?" He answered himself. "We don't. All we can do is run."

"Tell Webber to get his can back here," Camellion said to Major Moan. "We've got to make tracks away from this area—and fast."

Before Moan could speak into the W-T, Webber, who had heard the Death Merchant's voice, said, "I'm halfway back now. Don't worry. I'll catch up with you guys."

Duvane said scornfully, "The Ruskies can't have anymore commandos on board. "There's only so much room on even a big submarine."

"We don't know that," Roger Barnkoff, walking with the other men toward the weather station, said in a worried voice. "I can tell you one thing. If they do more of the *Morskaia Pekhota* ashore and they get to us, we'll have had it in spades."

"I'll buy that," agreed Will Donovan firmly. "The sooner we change into swimsuits and get in the water, the safer we'll all be."

"You mean if the Soviet sub doesn't decide to get even by sinking us," Merle Duvane intoned. "The Russians can be very vindictive when they want to, and we sure as hell have given them a good reason to be."

Intuition suddenly burned brightly in the Death Merchant's mind. The *Eugene Origen* wasn't moving in close— the sub could come within a mile of the south shore of Resolution Island—merely as an exercise.

"Major, get on your walkie-talkie and tell Lieutenant Altengid and the men with him to vacate the building—and fast!" Camellion said, his eyes on the commandos who were examining the three Russian civilians.

"I don't understand!" Moan sounded troubled as he reached for his walkie-talkie. "Why should—"

"Because that submarine will probably shell the building. Why else would she be coming in close?"

Another fifty feet and the Death Merchant and the rest of the men had reached the commandos and the three Russian civilians, one of whom was very still and lying face down in a pool of frozen blood. The .223 AUG bullet that had struck him in the leg had cut through the Femoral artery and Professor Josef Demokinin, the inventor of the L-Wave Disrupter, had bled to death.

"One of the Ruskies is dead," Dean Moffit, one of the commandos said, looking at Camellion. "None of them were armed except him." He pointed at Professor Egin Stalokov, who, with Professor Doctor Leon Kirensky, was sitting up, both men staring in fear and pain at the Americans and the Canadians.

"He had this little baby," Moffit said, showing Camellion a 9mm Makarov automatic pistol, which he then shoved into a pocket of his parka.

All of them heard the sound and looked upward—a weird, high-pitched shrieking. A 75mm shell was flying overhead. The *Eugene Origen* had fired off the first round from her deck gun. The shell arched downward and, with a monstrous sound and a flash of red and orange flame, exploded a hundred yards east of the weather station.

Camellion barked orders at the commandos. "Drag those two Russians out of here. Get to the northwest of the station." His eyes swept the intelligence officers. Merle, Roger, Charles—help me with this pallet. We're going to take the crate with us."

It took almost fifteen minutes for the Death Merchant and the whittled down force—carrying the two wounded Russians and the wooden platform on which rested the small crate—to reach the area northwest of the station where Lieutenant Buster Altengid and the rest of the commandos had gathered among snow-covered boulders that were strewn about.

During those tension-filled minutes, the Soviet submarine fired six more shells from her deck gun, but none touched the weather station. It was the seventh shell that blew the weather station into rubble that shot a hundred feet into the air before coming down and covering a wide area. And still the deck cannon continued to roar. Another tremendous explosion and the antenna tower southwest of the station fell to the ground.

"Come on, damn it!" urged Major Moan. He glanced anxiously toward the south, although from this distance he could not possibly see the *Eugene Origen.* "Let's get to the tents and the suits. Considering all the men we've lost, there's plenty of dry suits for everyone. We can even take the two Ruskies with us."

The Death Merchant, down on his haunches with Duvane, one of the commandos and Ursula Czerweny, hesitated, part of him watching the commando and Ursula Czerweny, both of whom were putting a fresh bandage on Dr. Davis' left leg. Once the bandage was in place, they would use four bayonets as splints and bind them tightly to the broken limb with belts. The other part of the Death Merchant was totally absorbed in escape. Some deeply buried instinct quietly informed him that once all of them were in the water in the Dragon Chariots, the Soviet submarine would seek them out. There was another horror. *Suppose the* Eugene Origen *goes after the* Amphitrite. *No, not likely. As angry as the Russians are, they won't risk our retaliating with a missile tipped with a nuclear warhead.*

Camellion put his thoughts into words. "There is a possibility that the submarine will come after us, once we're in the water."

A terrific explosion interrupted him. Another 75mm shell had exploded 250 feet to the east of their position.

"By now, the Russians on board the sub know we've wiped out the Russian commandos and that we must have sneaked in from the north in SDVs."

"What are you saying?" Major Moan sounded disgusted. "We've got to get back to *Amphitrite* and using the SDVs is the only way."

"I've been thinking along the same lines," Sam Bair said slowly.

"We can't remain here indefinitely." Roger Barnkoff looked up at the solid gray sky. "The wind has shifted and the temperature is dropping. We're going to need heat and food damned soon."

"There's a cold front moving in," Arnold Gulve, one of the Canadian weather station personnel, said mournfully.

There is perhaps a way we can extract ourselves from this dilemma."

The Death Merchant and the others looked intensely at Dr. Wayne Davis who had spoken in a voice colored by pain and emotional misery.

The scientist looked across at a skeptical Death Merchant. "Didn't I hear you say that you thought the Soviet psionic L-Wave Disrupter was in that crate the Russians had?"

"You did."

"It's possible that with the L-Wave Disrupter, I can destroy the Soviet submersible," Davis said. "I can't be positive, but it's worth the effort."

"Ridiculous!" Merle Duvane kept his voice low to control his uncertainty. "Hellfire! Whoever heard of destroying a submarine with a screwball device right out of science fiction?"

Doctor Davis gave Duvane a condescending look. "Young man, don't sneer at things you do not understand. You will only succeed in making a fool of yourself."

The Death Merchant couldn't help but smile—*"Young man!" That's rich. Davis is only Merle's senior by ten or eleven years!*

Studying the man Courtland Grojean had referred to as the "obstinate Puritan," Camellion said, "I thought you were a pacifist, Doctor Davis. Yet now you're willing to destroy the Russian sub. Why the change of heart? (*As if I didn't know!*)

"I know the Russians for what they really are," Davis said seriously. "During this past week, listening to the KGB agents talk, I know we can't trust the Soviet Union. We can't live in peace with them." He paused, then said fiercely, as if revealing an enormous secret. "Why, they want to conquer the world. They must be stopped."

Merle Duvane locked eyes with the Death Merchant. "He sounds like he has good sense, doesn't he?"

The Soviet L-Wave Disrupter was a metal box 20" long, 14" high, and 18" wide, the front filled with dials and several meters. An elastic and wire headband was plugged into a jack on the side of the box. Power was supplied by a dozen 12vDC batteries. The copper well plate was in the center top of the device, between the four telescoping antennae, which Dr. Davis, as excited as a child with a new toy, extended to full length.

"Ursula, have you noticed that this device is similar to my own Alpha One unit?" said Davis, running his fingers over the smooth metal well plate.

"Only larger," Ursula Czerweny said.

Dr. Davis glanced at Camellion, Moan, and Bair. "I'll need a piece of paper and a pencil," the scientist said, "to make an outline of the submarine."

"Weird," Duvane muttered. "Weird."

"I've a notebook and a ballpoint pen," said Sam Bair. "Will they do? . . ."

"Yes—and please hurry," Davis said.

Sitting flat on the frozen ground with the L-Wave Disrupter in front of him, between his legs, Doctor Davis accepted the pen and the notebook from Bair, tore a sheet from the notebook and, putting the small piece of paper on top of the metal box, proceeded to draw an outline of a submarine, after which he looked across at Camellion. "What is the name of the submarine?"

The *Eugene Origen*," offered Camellion.

"Spell it, please."

"E-U-G-E-N-E O-R-I-G-E-N!"

As Camellion spelled the name, Doctor Davis carefully printed the two words horizontally within the outline of the submarine he had drawn, much to the amusement of Merle Duvane, Fred Thumm and some of the other men whose smiles indicated their thoughts.

Doctor Davis handed the sheet of paper to the Death Merchant and returned the pen and notebook to Sam "Smokey" Bair.

"Please shoot the outline," Dr. Davis said to the Death Merchant." "By that I mean, put a bullet hole through the center of the drawing."

Duvane chuckled. Some of the others grinned. Others simply looked incredulous, as if they couldn't believe Dr. Davis was serious.

Davis, realizing that the men thought he was a crackpot of the first order, said irritably, "Whatever is done to a specimen that's placed on the well will also be done to the original object. You don't have to believe it; I don't expect any of you to."

"We don't!" Duvane declared.

"That's your privilege," Davis said. "The truth is that we haven't even scratched the surface of what can be accomplished with psionics. According to quantum physics all things are ultimately controlled by thought. As the Lamas and voodoo practitioners alike have proclaimed, if you believe it, it will be. In a nutshell, this Russian L-Wave device and my own Alpha One unit do the same things that are accomplished with ELF and UUHF waves, magnetic and ionic fields and much more in that they perform functions in the vast area of L-fields."

"Wayne, they don't believe you," Miss Czerweny sounded hurt. "Why bother to explain anything to them?"

"I think you're a brilliant man, Doctor," said Charles Fond. "But in all honesty, I think you've fooled yourself. I don't say that to be insulting either."

Dr. Davis grimaced in pain; yet he said in a controlled voice. "Yes, I know all of it sounds fantastic. Yet I have seen proof with my own eyes. For example, with a DeLaWarr device, one can actually take photographs of the past. This DeLaWarr unit uses coils inside chambers to enhance resonance or vibration of the specimen frequency. It's amazing. The seed of a lily was photographed and the dials set to produce a picture of a lily in full bloom! A pregnant woman three months gone produced a picture of a nine-month-old fetus. A few drops of blood of a man and his wife produced photographs of the two on their wedding day thirty years before; and there was the incident in which an electronic circuit at a powerhouse in Phoenix, Arizona, was repaired by inserting a whole or correct schematic into the psionic well and simply broadcasting the correct 'path' of the circuit. The malfunction was cleared up very shortly and the circuit *repaired itself*. This is not hearsay, gentlemen. I have absolute proof."

"Python poop!" sighed Duvane.

The Death Merchant had pulled a small Bauer autopistol from underneath his parka. He placed the small piece of paper on the ground and prevented the strong wind from blowing it away by placing a pebble at each corner of the drawing. He switched off the safety of the pistol, aimed, and pulled the trigger, the weapon cracking, the .25 caliber bullet going through the center of the drawing. Camellion bent down, picked up the paper and handed it to Dr. Davis, who carefully placed the sheet on the "well" of the Soviet L-Wave-D box, holding it in place by putting one of the sensor "wands" (4″ inches of round steel), connected to the box by a coiled wire, on the center of the drawing.

BERRRROOOOMMMMMMMMMM! Another 75mm shell from the Soviet submarine exploded, this burst only 200 feet to the north of where the small force was grouped.

"Those sons of bitches aren't ever going to quit!" Will Donovan said bitterly. "They sure intend to get even."

Dr. Davis pulled down the furred hood of his parka, slipped the headband over his head, turned on the L-Wave Disrupter, and said authoritatively, "Gentlemen, please move back."

"Look—" began Jacob Hall. "I—"

"Do as he says," Camellion ordered and stepped back. "At least, give Dr. Davis a chance—and all of you had damn well better hope he's right."

Dr. Davis, by noting the reaction of the GSR meter in the center of the front panel, could tell when he had found the correct frequency of the sub drawing he had placed on the well. He next began to adjust the Phase One and the Phase Two dials. All the time, he stroked the drawing on the "well plate" with the second sensor wand.

Finding the correct frequencies with the P-1 and the P-2 dials, Davis next began to tune the 3rd and the 4th "fine-tuning" dials. All the while, he stared at the GSR and the WV (Well-Vibration) meters, watching for the signal that would indicate that the full capability of the machine had been reached.

Desperately, Dr. Davis hoped that the Soviet device was, internally, similar to his own Alpha One unit. The more "fine tuning" you wanted, the more selective each resistor and each capacitor had to be. Instead of one that was variable from several ohms to several thousand ohms, you utilized individual ones in increments of say 10 each, that is, from 0-10 ohms, 10-20 ohms, 20-30 ohms, etc. Actually these would run more like 1-100, 100-1000, 1,000-10,000, etc.

The signal-strength was reached on both the GSR and the WVM.

Closing his eyes, Dr. Davis concentrated, centering all his thoughts, his entire consciousness, around picturing the submarine exploding—concentrated and held the sensor wand tightly in his left hand while he stroked the outline of the submarine, placed faced down on the well.

From ten feet away, Camellion, Ursula Czerweny, and the rest of the group watched and waited and wondered.

The L-Wave Disrupter hummed.

Dr. Davis concentrated and stroked the drawing on the well-plate.

A minute passed . . . two minutes . . . 240 seconds . . .

BBLAMMMMMMMMMM! Another 75mm shell, from the deck cannon of the submarine, exploded—three hundred feet to the west.

Not moving, sitting as quietly as a Buddha, Dr. Wayne Davis continued to concentrate, his eyes closed, his fingers stroking the drawing on the well plate.

Only the Death Merchant, Ursula Czerweny, and Roger Barnkoff weren't surprised when the explosion did come—a gigantic blast, several miles to the south, that made the ground quiver, a deep, internal crashing that could have only been an internal fulmination in a vessel.

Stunned, dumbfounded—with the exception of Camellion, Czerweny, and Barnkoff—the group knew that the *Eugene Origen* had been destroyed. The impossible had become possible. Fantasy had become fact.

Doctor Davis shut off the L-Wave Disrupter and removed the headband, a proud, self-satisfied look on his bearded face.

"I just don't believe it!" croaked Merle Duvane, staring toward the south.

"I can," the practical Camellion said. "But we have to be certain. Merle, let's you and I and Roger go have a look." He turned to a still speechless Major Moan. "Major, send some of your boys to where we have the suits and tents stashed. Have them bring back the HF transceiver. Once we're sure that the Soviet sub has gone to the bottom, we'll contact you by W-T. Then you can use the HF-T to radio Captain Beach. He can bring the *Amphitrite* to the south harbor."

Major Moan's face and the faces of the other men brightened.

"An excellent idea," Moan said. "The *Amphitrite* can get to us faster than we can get to her."

Offered Charles Fond, "And we can use the Soviet motor launches at the pier to get out to the *Amphitrite*."

Merle Duvane was still a Doubting Thomas. "Yeah . . . if the *Eugene Origen* has been destroyed."

"Let's go find out," suggested the Death Merchant.

Camellion, Duvane, and Barnkoff stood at the end of the pier, all three staring through binoculars, all three listening to the surging of the waves. The *Eugene Origen* was gone. Due to the stormy action of the waves, there wasn't any wreckage a mile off shore; yet some debris had been washed into the cove . . . foam cushions, pieces of wood, and some clothing. And three corpses dressed in Soviet "middie" uniforms, the three bodies floating face down, not far from the pier.

"I'll be damned!" Duvane muttered in awe. "That screwball Davis did it! He blew up the sub!"

"There isn't anything weird about psionics—the utilization of mind power," Barnkoff said. "It's the ultimate weapon of the future, and the future is now!"

Lowering his binoculars, Richard Camellion only half-heard the two men, his thoughts centered around the radio message he had received from Courtland Grojean—

Peacock. The Peoples Democratic Republic of Yemen.

The Death Merchant's mouth became as tight as a stretched steel cable. *Peacock!* The sign of Satan to the devil cult in Yemen. It would be the Night of the Peacock.

But only for a short while. I'll turn their night into the brightness of ten thousand suns. . . .

DEATH MERCHANT
by Joseph Rosenberger

More bestselling action/adventure from Pinnacle, America's #1 series publisher— Over 6 million copies in print!

☐ 41-345-9 Death Merchant #1	$1.95
☐ 41-346-7 Operation Overkill #2	$1.95
☐ 41-347-5 Psychotron Plot #3	$1.95
☐ 41-348-3 Chinese Conspiracy #4	$1.95
☐ 41-349-1 Satan Strike #5	$1.95
☐ 41-350-5 Albanian Connection #6	$1.95
☐ 41-351-3 Castro File #7	$1.95
☐ 41-352-1 Billionaire Mission #8	$1.95
☐ 41-353-X Laser War #9	$1.95
☐ 41-354-8 Mainline Plot #10	$1.95
☐ 40-816-1 Manhattan Wipeout #11	$1.75
☐ 40-817-X KGB Frame #12	$1.75
☐ 40-497-2 Mato Grosso Horror #13	$1.50
☐ 40-819-6 Vengeance: Golden Hawk #14	$1.75
☐ 22-823-6 Iron Swastika Plot #15	$1.25
☐ 22-857-0 Invasion of the Clones #16	$1.25
☐ 22-880-5 Zemlya Expedition #17	$1.25
☐ 22-911-9 Nightmare in Algeria #18	$1.25
☐ 40-460-3 Armageddon, USA! #19	$1.50
☐ 40-256-2 Hell in Hindu Land #20	$1.50
☐ 40-826-9 Pole Star Secret #21	$1.75
☐ 40-827-7 Kondrashev Chase #22	$1.75
☐ 40-078-0 Budapest Action #23	$1.25
☐ 40-352-6 Kronos Plot #24	$1.50
☐ 40-117-5 Enigma Project #25	$1.25
☐ 40-118-3 Mexican Hit #26	$1.50
☐ 40-119-1 Surinam Affair #27	$1.50
☐ 40-833-1 Nipponese Nightmare #28	$1.75
☐ 40-272-4 Fatal Formula #29	$1.50
☐ 40-385-2 Shambhala Strike #30	$1.50
☐ 40-392-5 Operation Thunderbolt #31	$1.50
☐ 40-475-1 Deadly Manhunt #32	$1.50
☐ 40-476-X Alaska Conspiracy #33	$1.50
☐ 41-378-5 Operation Mind-Murder #34	$1.95
☐ 40-478-6 Massacre in Rome #35	$1.50
☐ 41-380-7 Cosmic Reality Kill #36	$1.95
☐ 41-382-3 The Burning Blue Death #38	$1.95
☐ 41-383-1 The Fourth Reich #39	$1.95
☐ 41-020-4 High Command Murder #42	$1.95
☐ 41-021-2 Devil's Trashcan #43	$1.95
☐ 41-326-2 The Rim of Fire Conspiracy #45	$1.95
☐ 41-327-0 Blood Bath #46	$1.95
☐ 41-328-9 Operation Skyhook #47	$1.95
☐ 41-644-X The Psionics War #48	$1.95

Buy them at your local bookstore or use this handy coupon
Clip and mail this page with your order

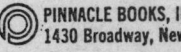 **PINNACLE BOOKS, INC.—Reader Service Dept.**
1430 Broadway, New York, NY 10018

Please send me the book(s) I have checked above. I am enclosing $_____ (please add 75¢ to cover postage and handling). Send check or money order only—no cash or C.O.D.'s.

Mr./Mrs./Miss _____

Address _____

City _____ State/Zip _____

Please allow six weeks for delivery. Prices subject to change without notice.